ROYAL OAK

JUN 06 2013

PUBLIC LIBRARY

STORY BY
BRIAN SMITH

ART BY
JACOB CHABOT

Voltron Force vol. 6: True Colors
Story by Brian Smith
Cover and Interior Art by Jacob Chabot
Colors by Michael Wiggam

Cover Art/Jacob Chabot
Letterer/Deron Bennett
Graphics and Cover Design/Sam Elzway
Editor/Traci N. Todd

Voltron Force ® & © World Events Productions
under license to Classic Media.

The stories, characters and incidents mentioned in this
publication are entirely fictional.

No portion of this book may be reproduced without written
permission from the copyright holders.

Printed in China

Published by VIZ Media, LLC
P.O. Box 77010
San Francisco, CA 94107

10 9 8 7 6 5 4 3 2 1
First printing, February 2013

3 9082 12360 9797

PARENTAL ADVISORY
VOLTRON FORCE VOL. 6: TRUE COLORS
is rated A and is suitable for readers
of all ages.
ratings.viz.com

www.vizkids.com

www.viz.com

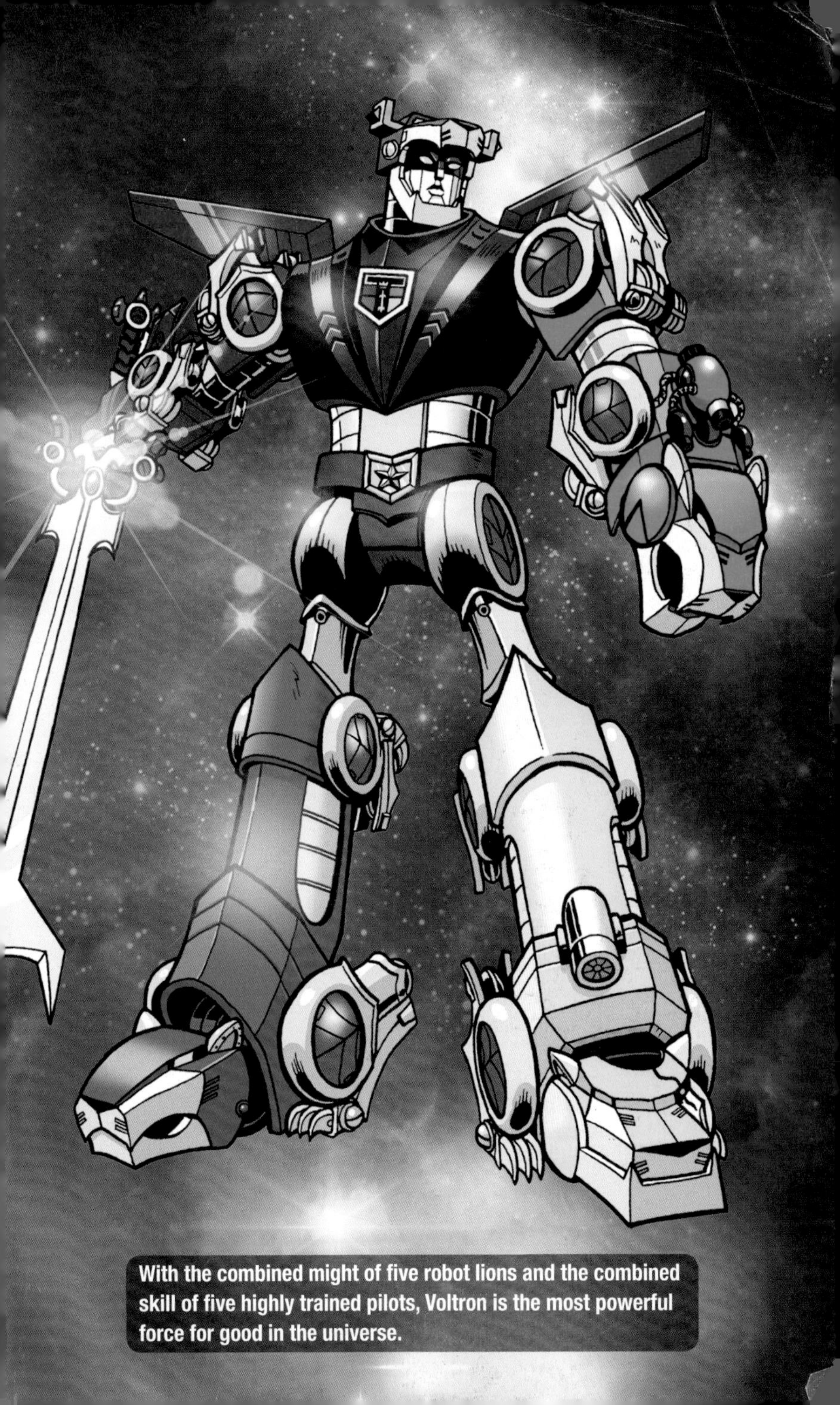

With the combined might of five robot lions and the combined skill of five highly trained pilots, Voltron is the most powerful force for good in the universe.

VOLTRON FORCE PILOTS

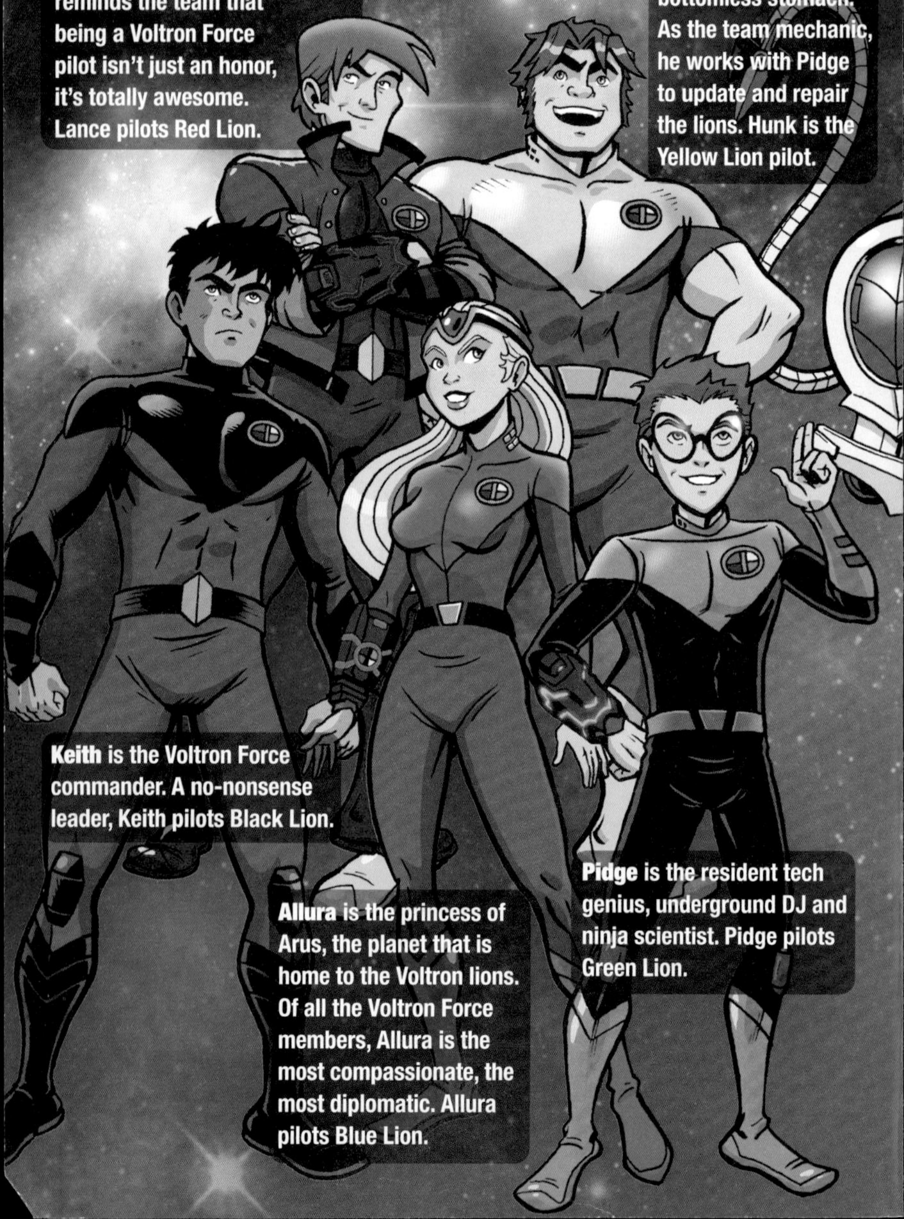

Quick with the one-liners and willing to bend the rules, **Lance** reminds the team that being a Voltron Force pilot isn't just an honor, it's totally awesome. Lance pilots Red Lion.

Hunk is a loveable goofball with a rock-and-roll heart and a bottomless stomach. As the team mechanic, he works with Pidge to update and repair the lions. Hunk is the Yellow Lion pilot.

Keith is the Voltron Force commander. A no-nonsense leader, Keith pilots Black Lion.

Allura is the princess of Arus, the planet that is home to the Voltron lions. Of all the Voltron Force members, Allura is the most compassionate, the most diplomatic. Allura pilots Blue Lion.

Pidge is the resident tech genius, underground DJ and ninja scientist. Pidge pilots Green Lion.

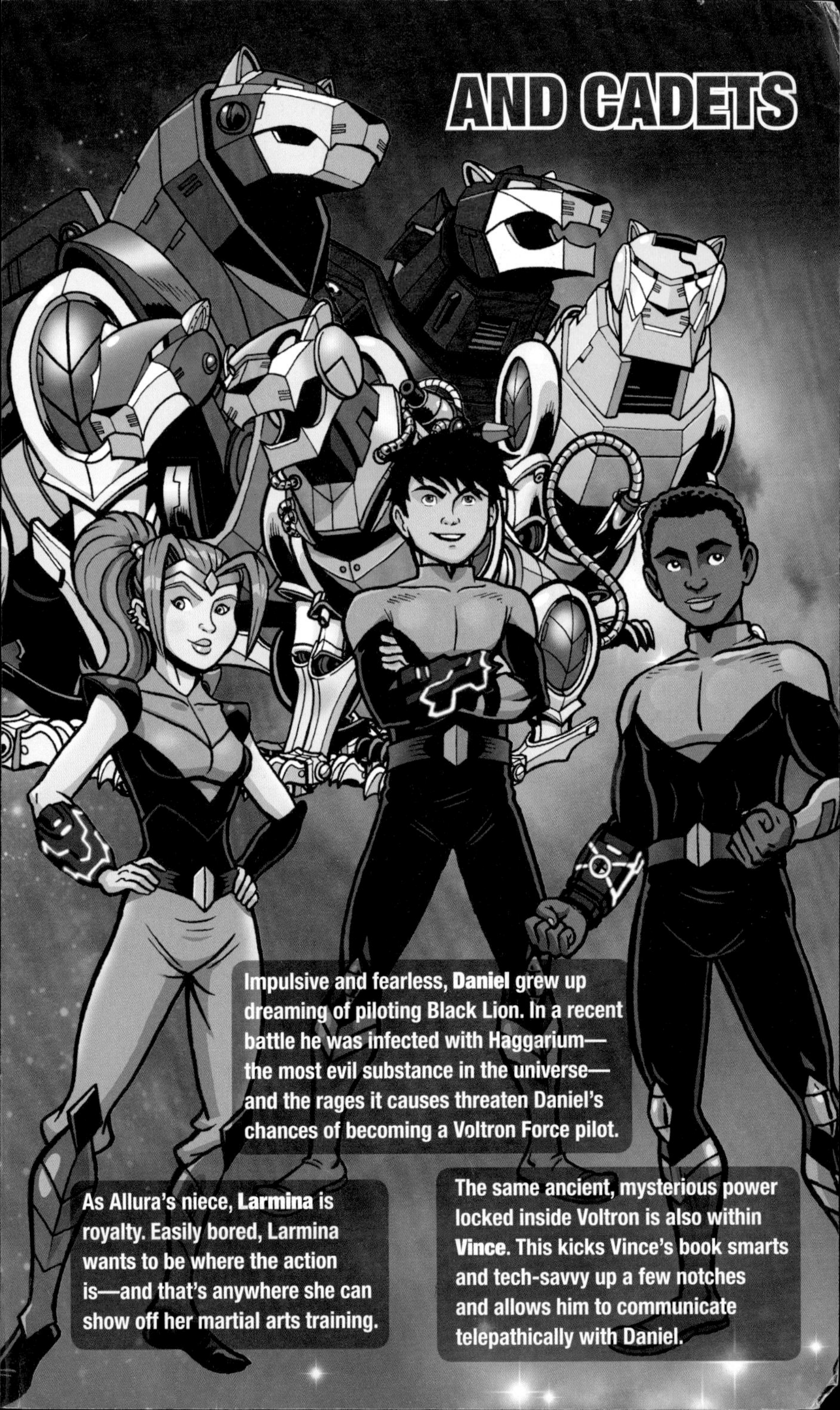
AND CADETS
Impulsive and fearless, **Daniel** grew up dreaming of piloting Black Lion. In a recent battle he was infected with Haggarium—the most evil substance in the universe—and the rages it causes threaten Daniel's chances of becoming a Voltron Force pilot.
As Allura's niece, **Larmina** is royalty. Easily bored, Larmina wants to be where the action is—and that's anywhere she can show off her martial arts training.
The same ancient, mysterious power locked inside Voltron is also within **Vince**. This kicks Vince's book smarts and tech-savvy up a few notches and allows him to communicate telepathically with Daniel.

VILLAINS

Lotor—the Drule king—is determined to do what his father never could: destroy Voltron. He boosts his evil energy with large doses of Haggarium, and while the horrible substance makes him unimaginably powerful, it is also driving him insane.

Maahox is a horrifyingly devious techno-scientist. He's the brains behind Lotor's whole operation, and as such, he wields the true power.

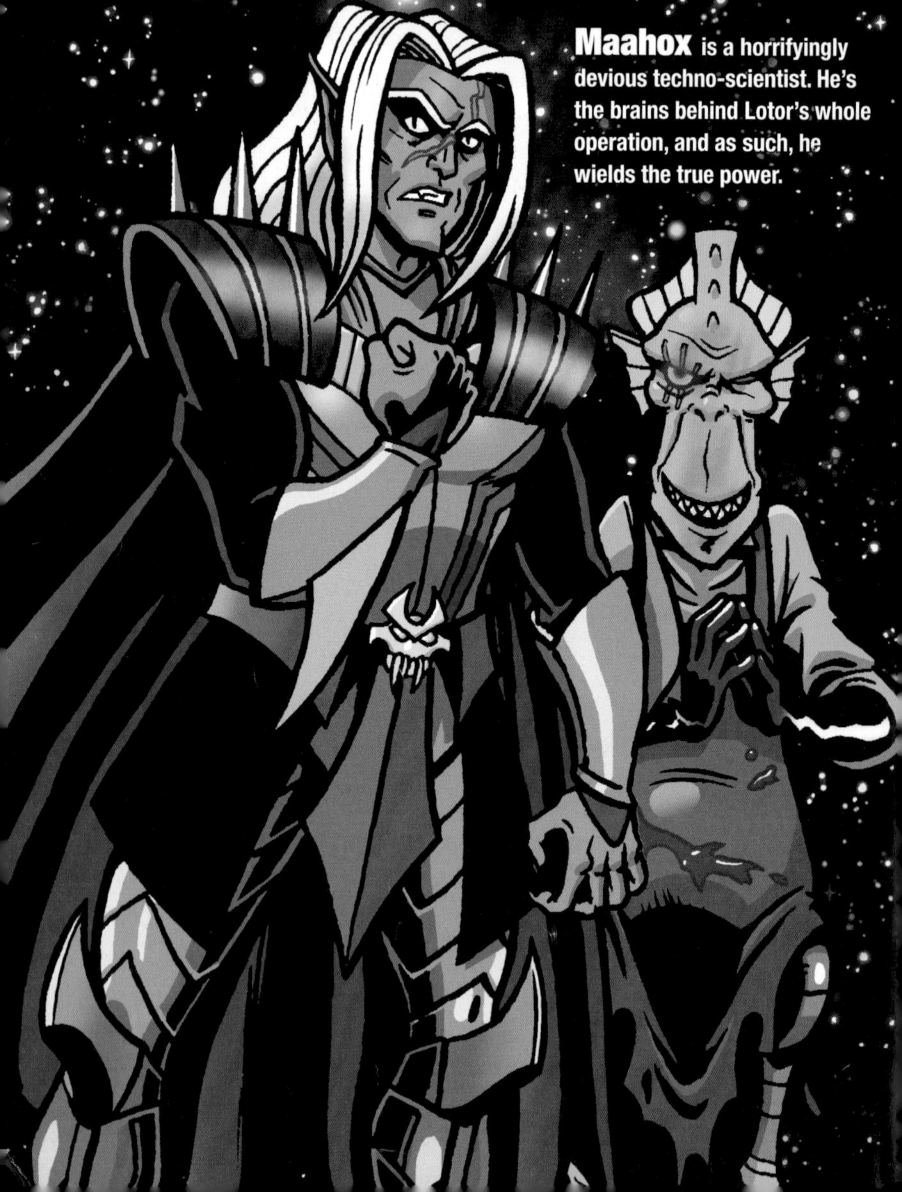

PLANET ARUS

ATTENTION, *CADETS.* BIG ANNOUNCEMENT INCOMING.

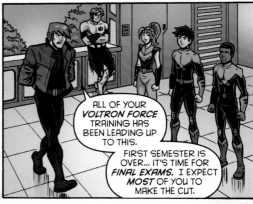

ALL OF YOUR *VOLTRON FORCE* TRAINING HAS BEEN LEADING UP TO THIS.

FIRST SEMESTER IS OVER... IT'S TIME FOR *FINAL EXAMS.* I EXPECT *MOST* OF YOU TO MAKE THE CUT.

MOST OF US? WE ALL KNOW WHO THE SUPERSTAR OF *THIS* GROUP IS, *LANCE.*

SOMETHING TO CONTRIBUTE *BESIDES JOKES,* DANIEL?

ERRR... MY *GOOD LOOKS?*

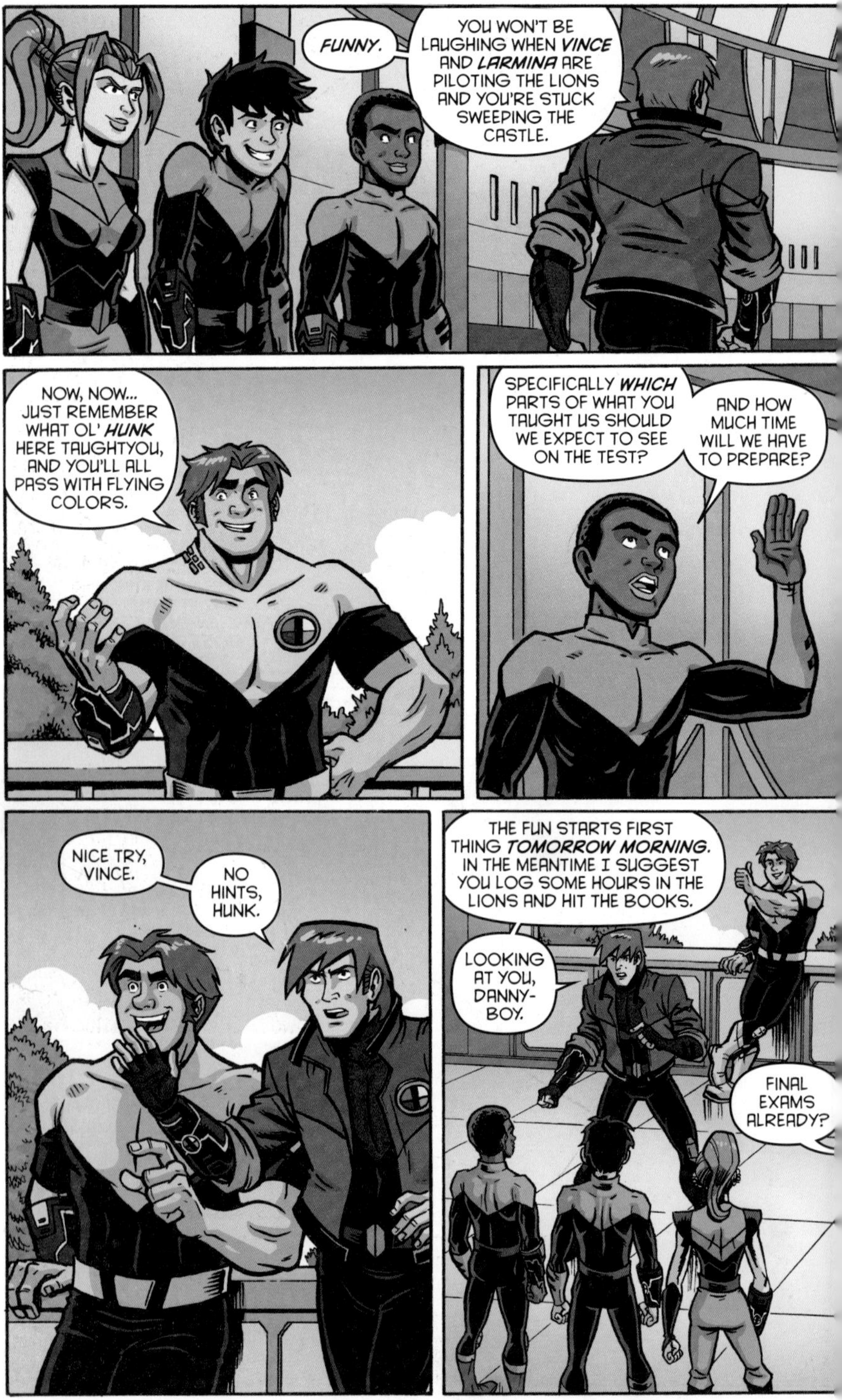
FUNNY.
YOU WON'T BE LAUGHING WHEN VINCE AND LARMINA ARE PILOTING THE LIONS AND YOU'RE STUCK SWEEPING THE CASTLE.
NOW, NOW... JUST REMEMBER WHAT OL' HUNK HERE TAUGHTYOU, AND YOU'LL ALL PASS WITH FLYING COLORS.
SPECIFICALLY WHICH PARTS OF WHAT YOU TAUGHT US SHOULD WE EXPECT TO SEE ON THE TEST?
AND HOW MUCH TIME WILL WE HAVE TO PREPARE?
NICE TRY, VINCE.
NO HINTS, HUNK.
THE FUN STARTS FIRST THING TOMORROW MORNING. IN THE MEANTIME I SUGGEST YOU LOG SOME HOURS IN THE LIONS AND HIT THE BOOKS.
LOOKING AT YOU, DANNY-BOY.
FINAL EXAMS ALREADY?

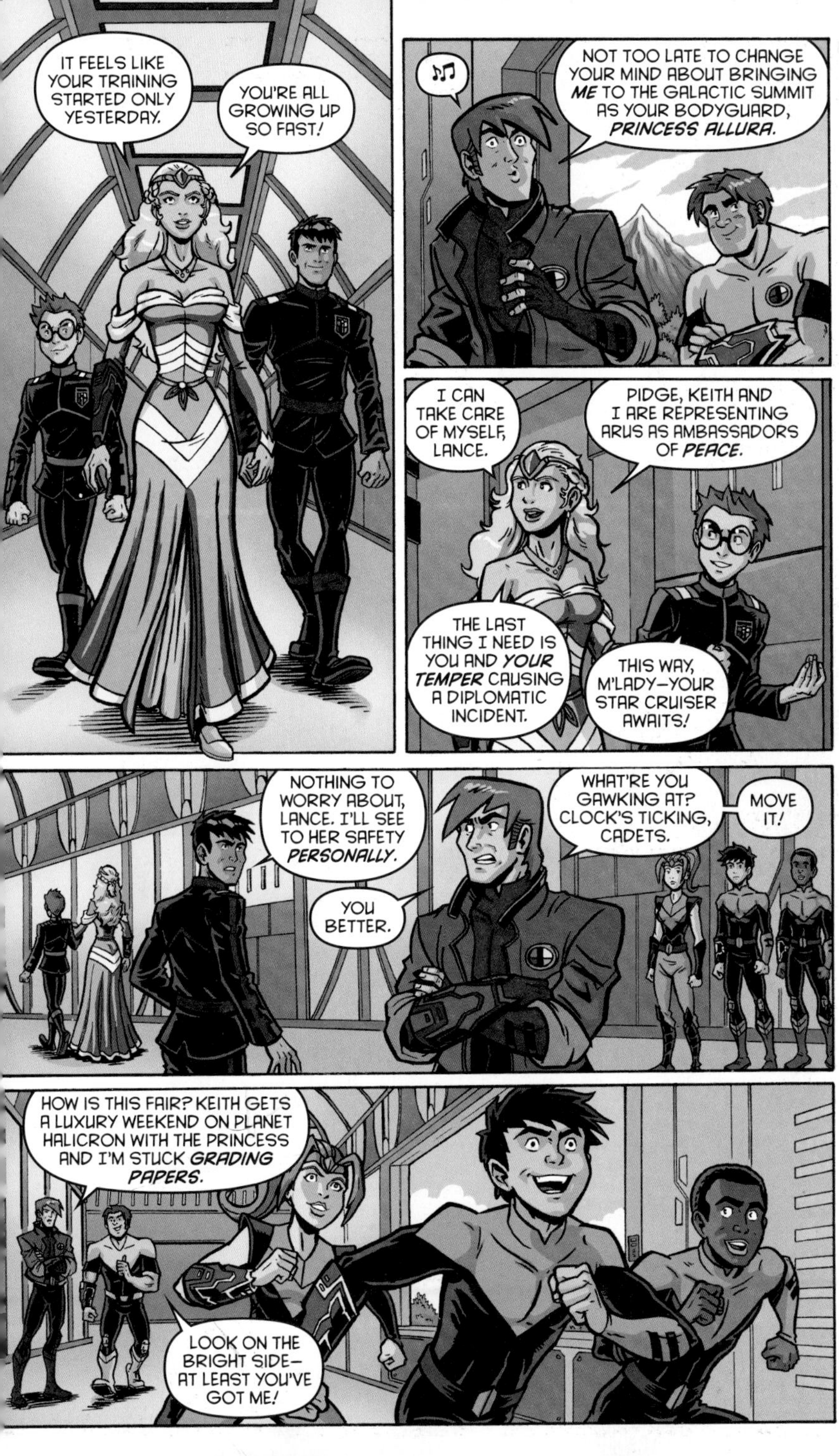
IT FEELS LIKE YOUR TRAINING STARTED ONLY YESTERDAY.
YOU'RE ALL GROWING UP SO FAST!
♫
NOT TOO LATE TO CHANGE YOUR MIND ABOUT BRINGING *ME* TO THE GALACTIC SUMMIT AS YOUR BODYGUARD, *PRINCESS ALLURA.*
I CAN TAKE CARE OF MYSELF, LANCE.
PIDGE, KEITH AND I ARE REPRESENTING ARUS AS AMBASSADORS OF *PEACE.*
THE LAST THING I NEED IS YOU AND *YOUR TEMPER* CAUSING A DIPLOMATIC INCIDENT.
THIS WAY, M'LADY—YOUR STAR CRUISER AWAITS!
NOTHING TO WORRY ABOUT, LANCE. I'LL SEE TO HER SAFETY *PERSONALLY.*
YOU BETTER.
WHAT'RE YOU GAWKING AT? CLOCK'S TICKING, CADETS.
MOVE IT!
HOW IS THIS FAIR? KEITH GETS A LUXURY WEEKEND ON PLANET HALICRON WITH THE PRINCESS AND I'M STUCK *GRADING PAPERS.*
LOOK ON THE BRIGHT SIDE— AT LEAST YOU'VE GOT ME!

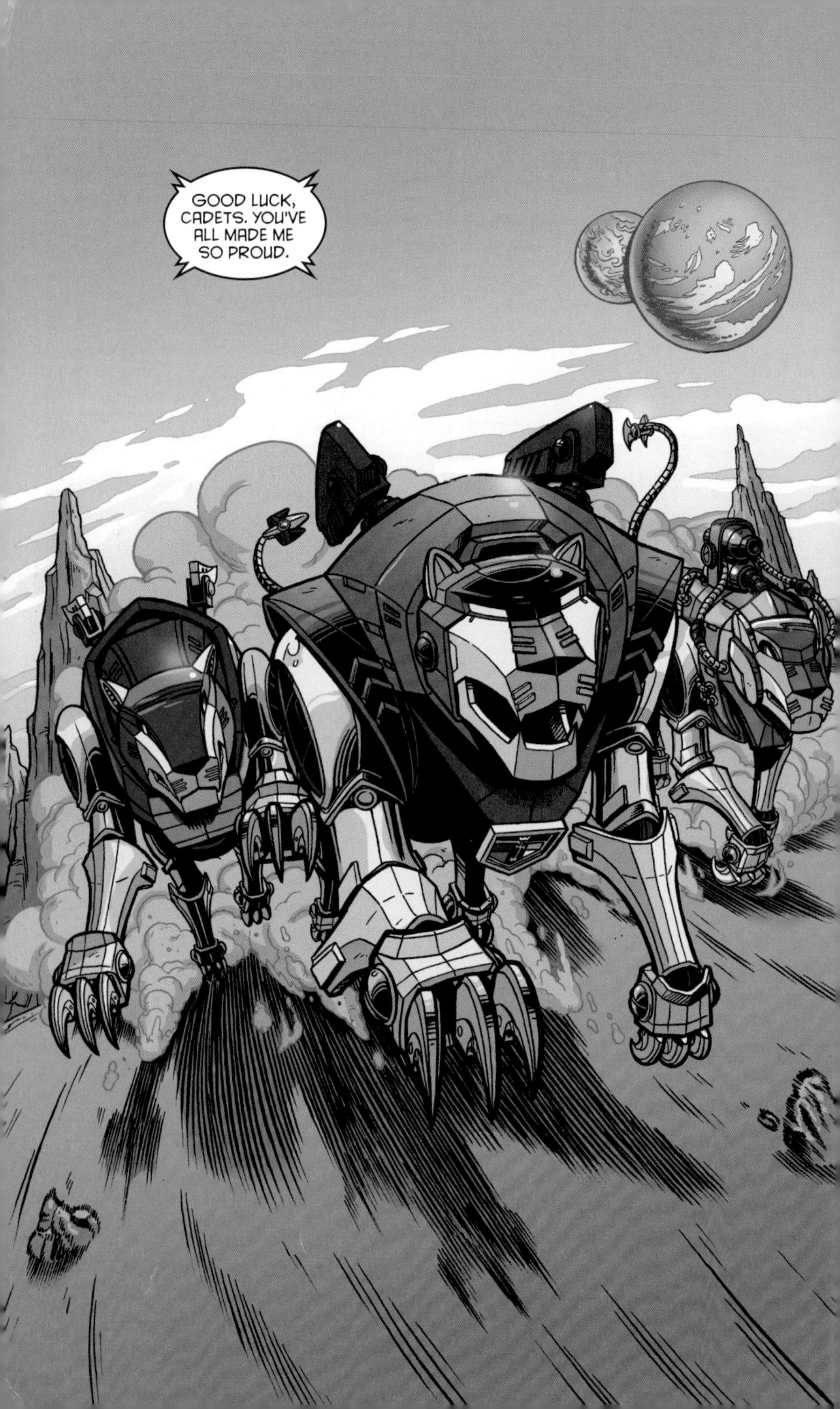
GOOD LUCK, CADETS. YOU'VE ALL MADE ME SO PROUD.

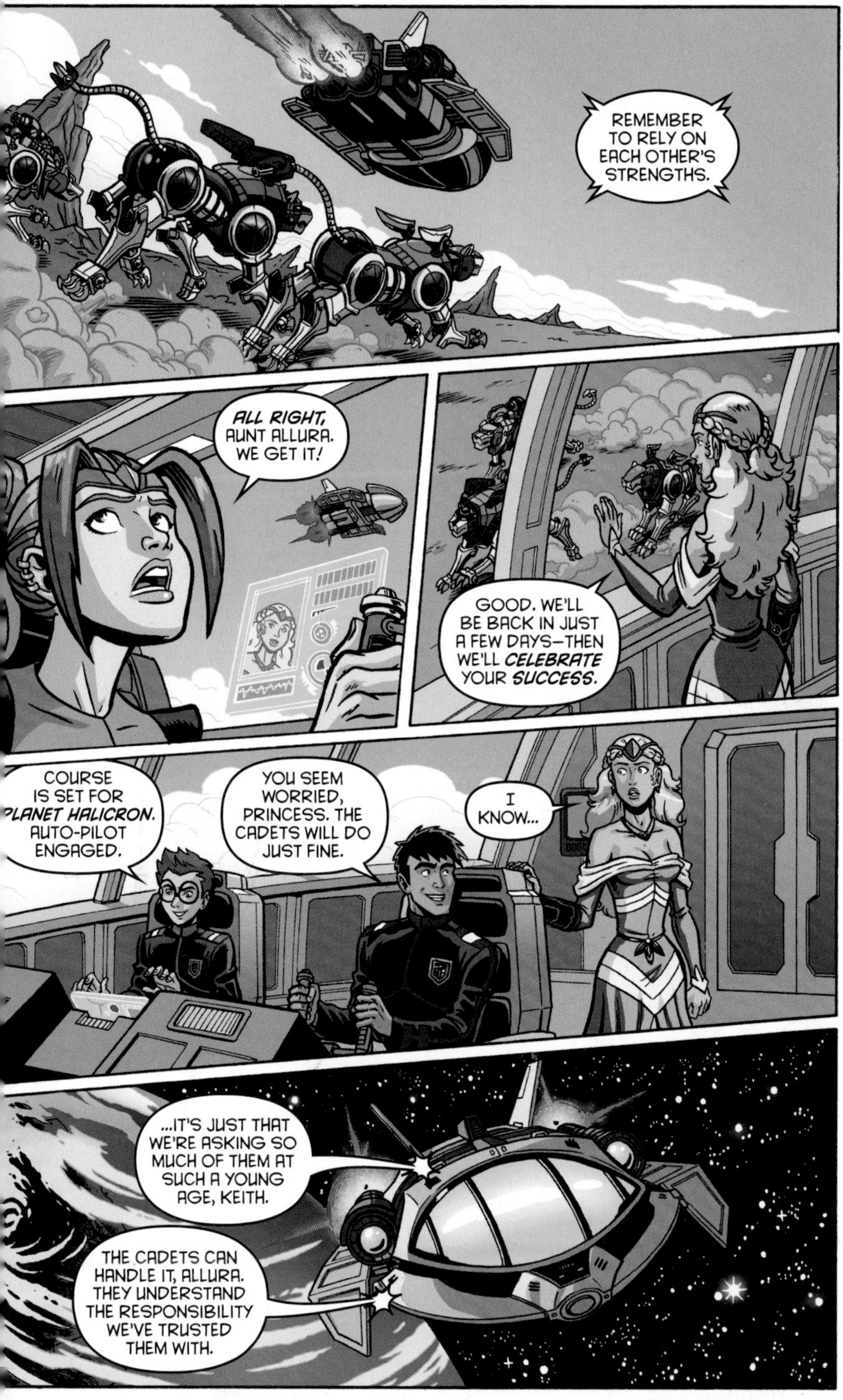
REMEMBER TO RELY ON EACH OTHER'S STRENGTHS.
ALL RIGHT, AUNT ALLURA. WE GET IT!
GOOD. WE'LL BE BACK IN JUST A FEW DAYS—THEN WE'LL CELEBRATE YOUR SUCCESS.
COURSE IS SET FOR PLANET HALICRON. AUTO-PILOT ENGAGED.
YOU SEEM WORRIED, PRINCESS. THE CADETS WILL DO JUST FINE.
I KNOW...
...IT'S JUST THAT WE'RE ASKING SO MUCH OF THEM AT SUCH A YOUNG AGE, KEITH.
THE CADETS CAN HANDLE IT, ALLURA. THEY UNDERSTAND THE RESPONSIBILITY WE'VE TRUSTED THEM WITH.

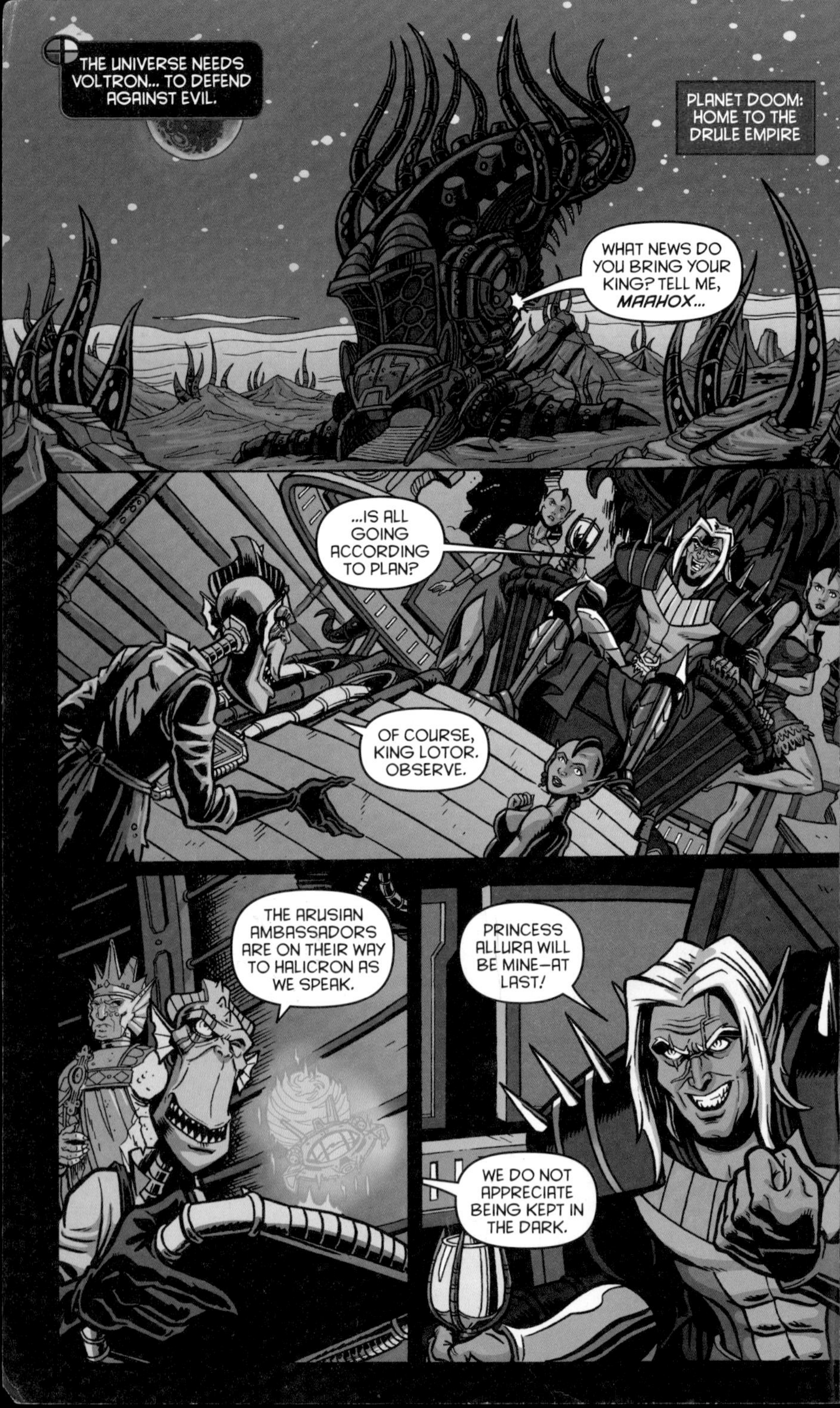
THE UNIVERSE NEEDS VOLTRON... TO DEFEND AGAINST EVIL.
PLANET DOOM: HOME TO THE DRULE EMPIRE
WHAT NEWS DO YOU BRING YOUR KING? TELL ME, *MAAHOX*...
...IS ALL GOING ACCORDING TO PLAN?
OF COURSE, KING LOTOR. OBSERVE.
THE ARUSIAN AMBASSADORS ARE ON THEIR WAY TO HALICRON AS WE SPEAK.
PRINCESS ALLURA WILL BE MINE—AT LAST!
WE DO NOT APPRECIATE BEING KEPT IN THE DARK.

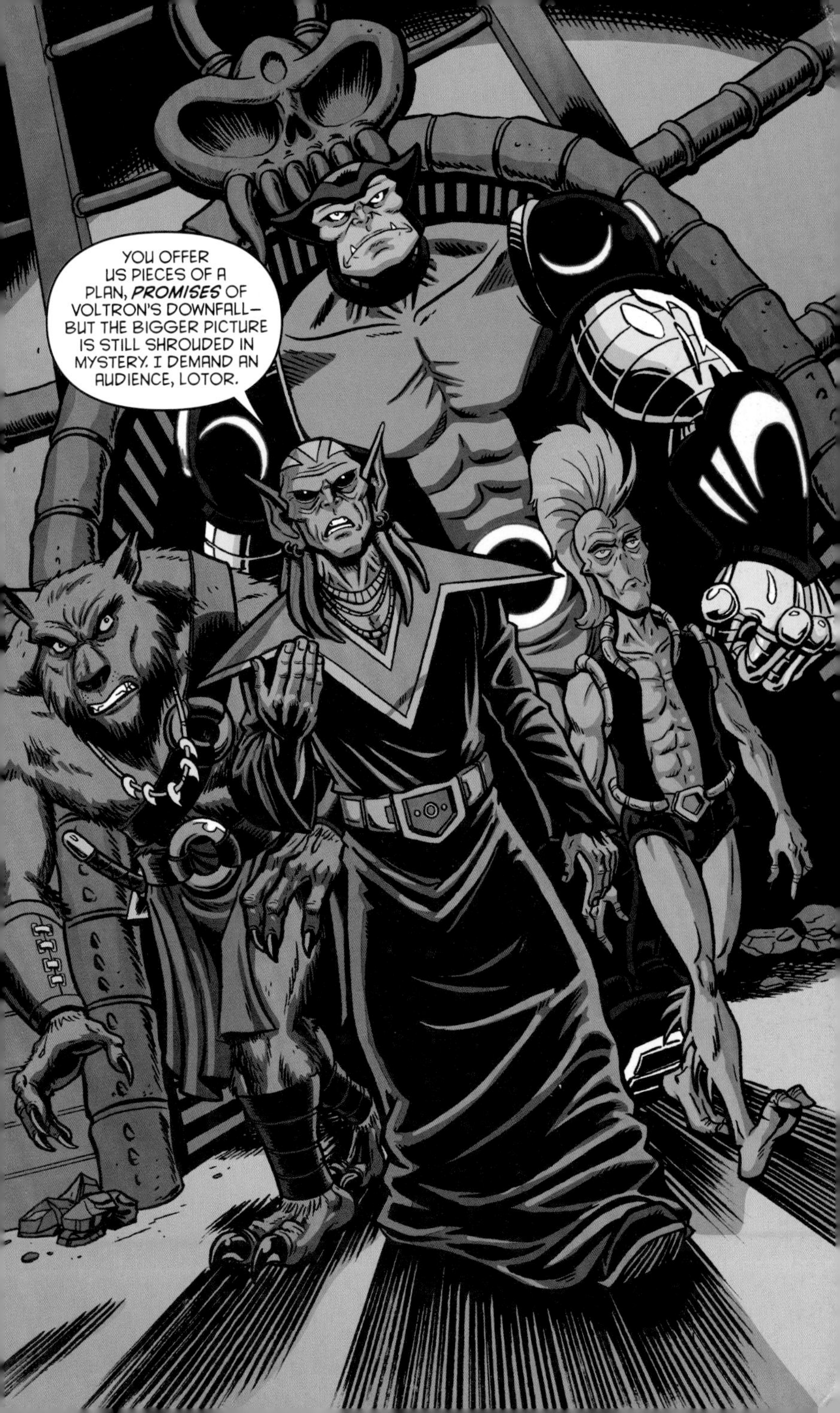
YOU OFFER US PIECES OF A PLAN, PROMISES OF VOLTRON'S DOWNFALL— BUT THE BIGGER PICTURE IS STILL SHROUDED IN MYSTERY. I DEMAND AN AUDIENCE, LOTOR.

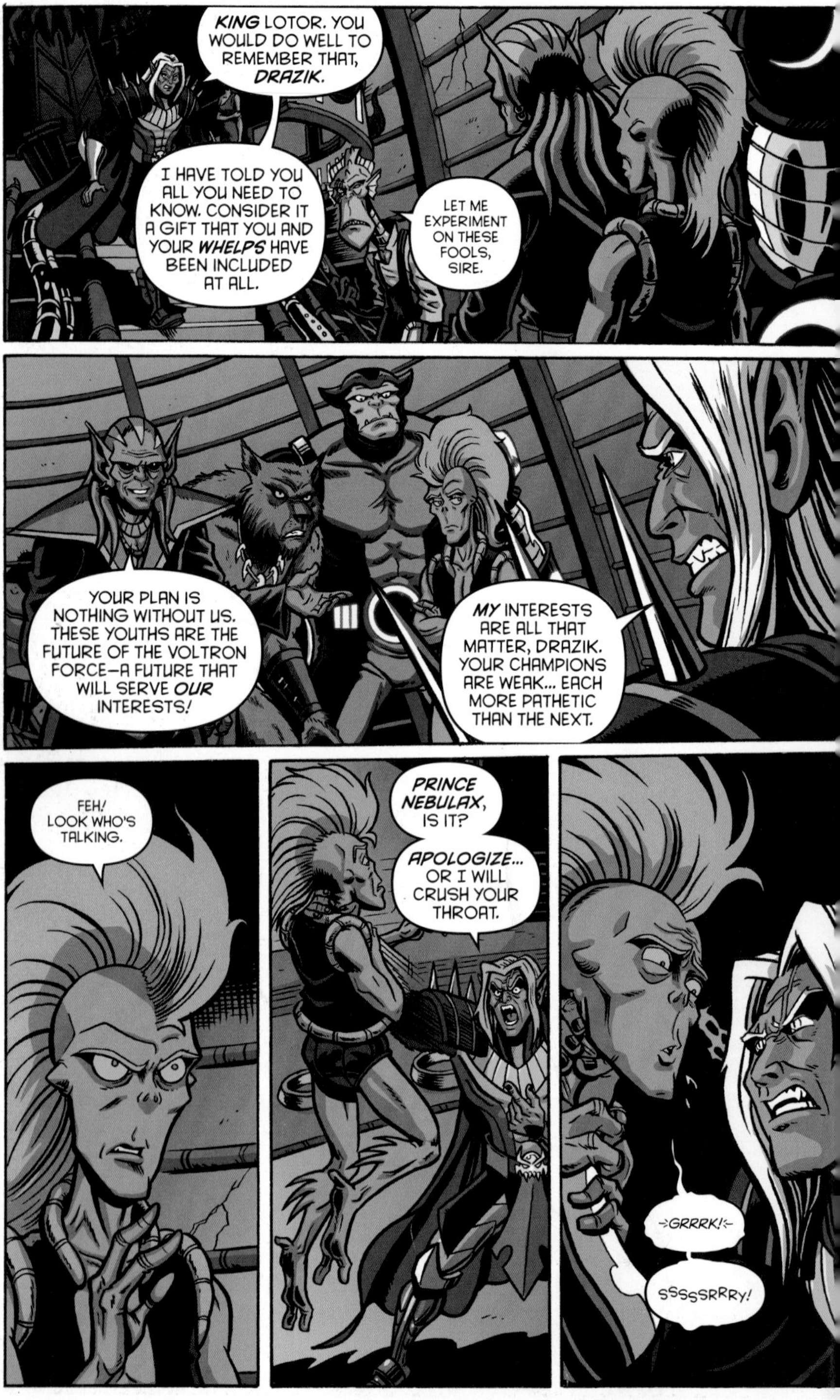
KING LOTOR. YOU WOULD DO WELL TO REMEMBER THAT, DRAZIK.
I HAVE TOLD YOU ALL YOU NEED TO KNOW. CONSIDER IT A GIFT THAT YOU AND YOUR WHELPS HAVE BEEN INCLUDED AT ALL.
LET ME EXPERIMENT ON THESE FOOLS, SIRE.
YOUR PLAN IS NOTHING WITHOUT US. THESE YOUTHS ARE THE FUTURE OF THE VOLTRON FORCE—A FUTURE THAT WILL SERVE OUR INTERESTS!
MY INTERESTS ARE ALL THAT MATTER, DRAZIK. YOUR CHAMPIONS ARE WEAK... EACH MORE PATHETIC THAN THE NEXT.
FEH! LOOK WHO'S TALKING.
PRINCE NEBULAX, IS IT?
APOLOGIZE... OR I WILL CRUSH YOUR THROAT.
GRRRK!
SSSSSRRRY!

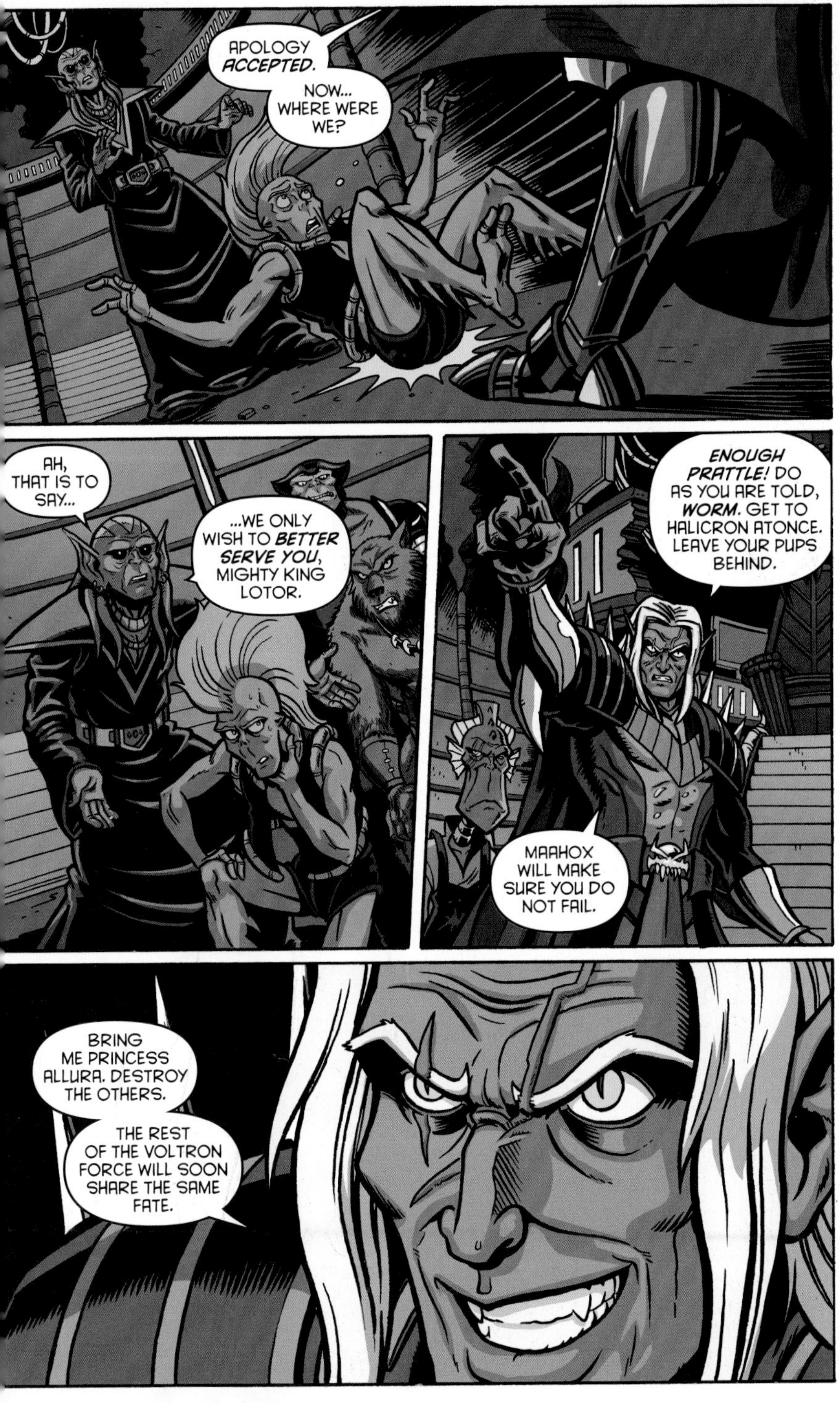
APOLOGY *ACCEPTED.*
NOW... WHERE WERE WE?
AH, THAT IS TO SAY...
...WE ONLY WISH TO *BETTER SERVE YOU*, MIGHTY KING LOTOR.
ENOUGH PRATTLE! DO AS YOU ARE TOLD, *WORM.* GET TO HALICRON ATONCE. LEAVE YOUR PUPS BEHIND.
MAAHOX WILL MAKE SURE YOU DO NOT FAIL.
BRING ME PRINCESS ALLURA. DESTROY THE OTHERS.
THE REST OF THE VOLTRON FORCE WILL SOON SHARE THE SAME FATE.

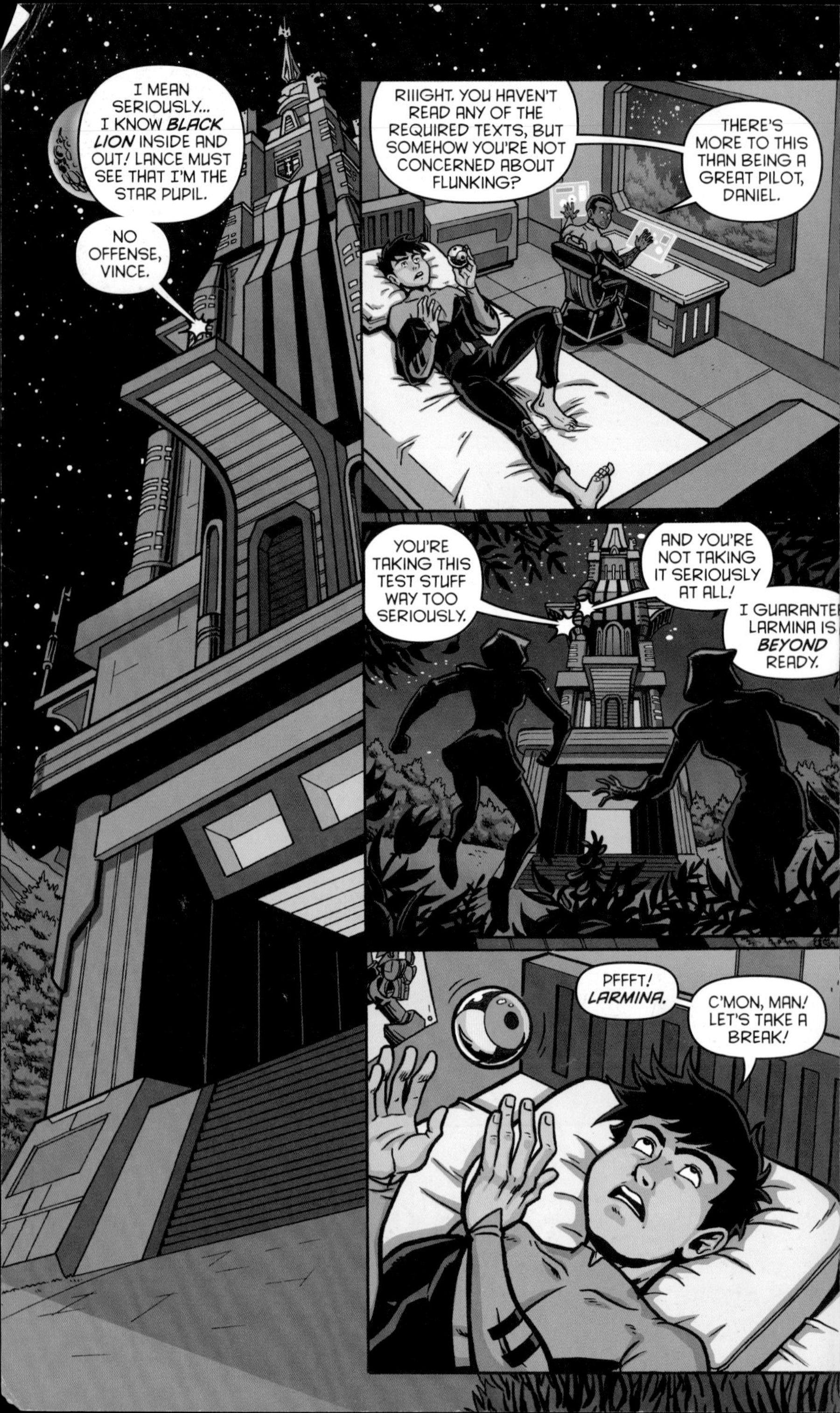
I MEAN SERIOUSLY... I KNOW *BLACK LION* INSIDE AND OUT! LANCE MUST SEE THAT I'M THE STAR PUPIL.
NO OFFENSE, VINCE.
RIIIGHT. YOU HAVEN'T READ ANY OF THE REQUIRED TEXTS, BUT SOMEHOW YOU'RE NOT CONCERNED ABOUT FLUNKING?
THERE'S MORE TO THIS THAN BEING A GREAT PILOT, DANIEL.
YOU'RE TAKING THIS TEST STUFF WAY TOO SERIOUSLY.
AND YOU'RE NOT TAKING IT SERIOUSLY AT ALL!
I GUARANTE LARMINA IS *BEYOND* READY.
PFFFT! *LARMINA.*
C'MON, MAN! LET'S TAKE A BREAK!

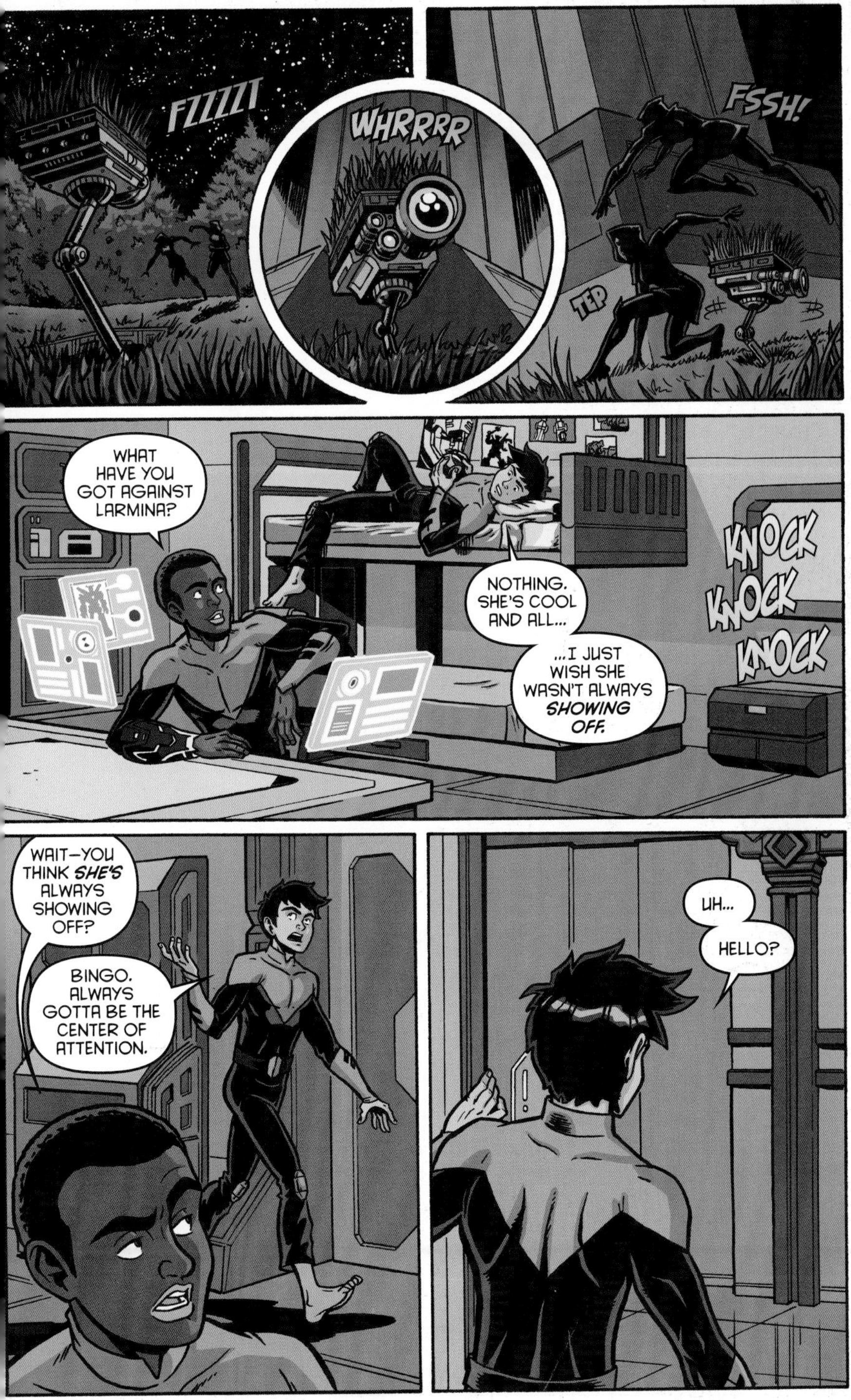
FZZZZT
WHRRRR
FSSH!
TEP
WHAT HAVE YOU GOT AGAINST LARMINA?
NOTHING. SHE'S COOL AND ALL...
...I JUST WISH SHE WASN'T ALWAYS SHOWING OFF.
KNOCK KNOCK KNOCK
WAIT—YOU THINK SHE'S ALWAYS SHOWING OFF?
BINGO. ALWAYS GOTTA BE THE CENTER OF ATTENTION.
UH...
HELLO?

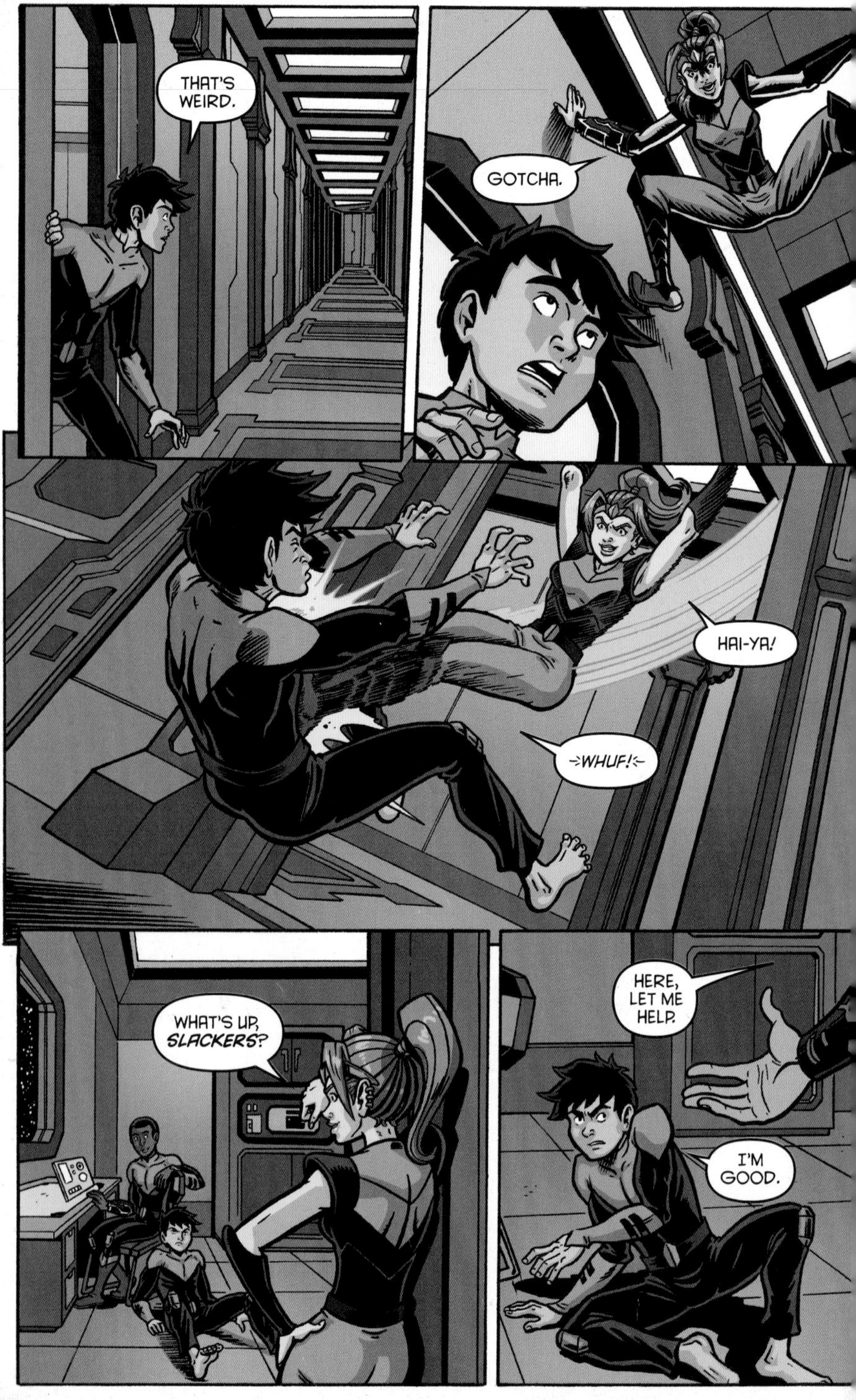
THAT'S WEIRD.
GOTCHA.
HAI-YA!
WHUF!
WHAT'S UP, SLACKERS?
HERE, LET ME HELP.
I'M GOOD.

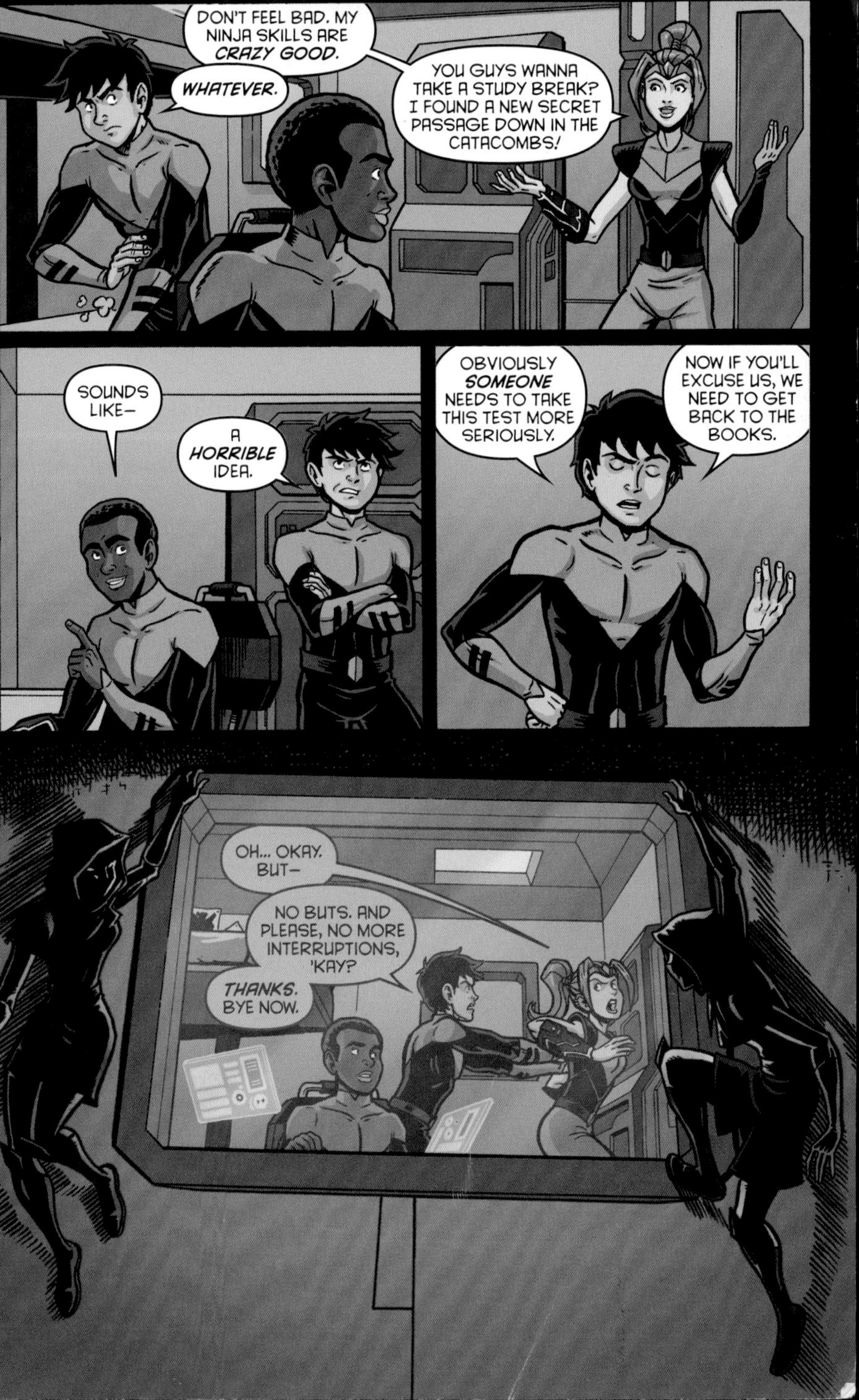
DON'T FEEL BAD. MY NINJA SKILLS ARE CRAZY GOOD.
WHATEVER.
YOU GUYS WANNA TAKE A STUDY BREAK? I FOUND A NEW SECRET PASSAGE DOWN IN THE CATACOMBS!
SOUNDS LIKE—
A HORRIBLE IDEA.
OBVIOUSLY SOMEONE NEEDS TO TAKE THIS TEST MORE SERIOUSLY.
NOW IF YOU'LL EXCUSE US, WE NEED TO GET BACK TO THE BOOKS.
OH... OKAY. BUT—
NO BUTS. AND PLEASE, NO MORE INTERRUPTIONS, 'KAY?
THANKS. BYE NOW.

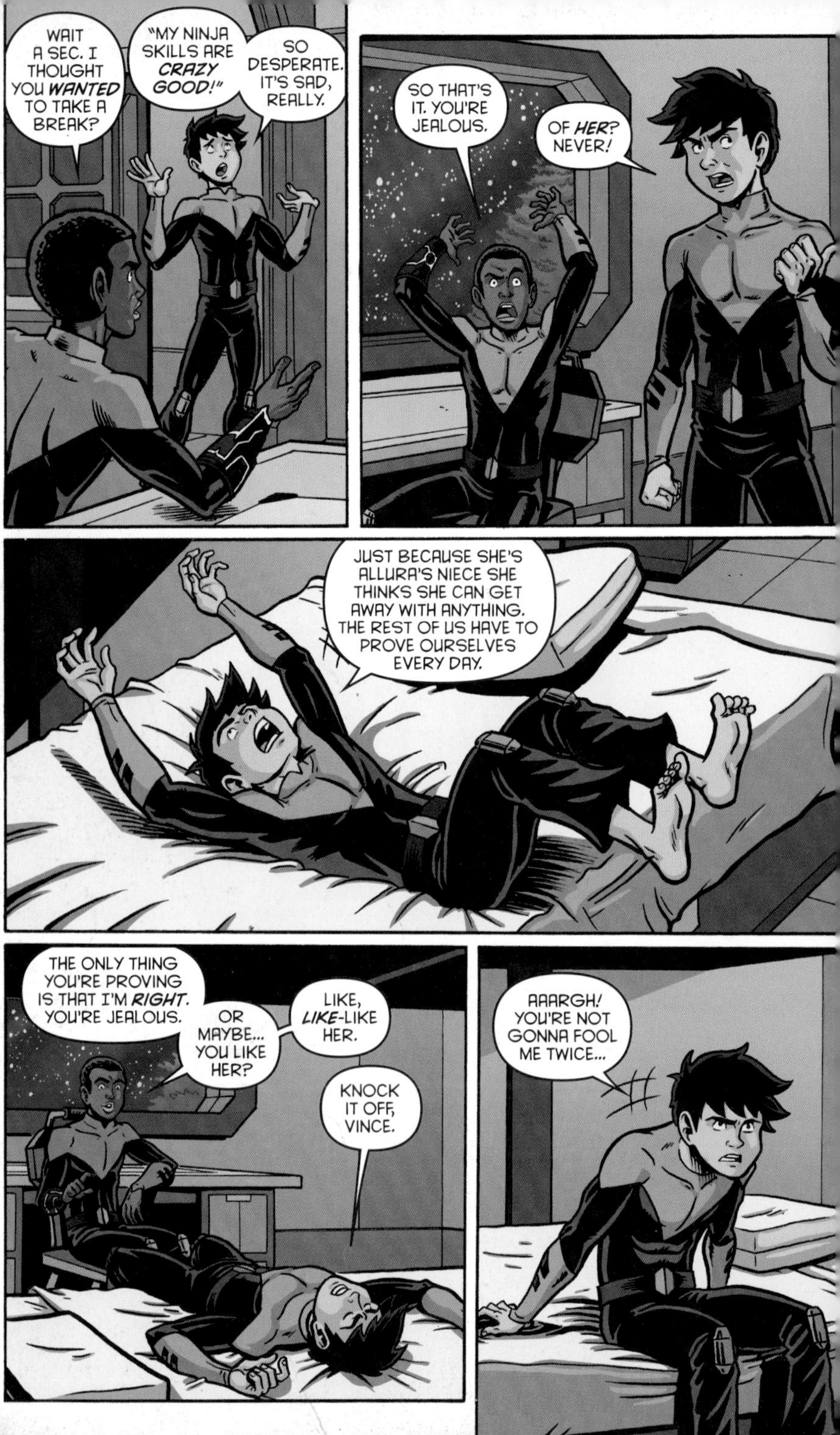
WAIT A SEC. I THOUGHT YOU *WANTED* TO TAKE A BREAK?
"MY NINJA SKILLS ARE *CRAZY GOOD!*"
SO DESPERATE. IT'S SAD, REALLY.
SO THAT'S IT. YOU'RE JEALOUS.
OF *HER*? NEVER!
JUST BECAUSE SHE'S ALLURA'S NIECE SHE THINKS SHE CAN GET AWAY WITH ANYTHING. THE REST OF US HAVE TO PROVE OURSELVES EVERY DAY.
THE ONLY THING YOU'RE PROVING IS THAT I'M *RIGHT*. YOU'RE JEALOUS.
OR MAYBE... YOU LIKE HER?
LIKE, *LIKE*-LIKE HER.
KNOCK IT OFF, VINCE.
AAARGH! YOU'RE NOT GONNA FOOL ME TWICE...

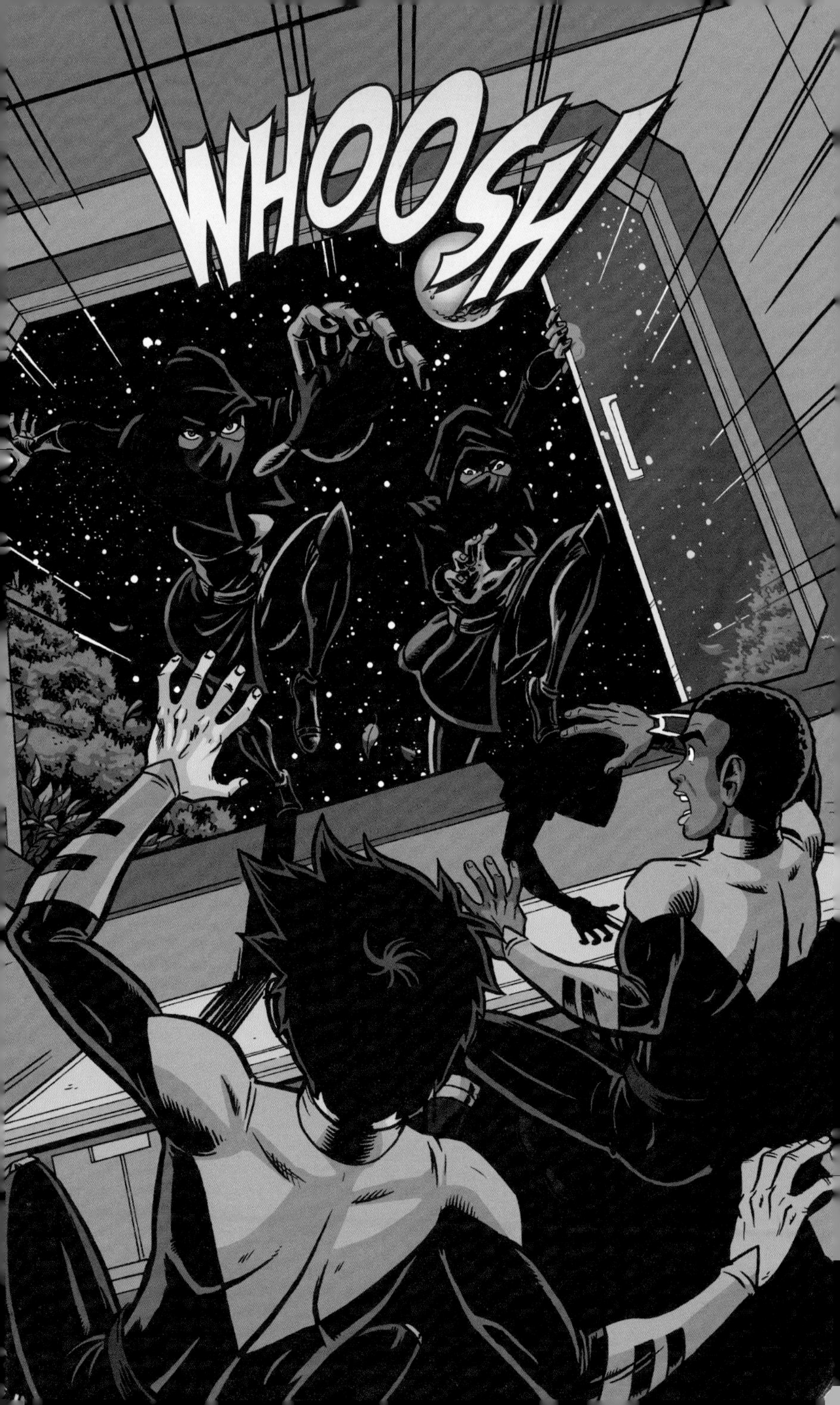
WHOOSH

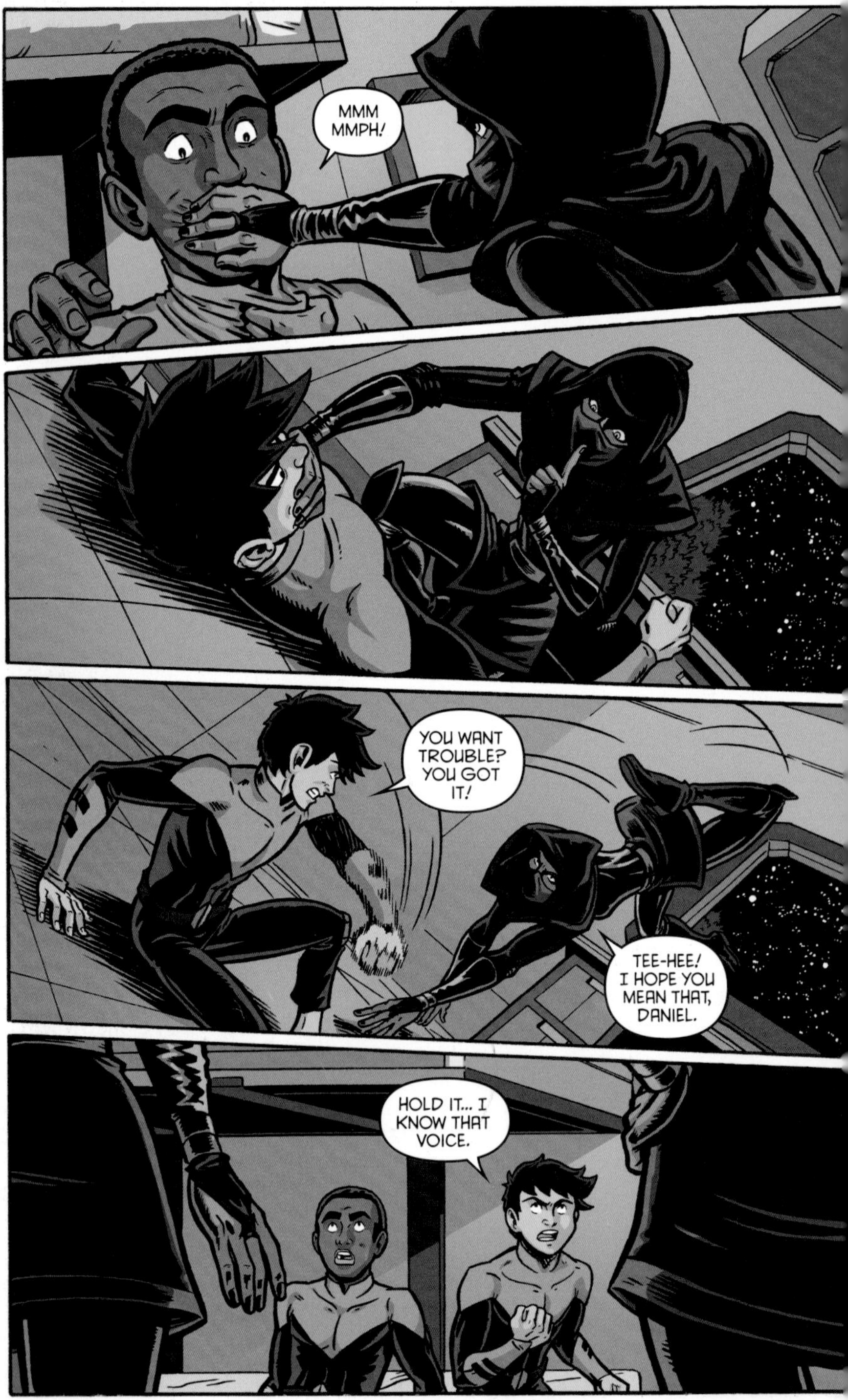
MMM MMPH!
YOU WANT TROUBLE? YOU GOT IT!
TEE-HEE! I HOPE YOU MEAN THAT, DANIEL.
HOLD IT... I KNOW THAT VOICE.

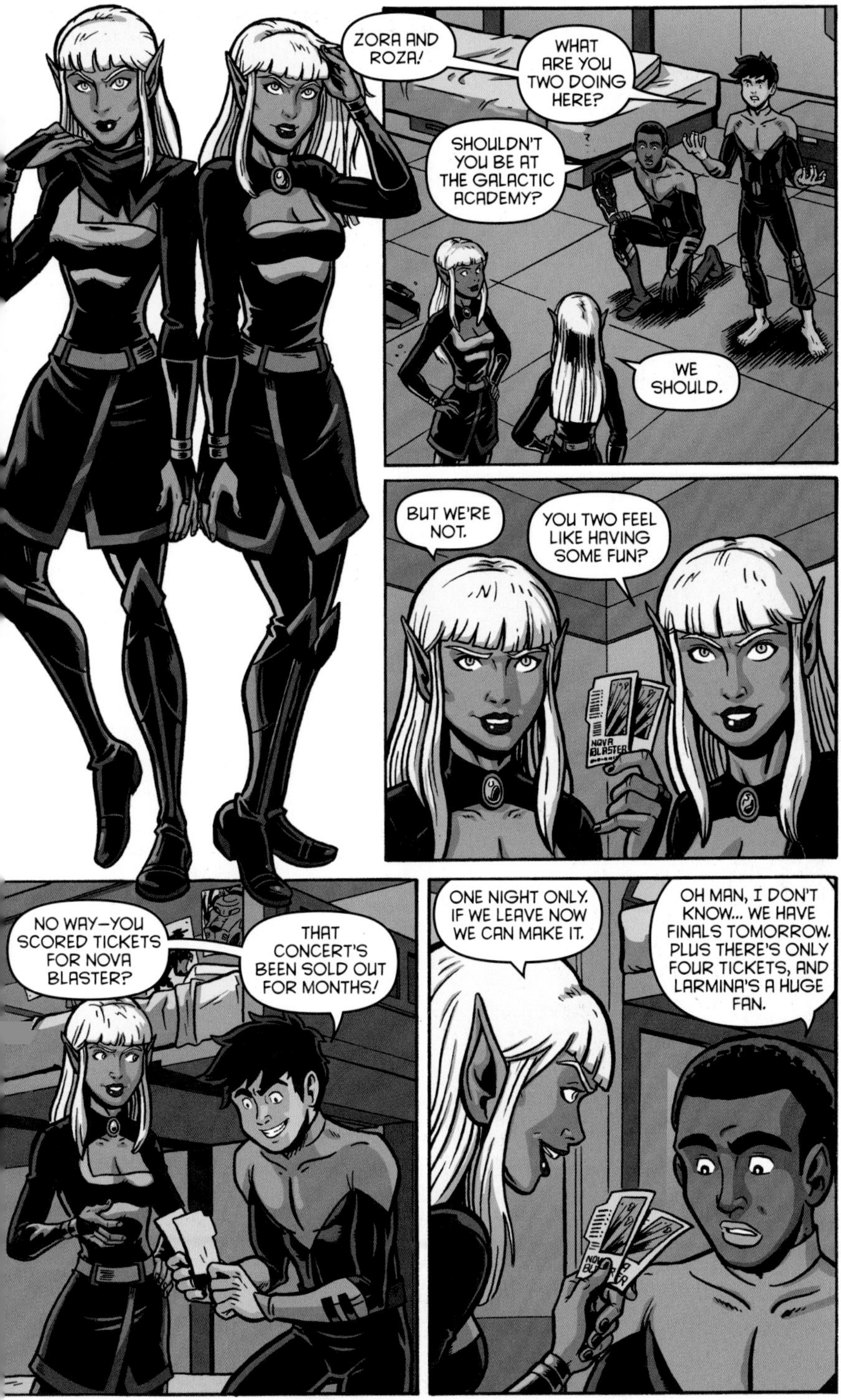
ZORA AND ROZA!
WHAT ARE YOU TWO DOING HERE?
SHOULDN'T YOU BE AT THE GALACTIC ACADEMY?
WE SHOULD.
BUT WE'RE NOT.
YOU TWO FEEL LIKE HAVING SOME FUN?
NOVA BLASTER
NO WAY—YOU SCORED TICKETS FOR NOVA BLASTER?
THAT CONCERT'S BEEN SOLD OUT FOR MONTHS!
ONE NIGHT ONLY. IF WE LEAVE NOW WE CAN MAKE IT.
OH MAN, I DON'T KNOW... WE HAVE FINALS TOMORROW. PLUS THERE'S ONLY FOUR TICKETS, AND LARMINA'S A HUGE FAN.

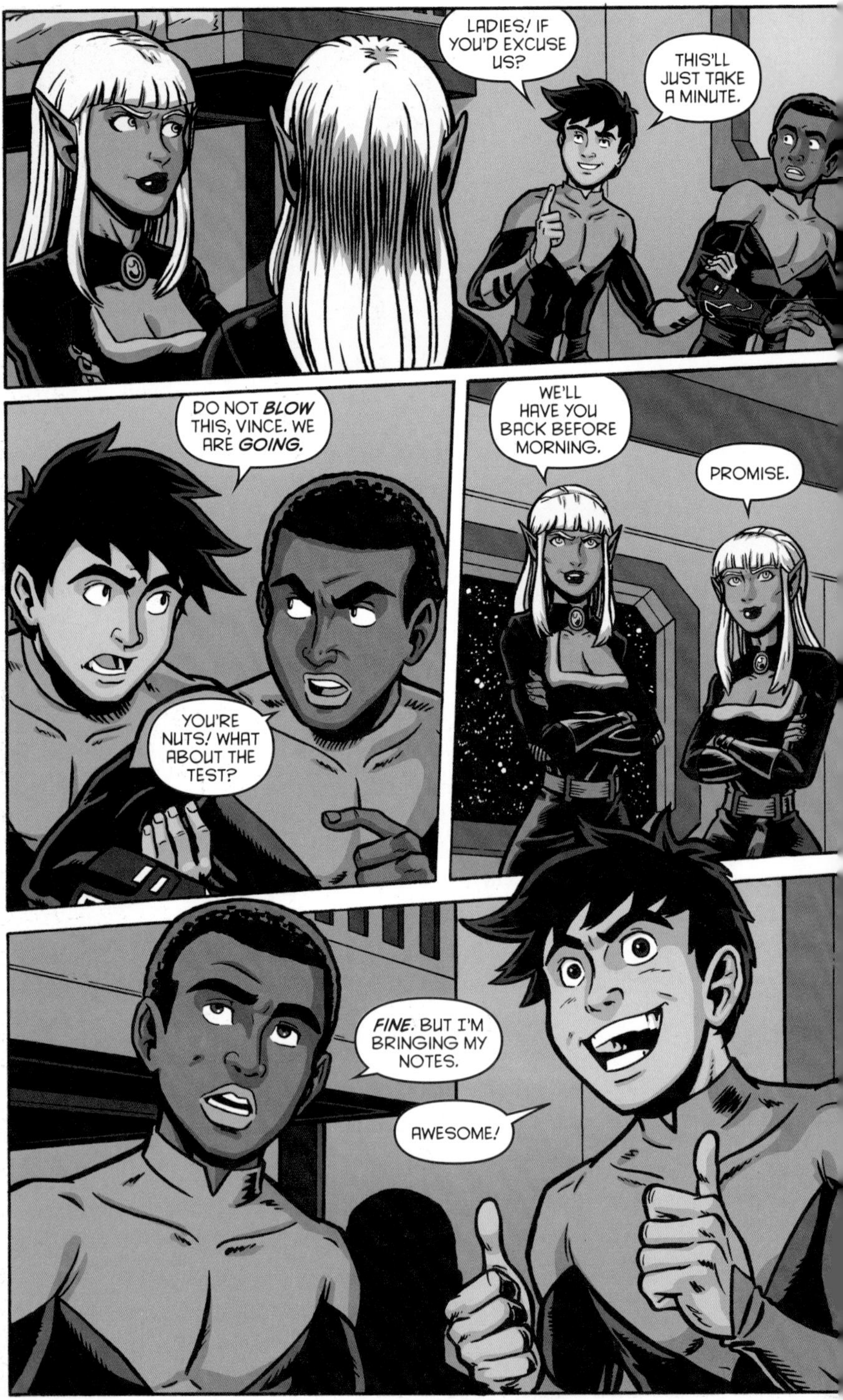
LADIES! IF YOU'D EXCUSE US?
THIS'LL JUST TAKE A MINUTE.
DO NOT **BLOW** THIS, VINCE. WE ARE **GOING.**
YOU'RE NUTS! WHAT ABOUT THE TEST?
WE'LL HAVE YOU BACK BEFORE MORNING.
PROMISE.
FINE. BUT I'M BRINGING MY NOTES.
AWESOME!

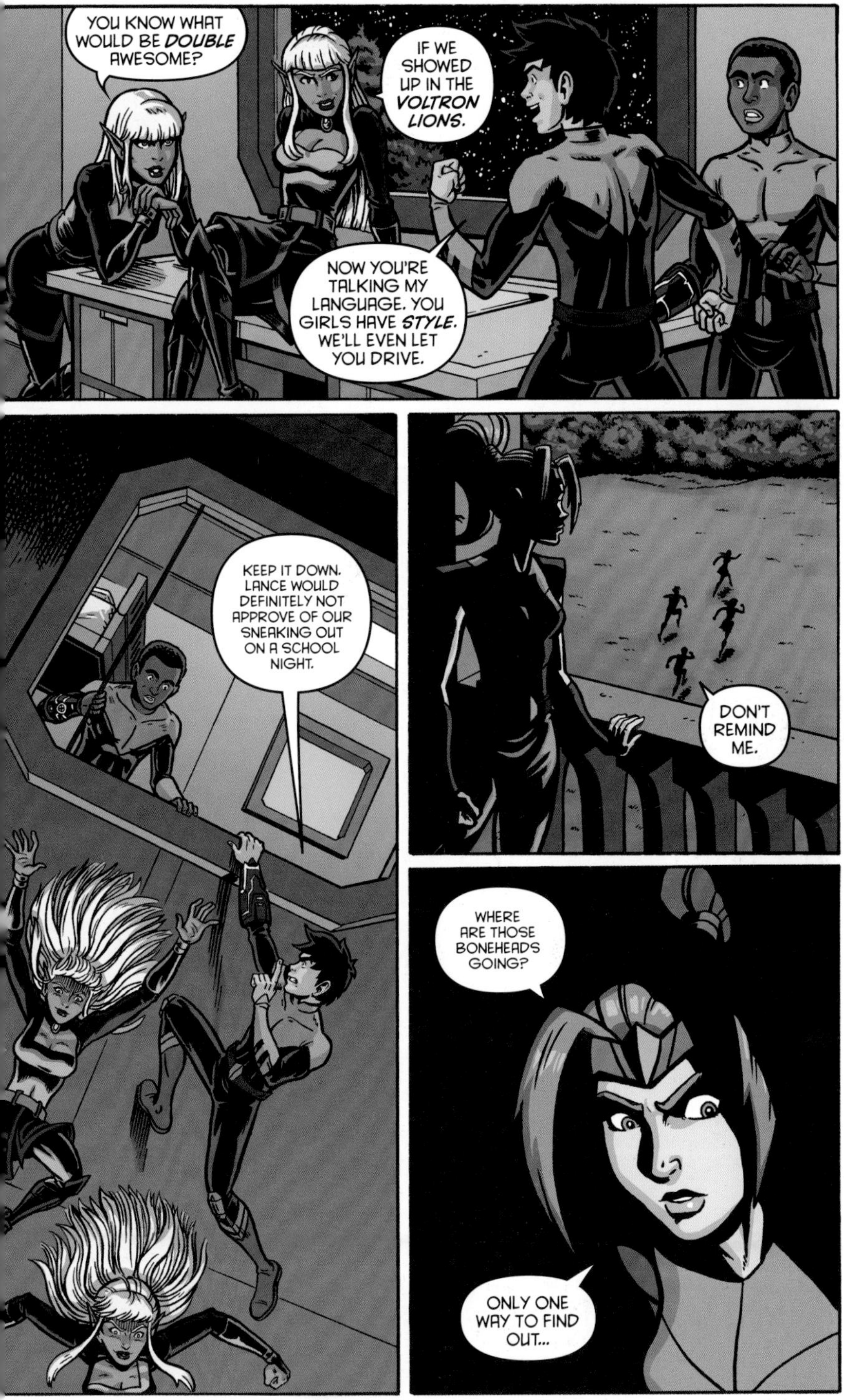
YOU KNOW WHAT WOULD BE DOUBLE AWESOME?
IF WE SHOWED UP IN THE VOLTRON LIONS.
NOW YOU'RE TALKING MY LANGUAGE. YOU GIRLS HAVE STYLE. WE'LL EVEN LET YOU DRIVE.
KEEP IT DOWN. LANCE WOULD DEFINITELY NOT APPROVE OF OUR SNEAKING OUT ON A SCHOOL NIGHT.
DON'T REMIND ME.
WHERE ARE THOSE BONEHEADS GOING?
ONLY ONE WAY TO FIND OUT...

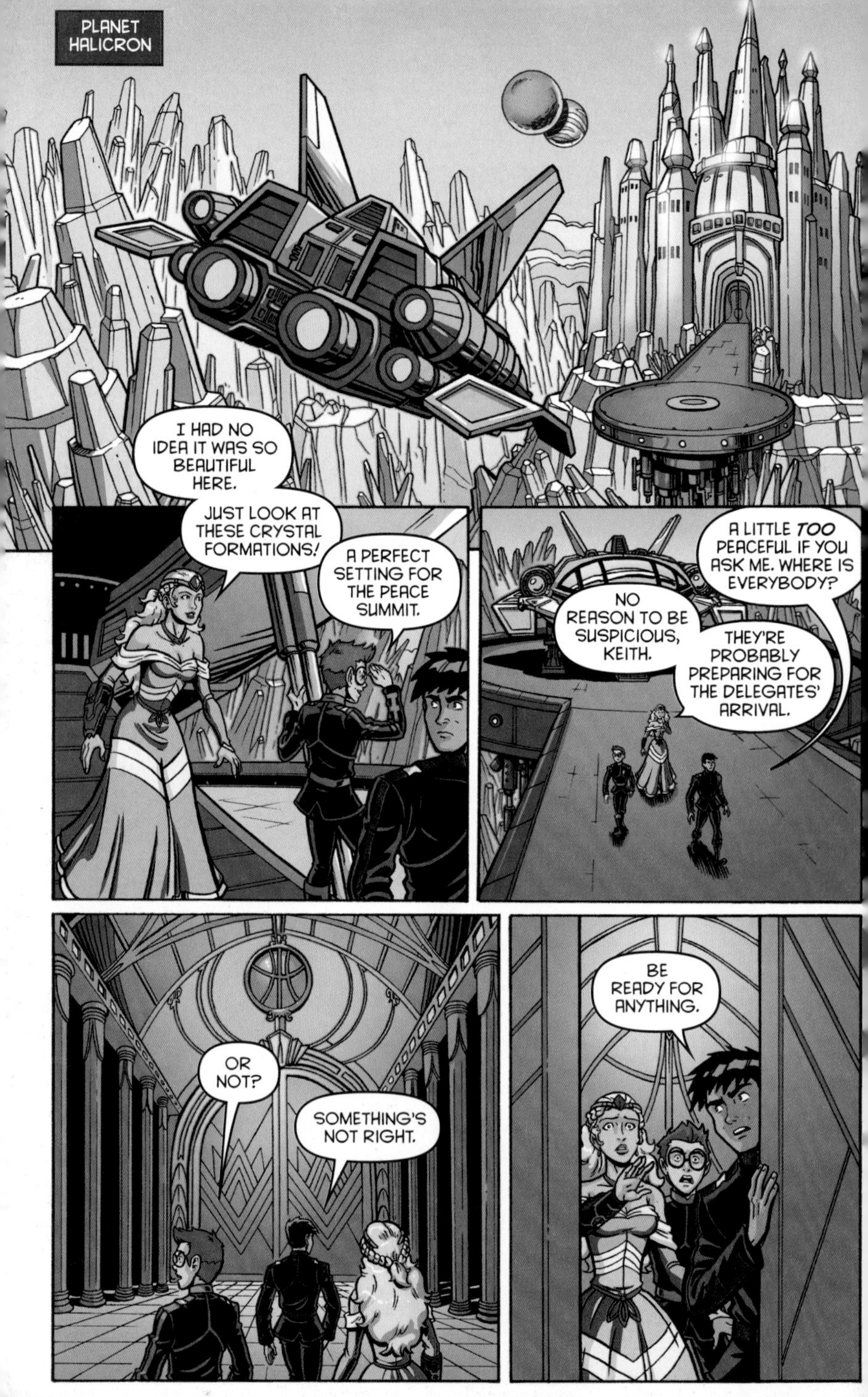
PLANET HALICRON
I HAD NO IDEA IT WAS SO BEAUTIFUL HERE.
JUST LOOK AT THESE CRYSTAL FORMATIONS!
A PERFECT SETTING FOR THE PEACE SUMMIT.
A LITTLE *TOO* PEACEFUL IF YOU ASK ME. WHERE IS EVERYBODY?
NO REASON TO BE SUSPICIOUS, KEITH.
THEY'RE PROBABLY PREPARING FOR THE DELEGATES' ARRIVAL.
OR NOT?
SOMETHING'S NOT RIGHT.
BE READY FOR ANYTHING.

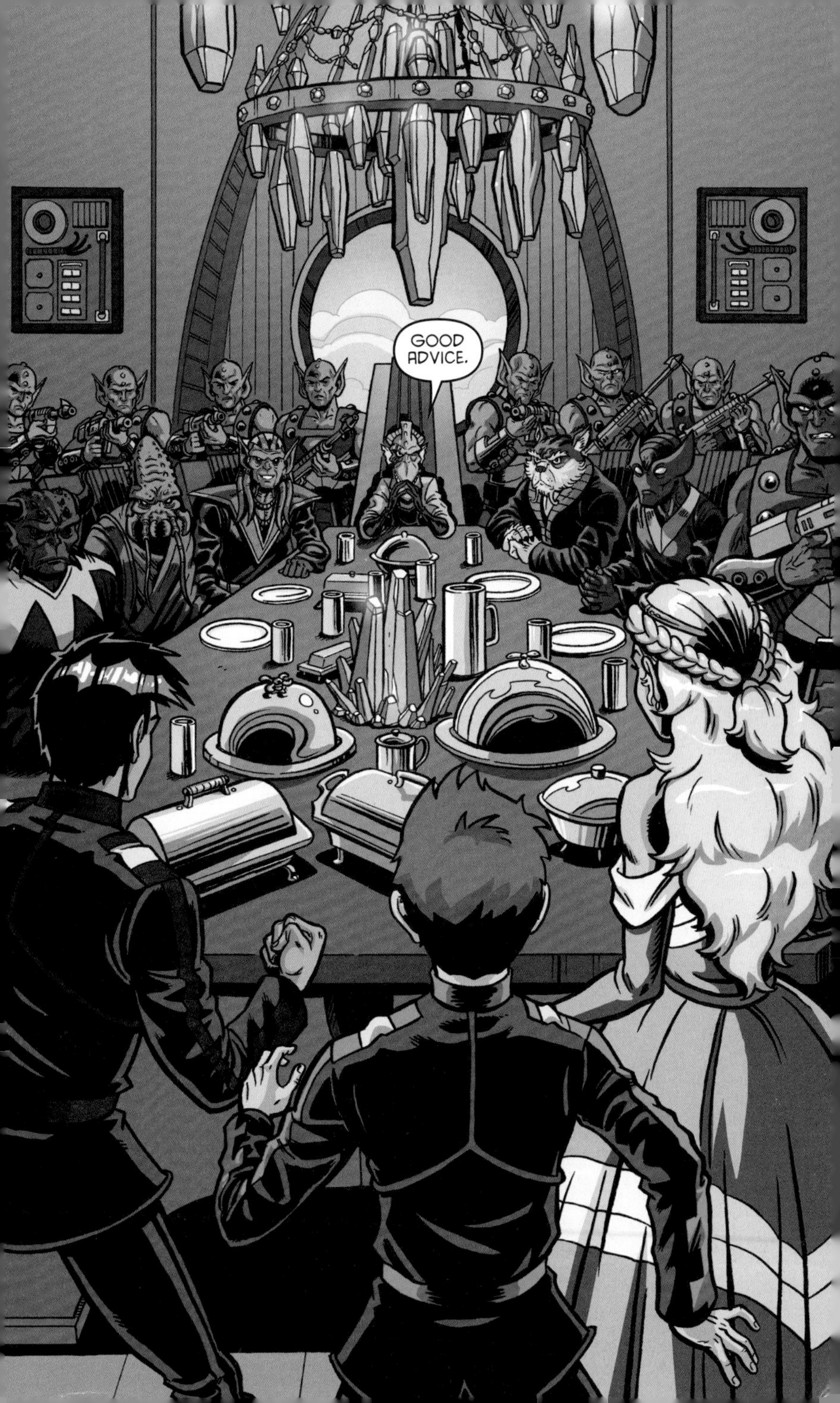
GOOD ADVICE.

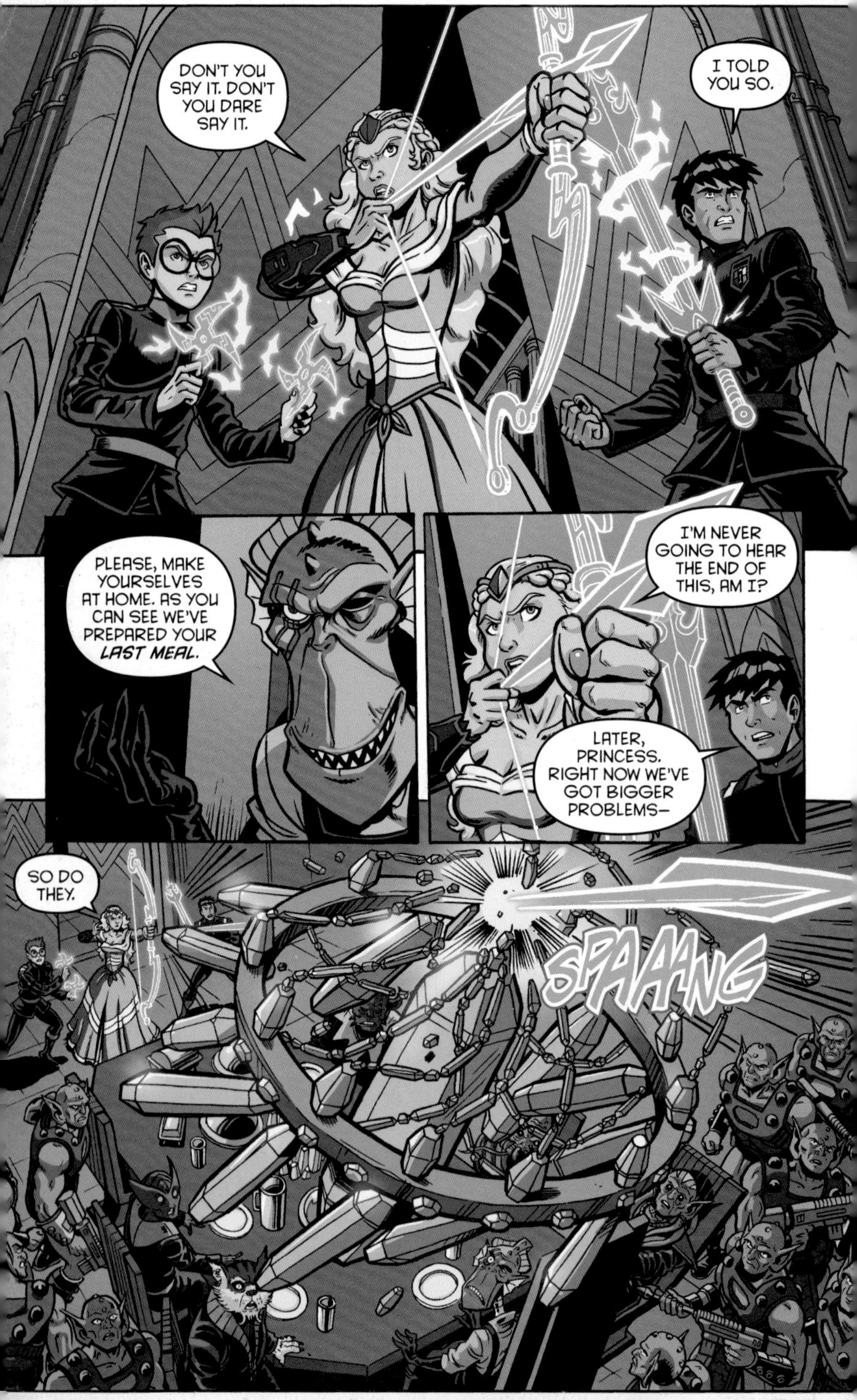
DON'T YOU SAY IT. DON'T YOU DARE SAY IT.
I TOLD YOU SO.
PLEASE, MAKE YOURSELVES AT HOME. AS YOU CAN SEE WE'VE PREPARED YOUR *LAST MEAL.*
I'M NEVER GOING TO HEAR THE END OF THIS, AM I?
LATER, PRINCESS. RIGHT NOW WE'VE GOT BIGGER PROBLEMS—
SO DO THEY.
SPAAANG

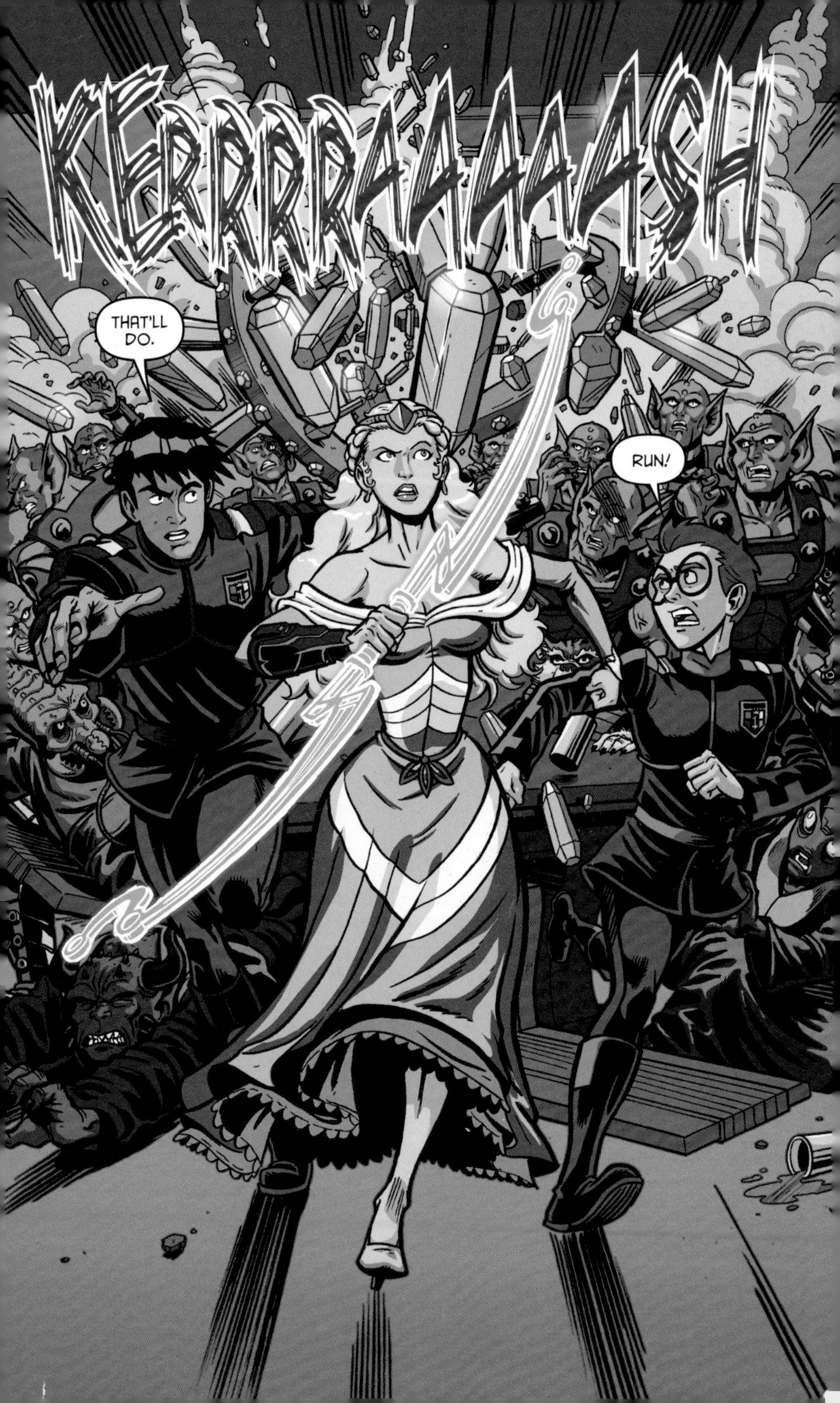
KERRRRAAAAASH
THAT'LL DO.
RUN!

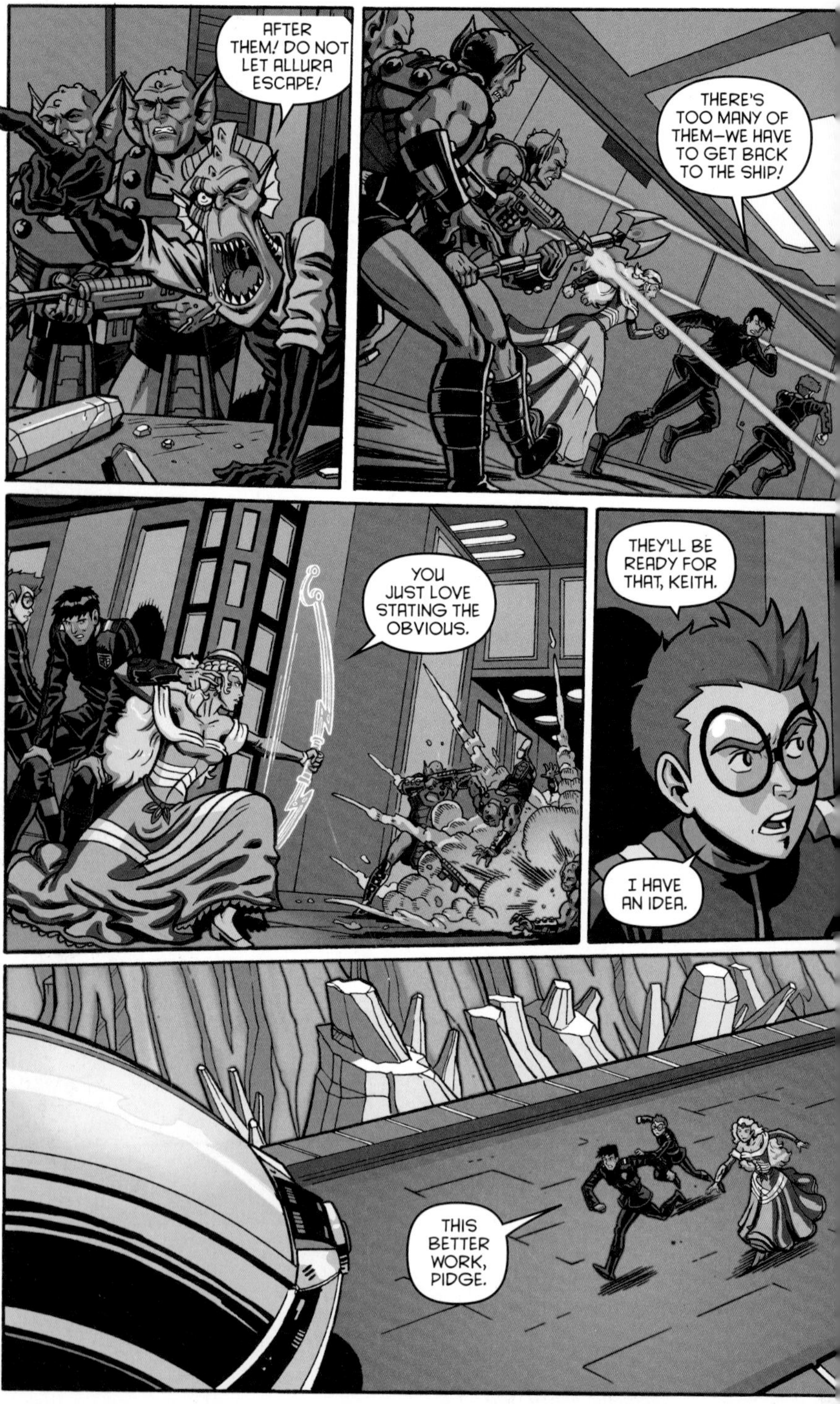
AFTER THEM! DO NOT LET ALLURA ESCAPE!
THERE'S TOO MANY OF THEM—WE HAVE TO GET BACK TO THE SHIP!
YOU JUST LOVE STATING THE OBVIOUS.
THEY'LL BE READY FOR THAT, KEITH.
I HAVE AN IDEA.
THIS BETTER WORK, PIDGE.

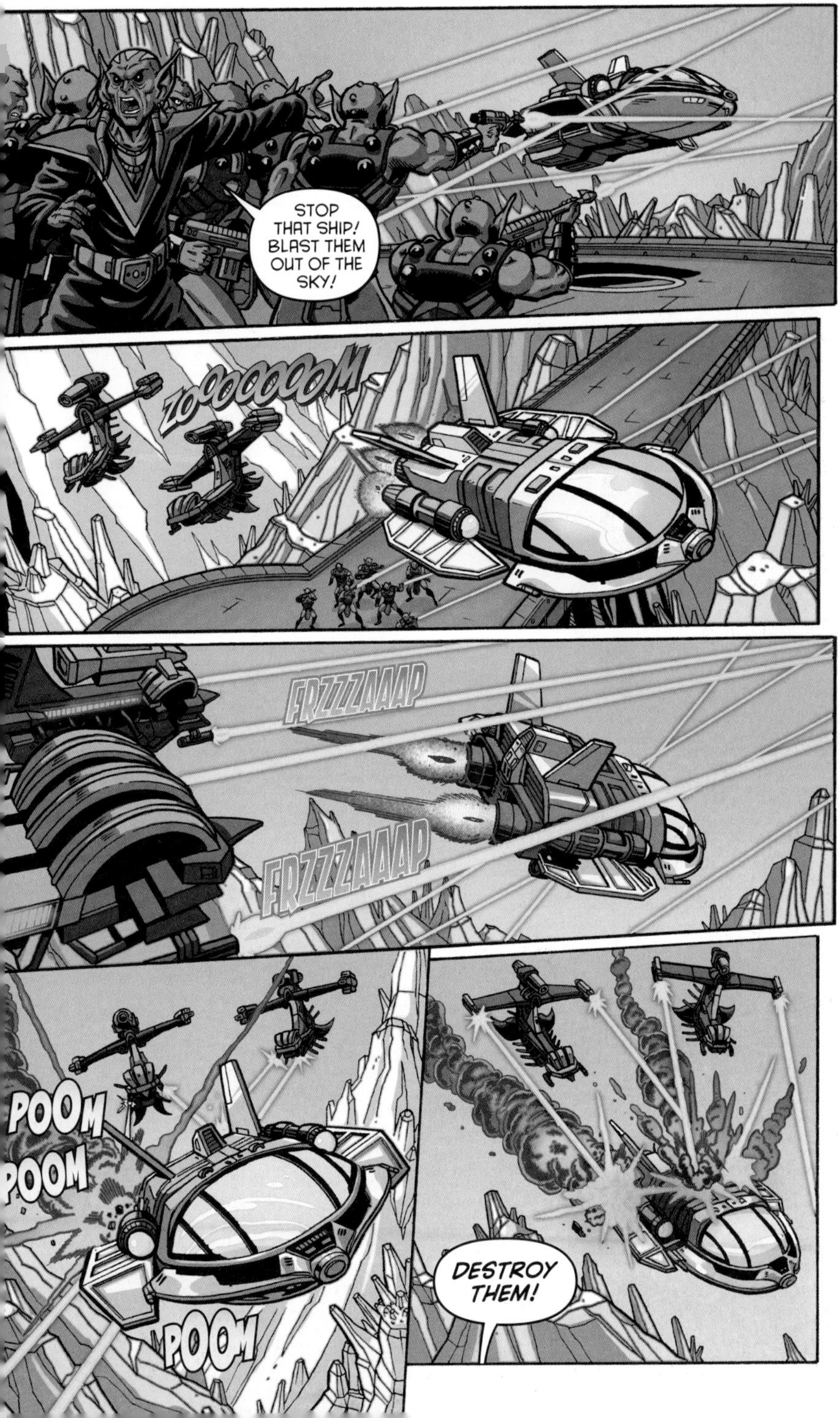
STOP THAT SHIP! BLAST THEM OUT OF THE SKY!
ZOOOOOOOOM
FRZZZAAAP
FRZZZAAAP
POOM
POOM
POOM
DESTROY THEM!

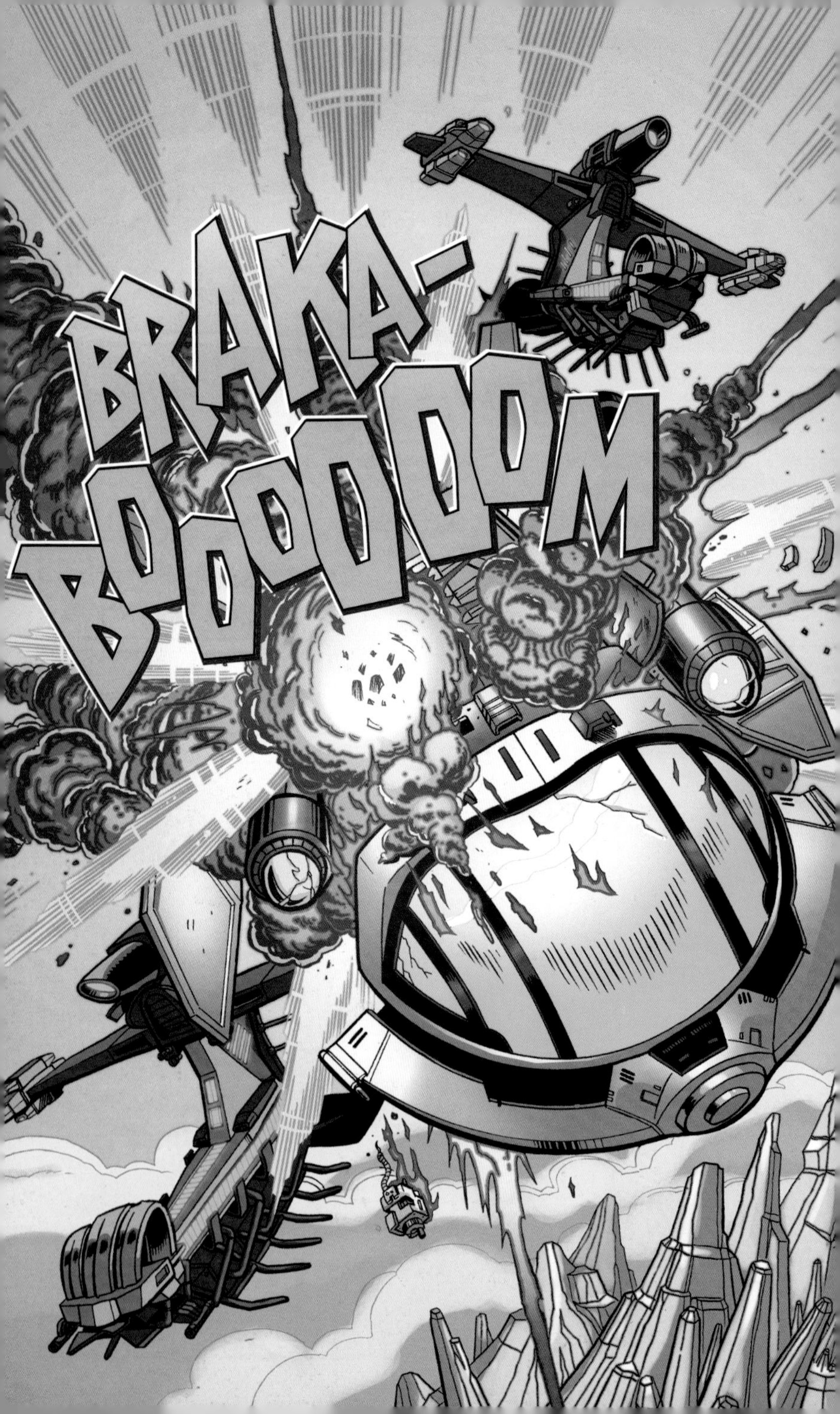
BRAKA-
BOOOOOOM

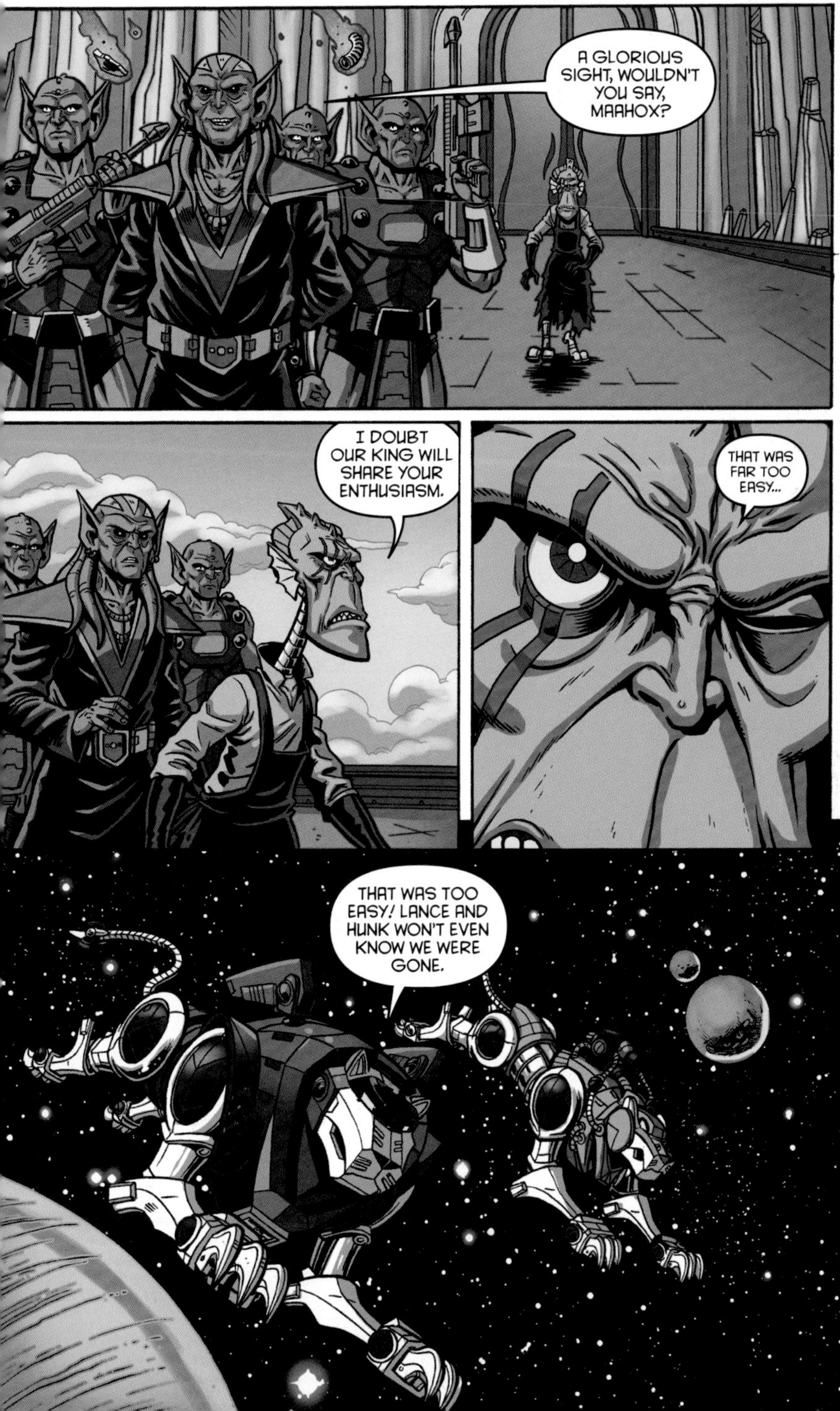
A GLORIOUS SIGHT, WOULDN'T YOU SAY, MAAHOX?
I DOUBT OUR KING WILL SHARE YOUR ENTHUSIASM.
THAT WAS FAR TOO EASY...
THAT WAS TOO EASY! LANCE AND HUNK WON'T EVEN KNOW WE WERE GONE.

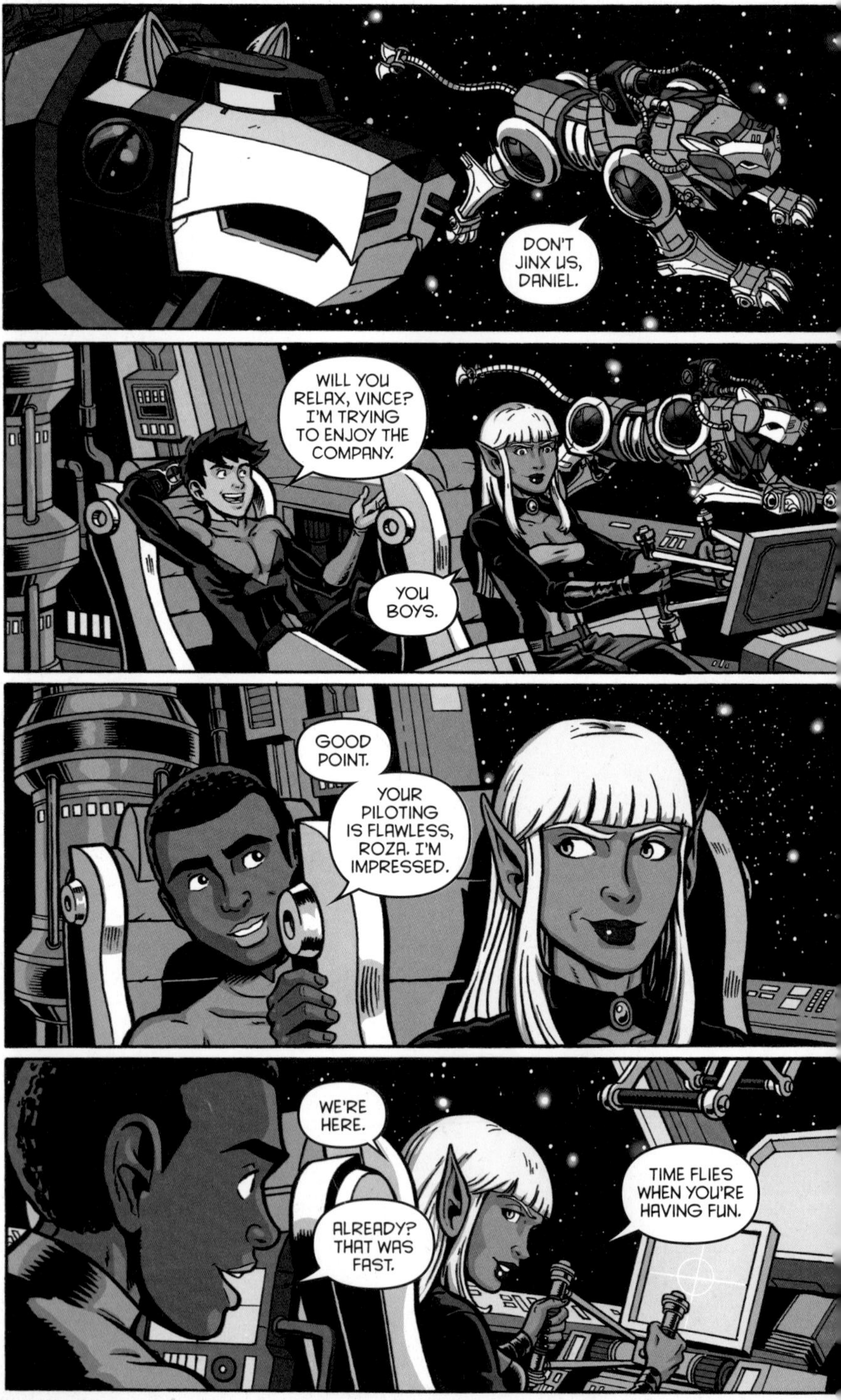
DON'T JINX US, DANIEL.
WILL YOU RELAX, VINCE? I'M TRYING TO ENJOY THE COMPANY.
YOU BOYS.
GOOD POINT.
YOUR PILOTING IS FLAWLESS, ROZA. I'M IMPRESSED.
WE'RE HERE.
ALREADY? THAT WAS FAST.
TIME FLIES WHEN YOU'RE HAVING FUN.

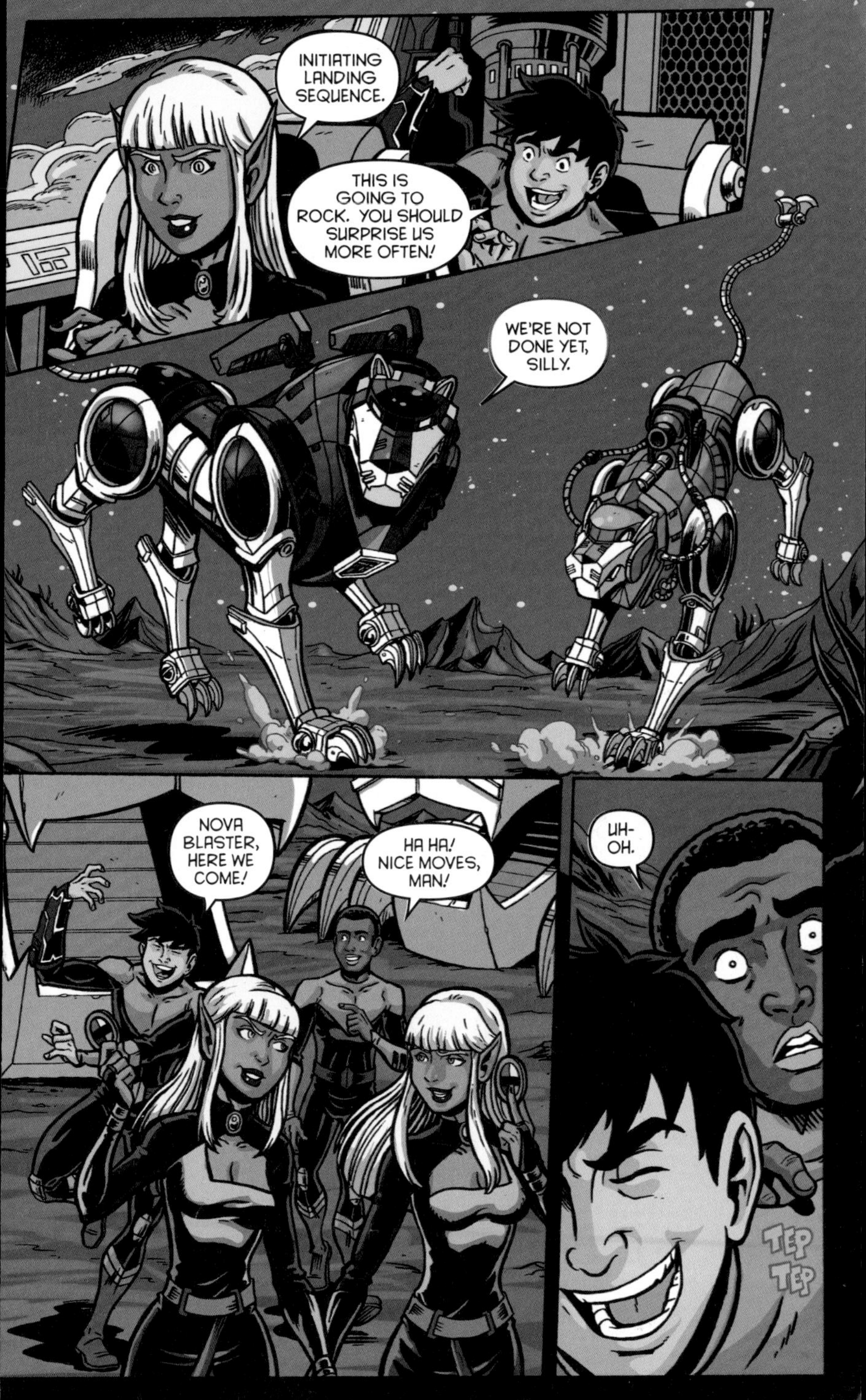
INITIATING LANDING SEQUENCE.
THIS IS GOING TO ROCK. YOU SHOULD SURPRISE US MORE OFTEN!
WE'RE NOT DONE YET, SILLY.
NOVA BLASTER, HERE WE COME!
HA HA! NICE MOVES, MAN!
UH-OH.
TEP TEP

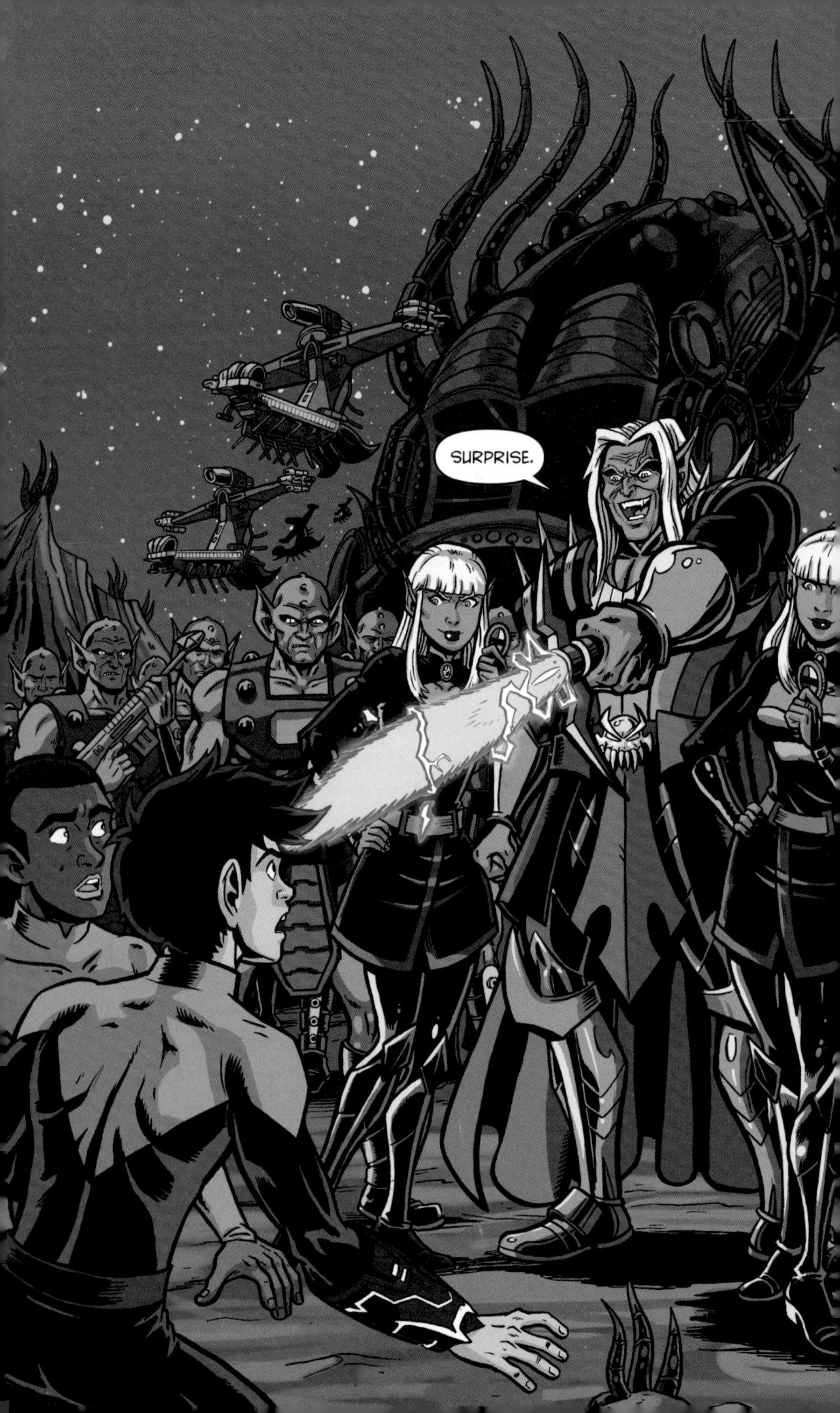
SURPRISE.

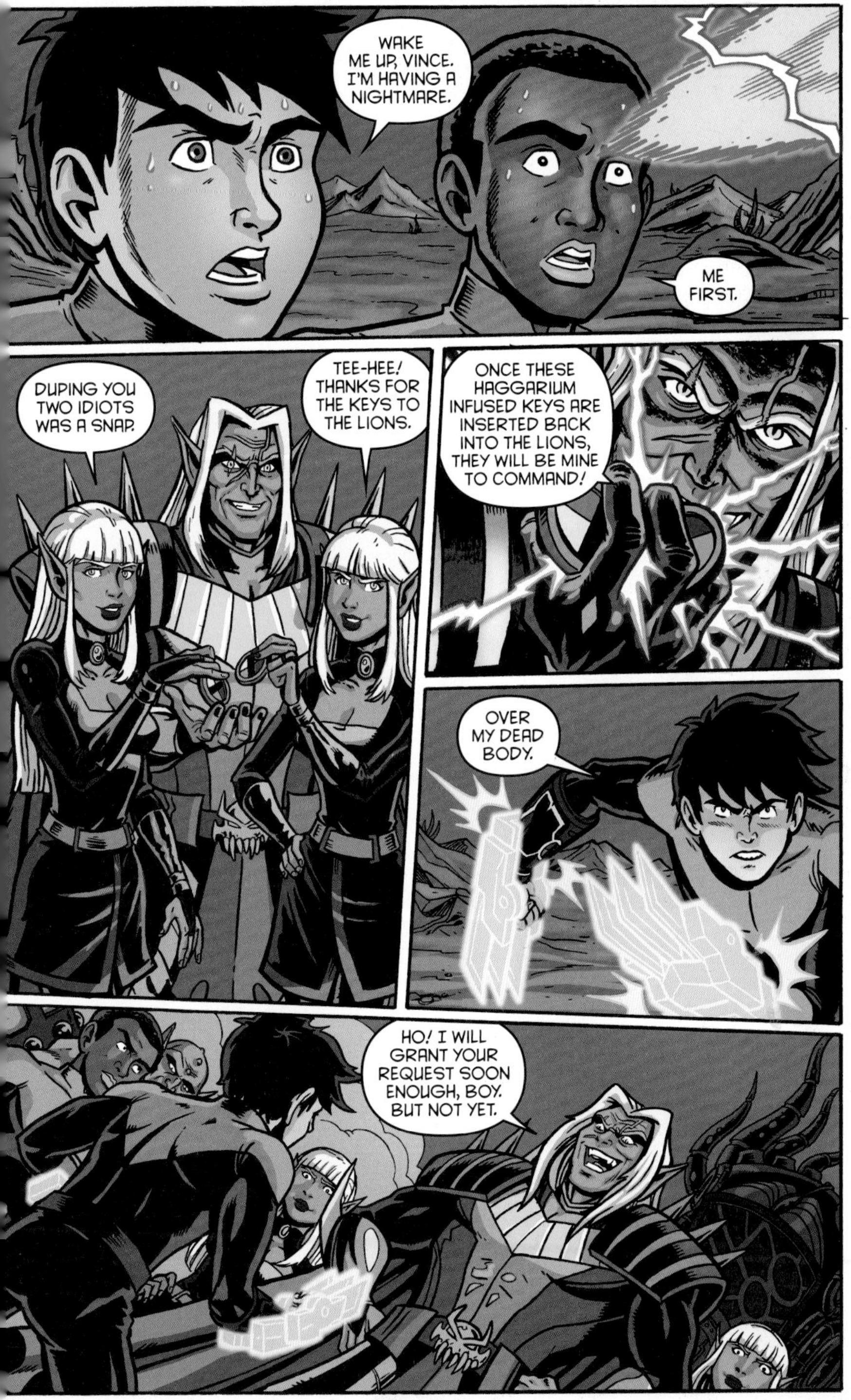
WAKE ME UP, VINCE. I'M HAVING A NIGHTMARE.
ME FIRST.
DUPING YOU TWO IDIOTS WAS A SNAP.
TEE-HEE! THANKS FOR THE KEYS TO THE LIONS.
ONCE THESE HAGGARIUM INFUSED KEYS ARE INSERTED BACK INTO THE LIONS, THEY WILL BE MINE TO COMMAND!
OVER MY DEAD BODY.
HO! I WILL GRANT YOUR REQUEST SOON ENOUGH, BOY. BUT NOT YET.

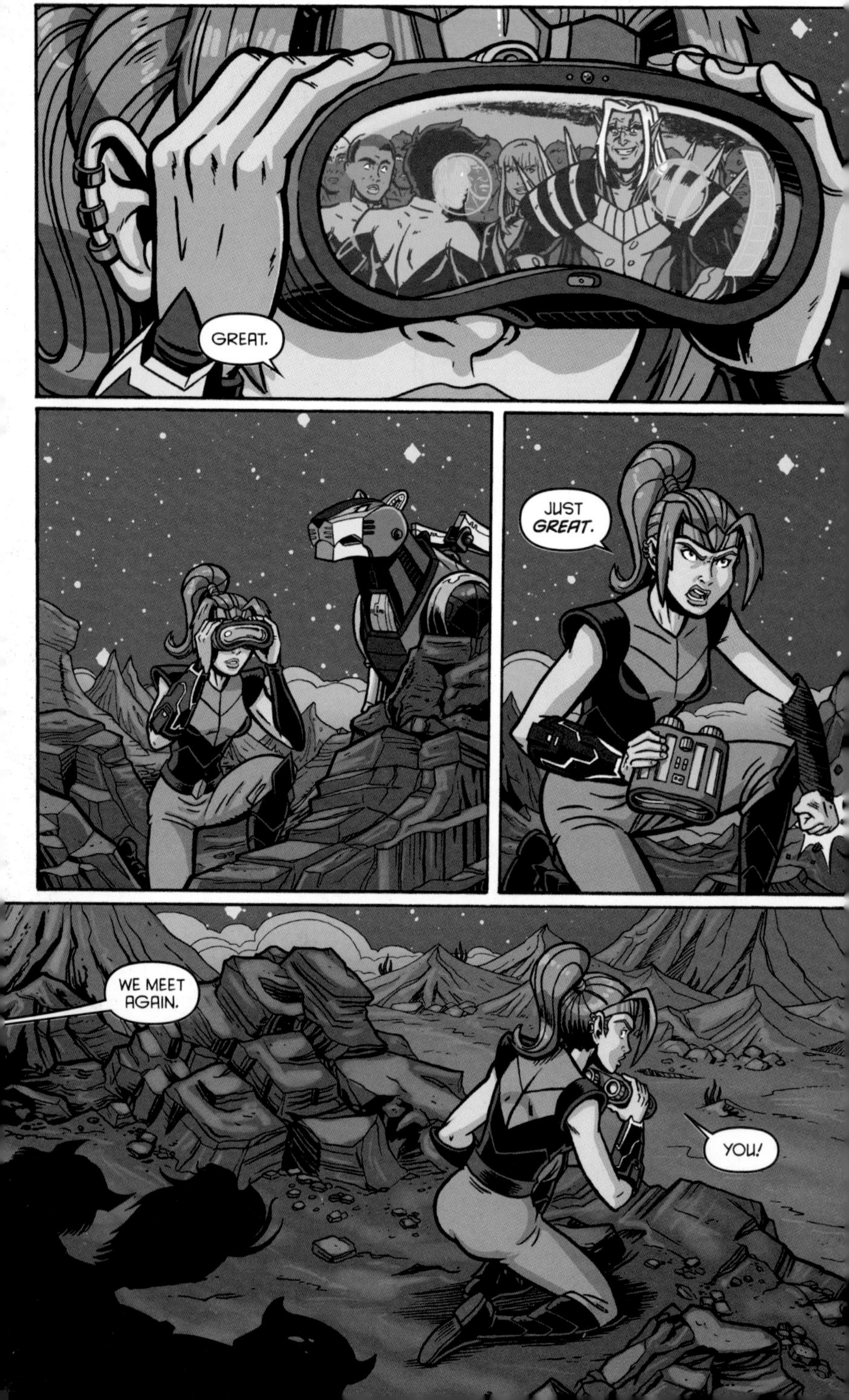
GREAT.
JUST GREAT.
WE MEET AGAIN.
YOU!

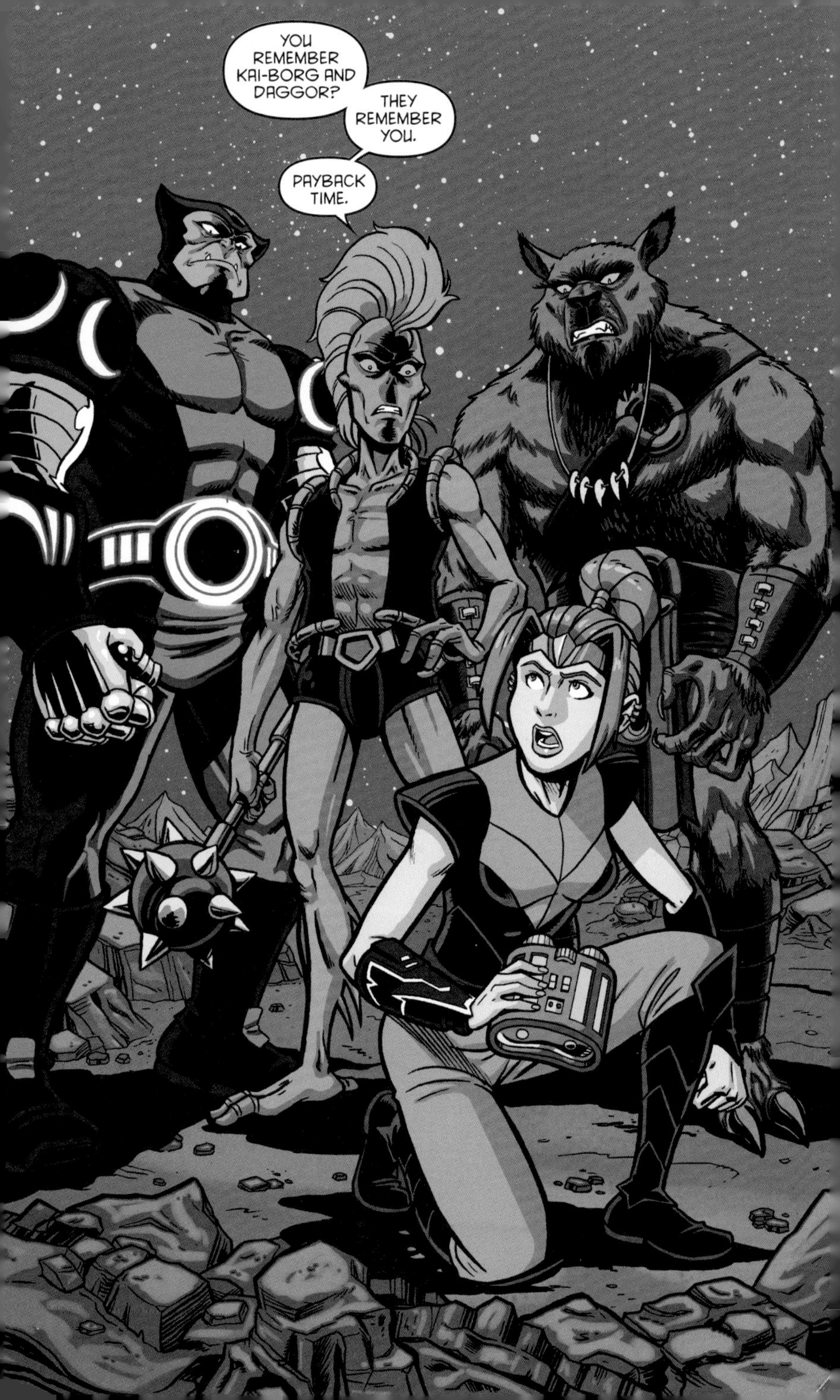
YOU REMEMBER KAI-BORG AND DAGGOR?
THEY REMEMBER YOU.
PAYBACK TIME.

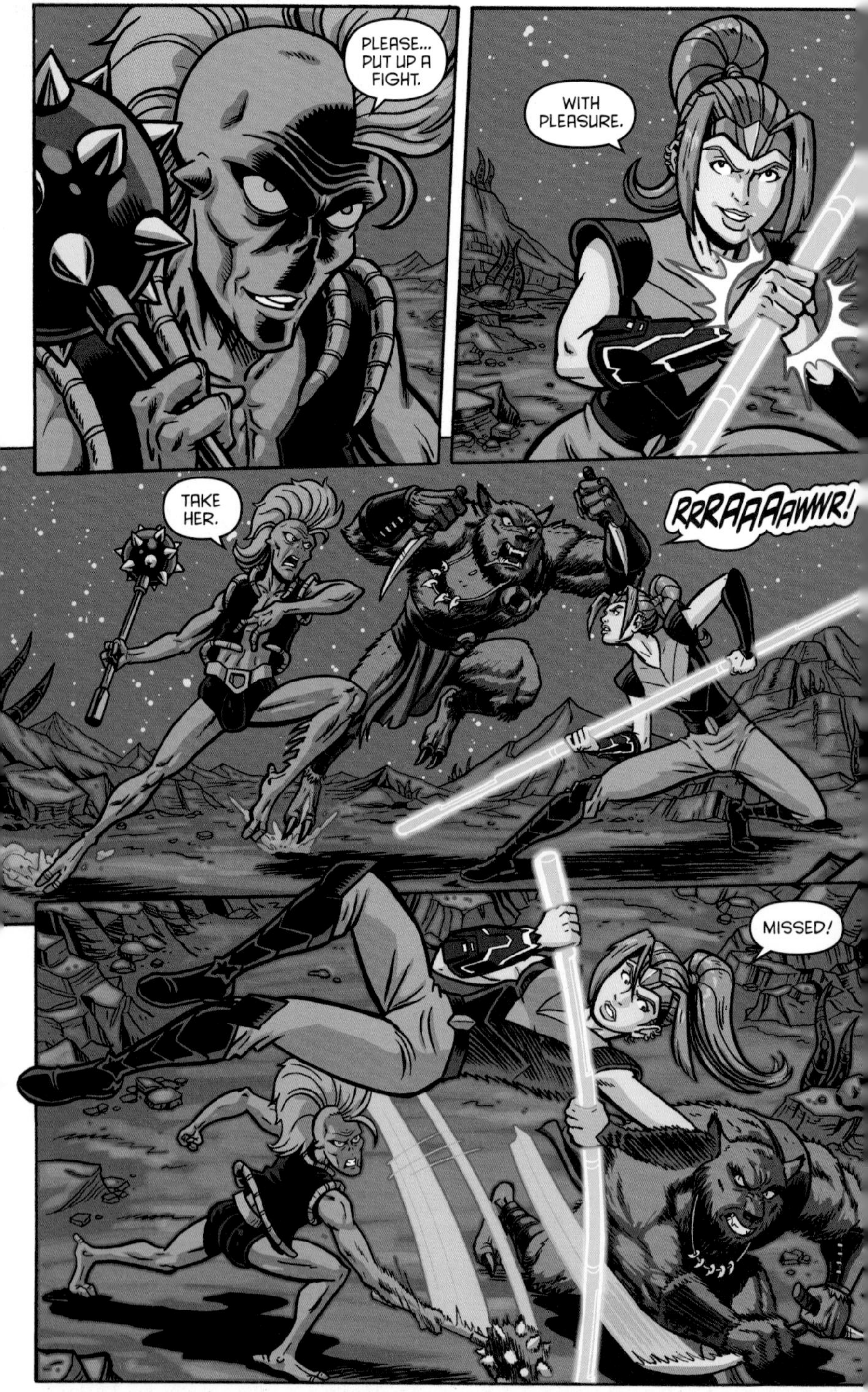
PLEASE... PUT UP A FIGHT.
WITH PLEASURE.
TAKE HER.
RRRAAAAAWWR!
MISSED!

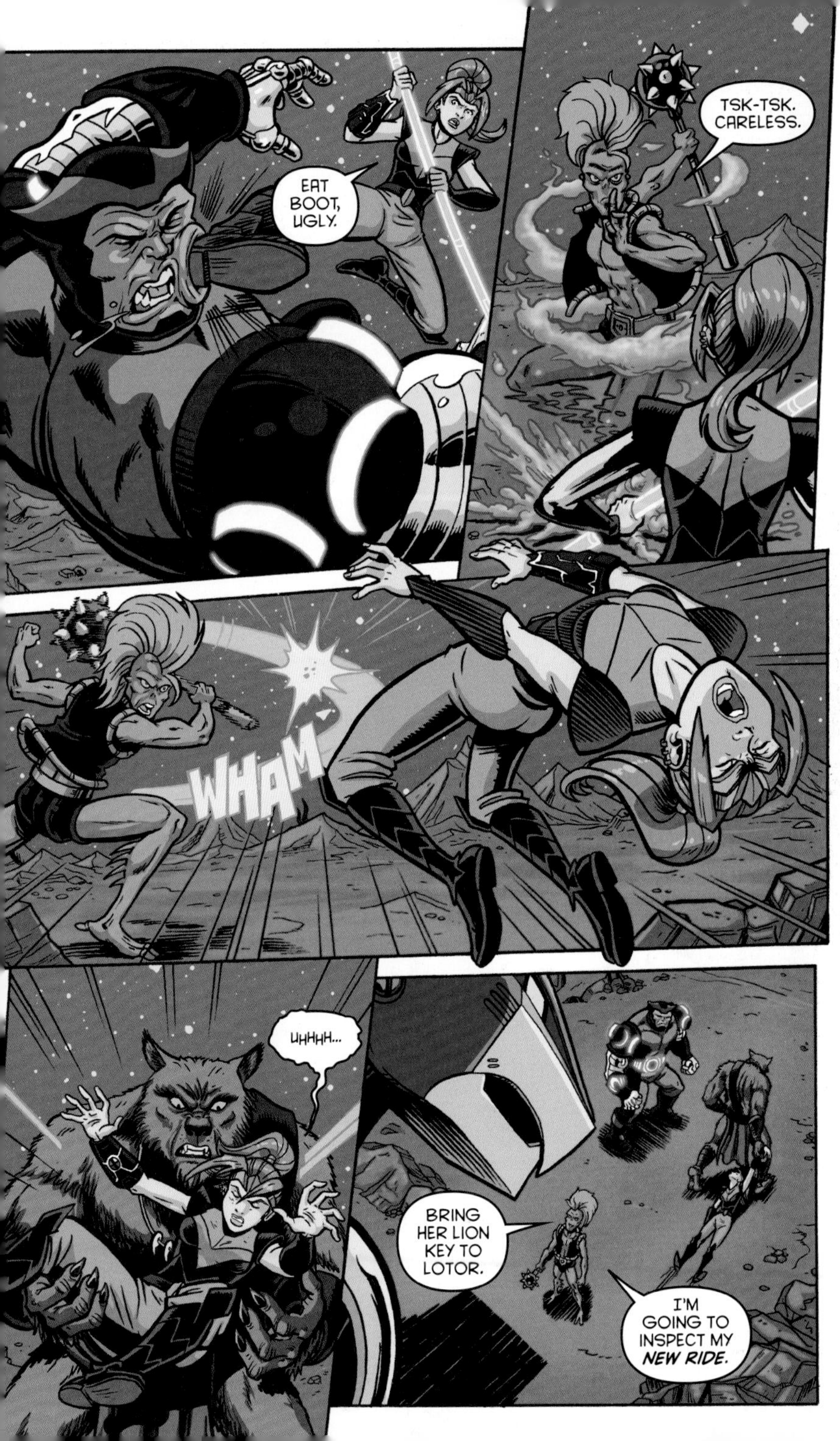
EAT BOOT, UGLY.
TSK-TSK. CARELESS.
WHAM
UHHHH...
BRING HER LION KEY TO LOTOR.
I'M GOING TO INSPECT MY NEW RIDE.

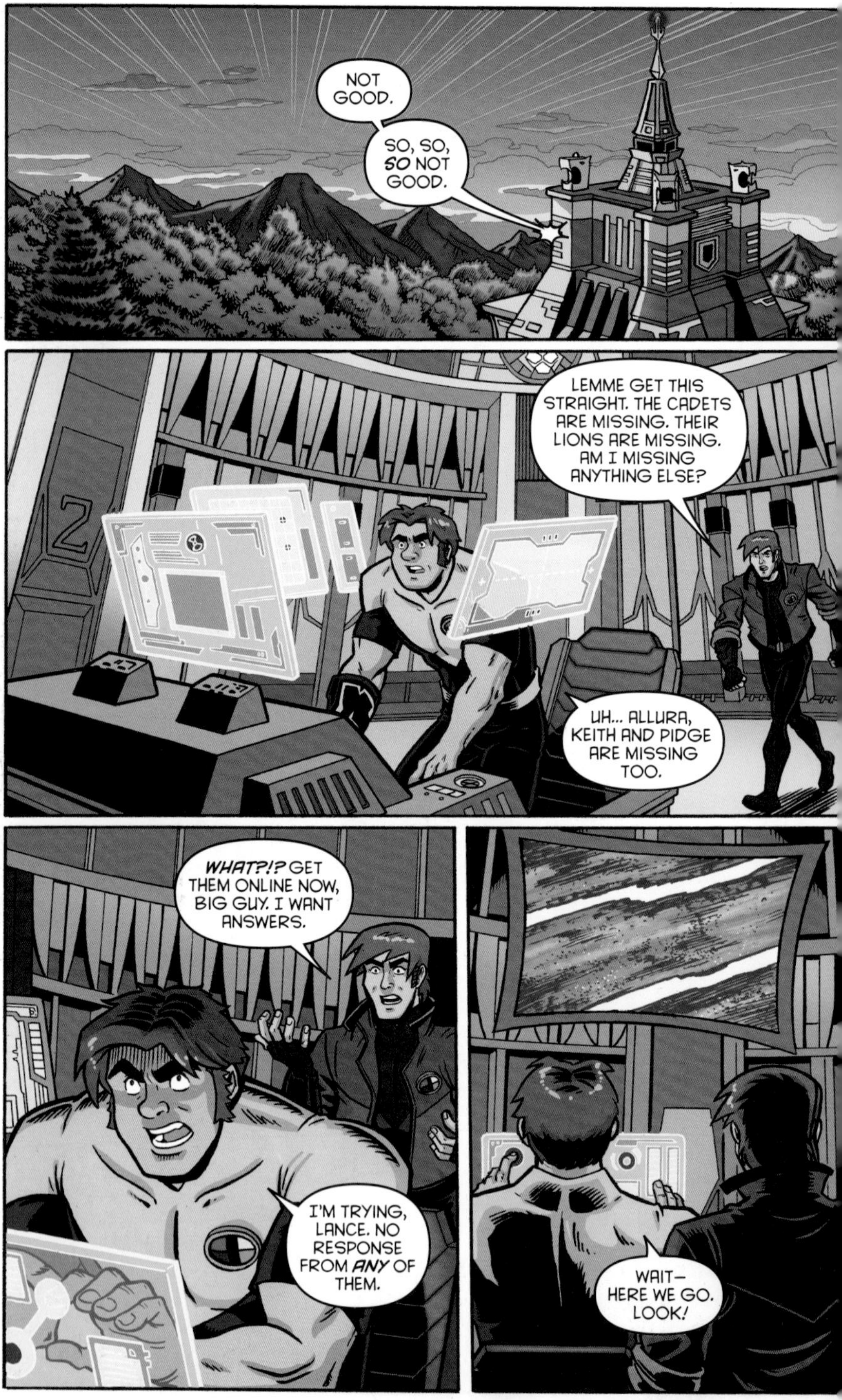
NOT GOOD.
SO, SO, SO NOT GOOD.
LEMME GET THIS STRAIGHT. THE CADETS ARE MISSING. THEIR LIONS ARE MISSING. AM I MISSING ANYTHING ELSE?
UH... ALLURA, KEITH AND PIDGE ARE MISSING TOO.
WHAT?!? GET THEM ONLINE NOW, BIG GUY. I WANT ANSWERS.
I'M TRYING, LANCE. NO RESPONSE FROM ANY OF THEM.
WAIT— HERE WE GO. LOOK!

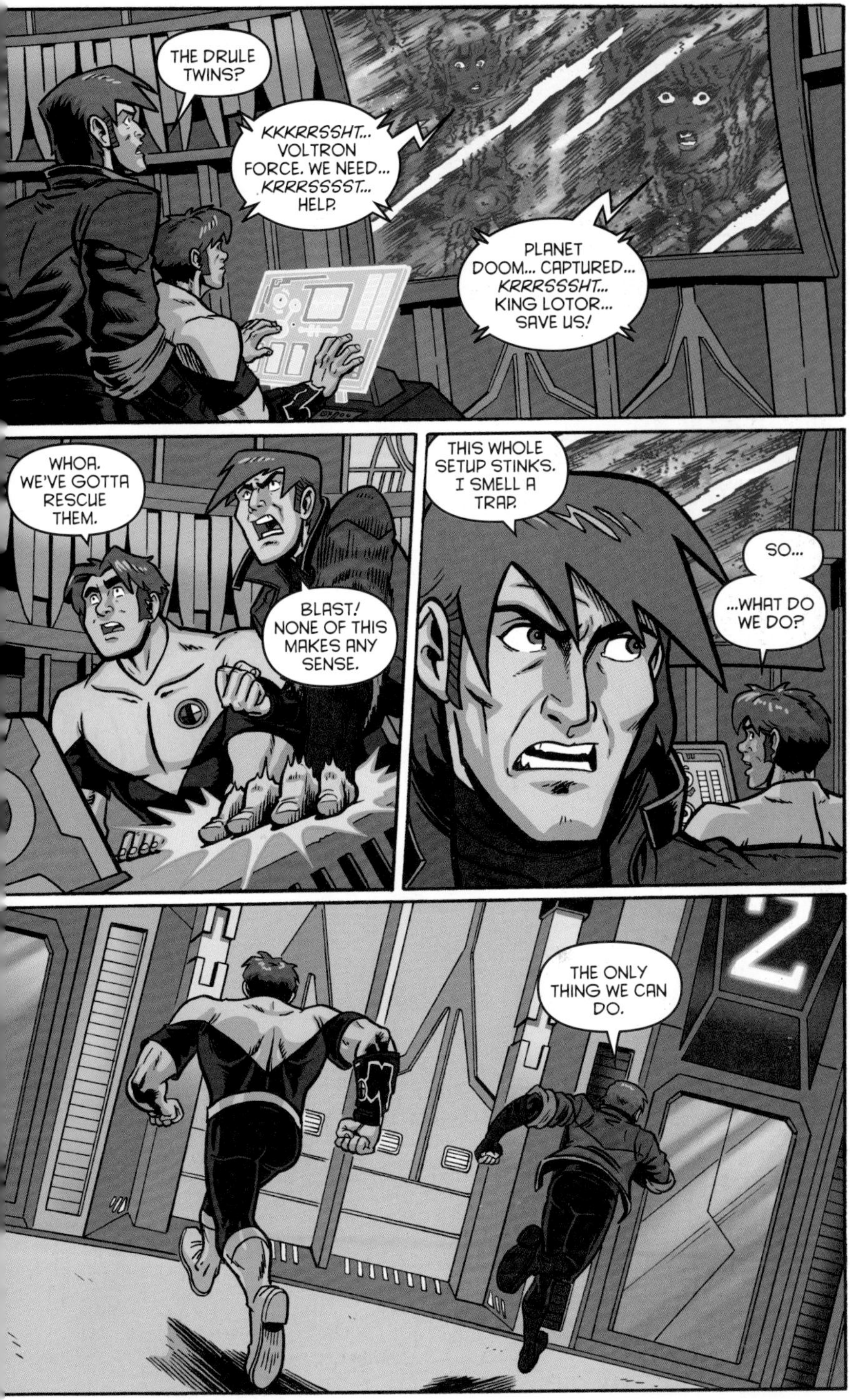
THE DRULE TWINS?
KKKRRSSHT... VOLTRON FORCE. WE NEED... KRRRSSSST... HELP.
PLANET DOOM... CAPTURED... KRRRSSSHT... KING LOTOR... SAVE US!
WHOA. WE'VE GOTTA RESCUE THEM.
BLAST! NONE OF THIS MAKES ANY SENSE.
THIS WHOLE SETUP STINKS. I SMELL A TRAP.
SO...
...WHAT DO WE DO?
THE ONLY THING WE CAN DO.

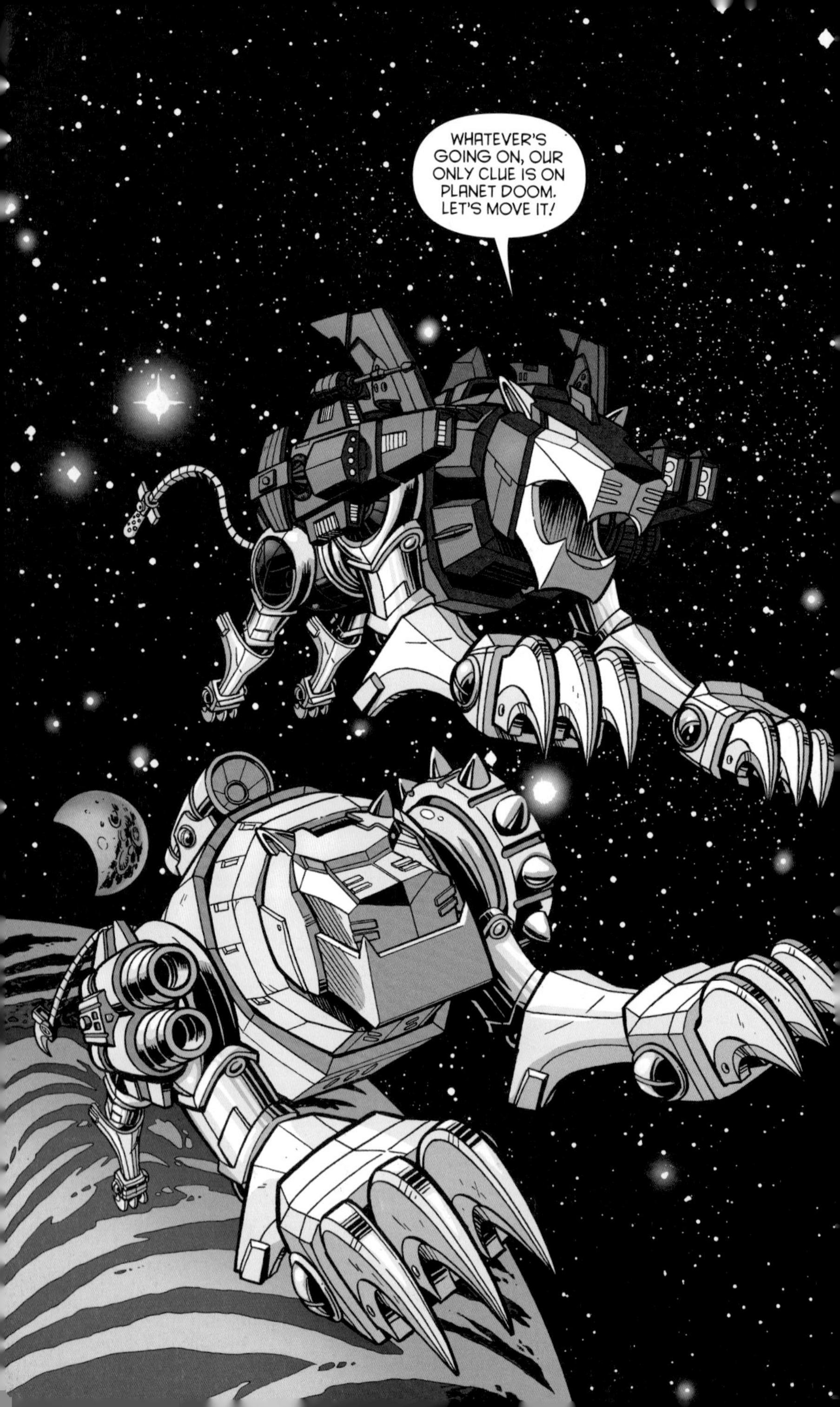
WHATEVER'S GOING ON, OUR ONLY CLUE IS ON PLANET DOOM. LET'S MOVE IT!

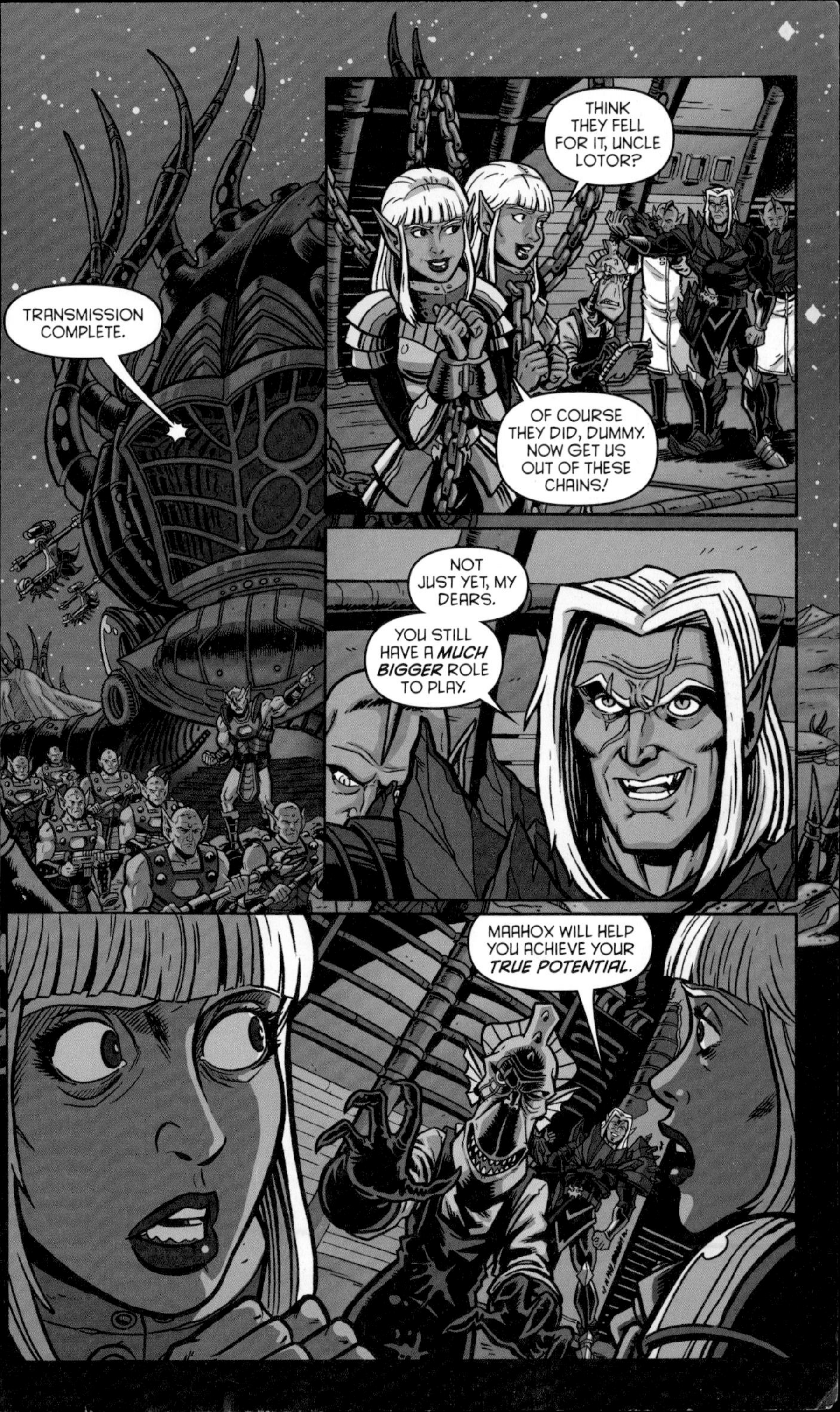

TRANSMISSION COMPLETE.
THINK THEY FELL FOR IT, UNCLE LOTOR?
OF COURSE THEY DID, DUMMY. NOW GET US OUT OF THESE CHAINS!
NOT JUST YET, MY DEARS.
YOU STILL HAVE A *MUCH BIGGER* ROLE TO PLAY.
MAAHOX WILL HELP YOU ACHIEVE YOUR *TRUE POTENTIAL*.

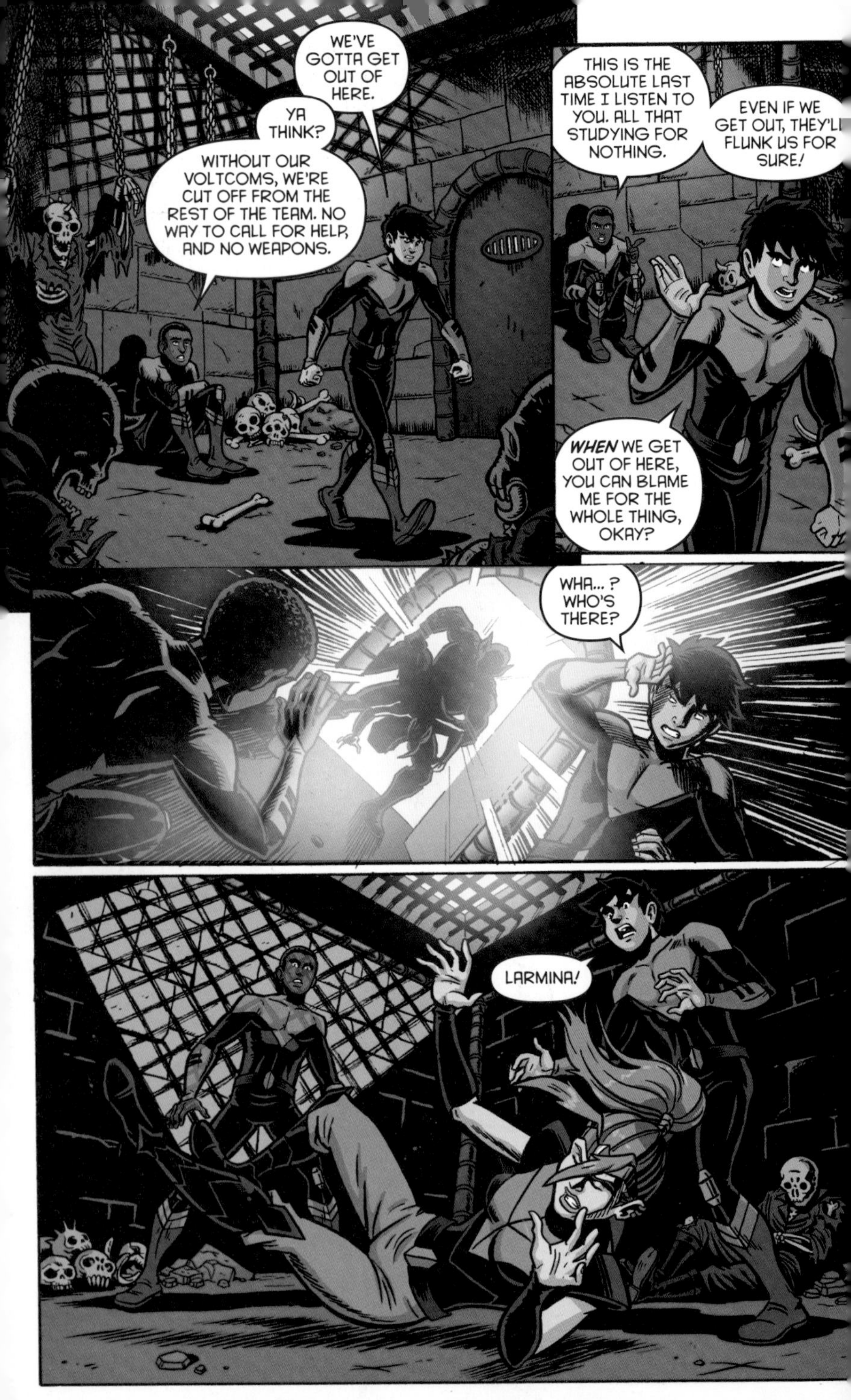
WE'VE GOTTA GET OUT OF HERE.
YA THINK?
WITHOUT OUR VOLTCOMS, WE'RE CUT OFF FROM THE REST OF THE TEAM. NO WAY TO CALL FOR HELP, AND NO WEAPONS.
THIS IS THE ABSOLUTE LAST TIME I LISTEN TO YOU. ALL THAT STUDYING FOR NOTHING.
EVEN IF WE GET OUT, THEY'LL FLUNK US FOR SURE!
WHEN WE GET OUT OF HERE, YOU CAN BLAME ME FOR THE WHOLE THING, OKAY?
WHA... ? WHO'S THERE?
LARMINA!

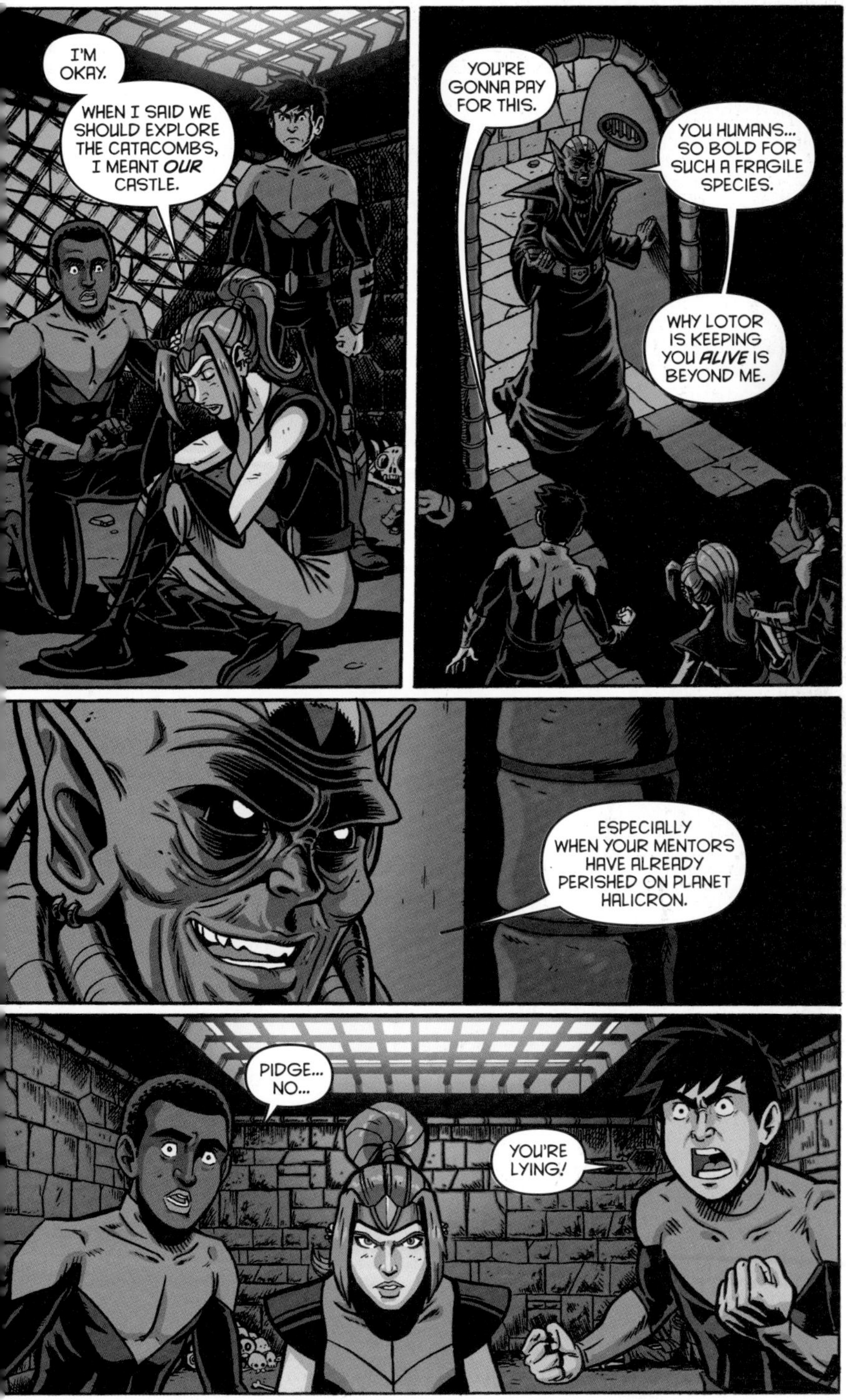
I'M OKAY.
WHEN I SAID WE SHOULD EXPLORE THE CATACOMBS, I MEANT *OUR* CASTLE.
YOU'RE GONNA PAY FOR THIS.
YOU HUMANS... SO BOLD FOR SUCH A FRAGILE SPECIES.
WHY LOTOR IS KEEPING YOU *ALIVE* IS BEYOND ME.
ESPECIALLY WHEN YOUR MENTORS HAVE ALREADY PERISHED ON PLANET HALICRON.
PIDGE... NO...
YOU'RE LYING!

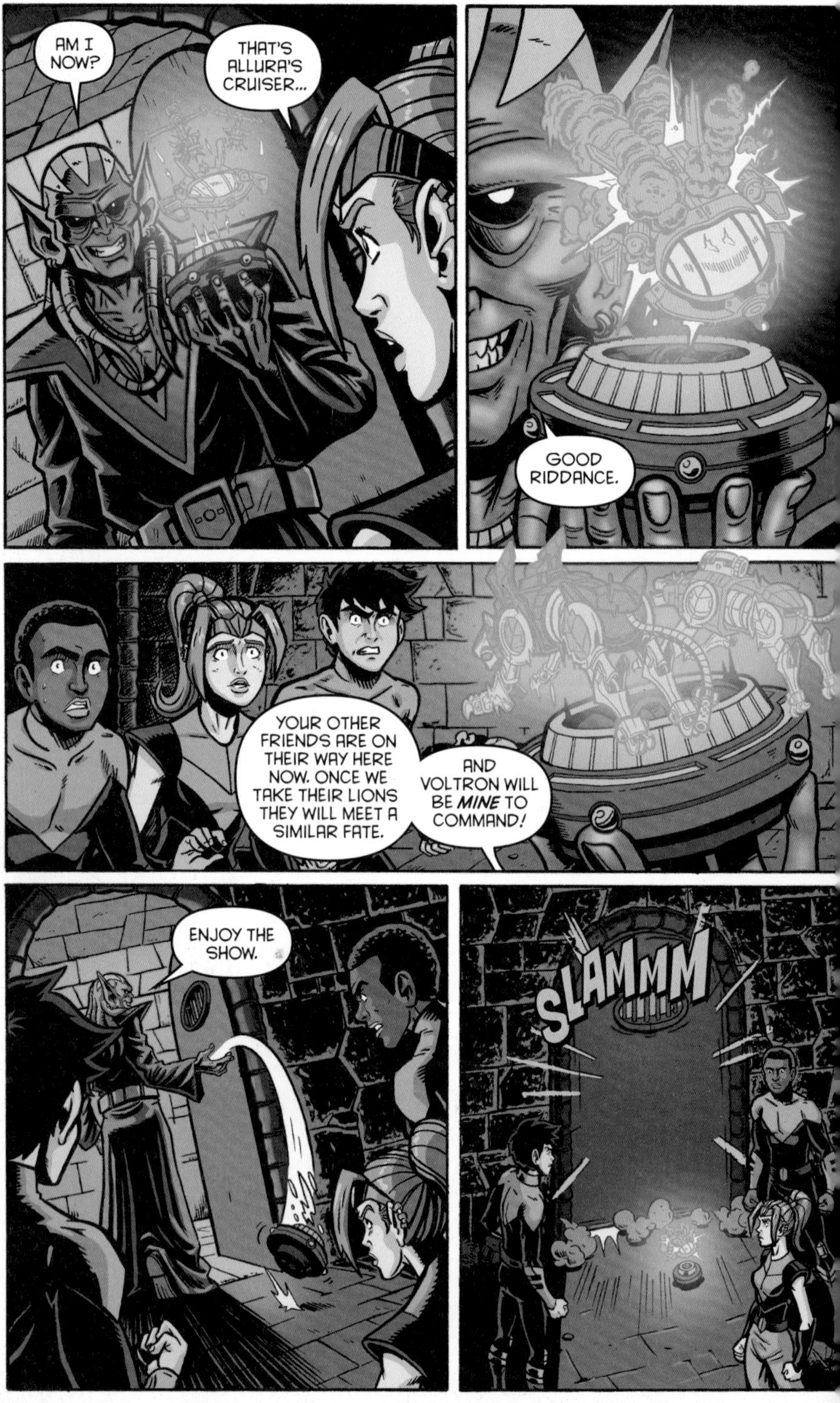

AM I NOW?
THAT'S ALLURA'S CRUISER...
GOOD RIDDANCE.
YOUR OTHER FRIENDS ARE ON THEIR WAY HERE NOW. ONCE WE TAKE THEIR LIONS THEY WILL MEET A SIMILAR FATE.
AND VOLTRON WILL BE *MINE* TO COMMAND!
ENJOY THE SHOW.
SLAMMM

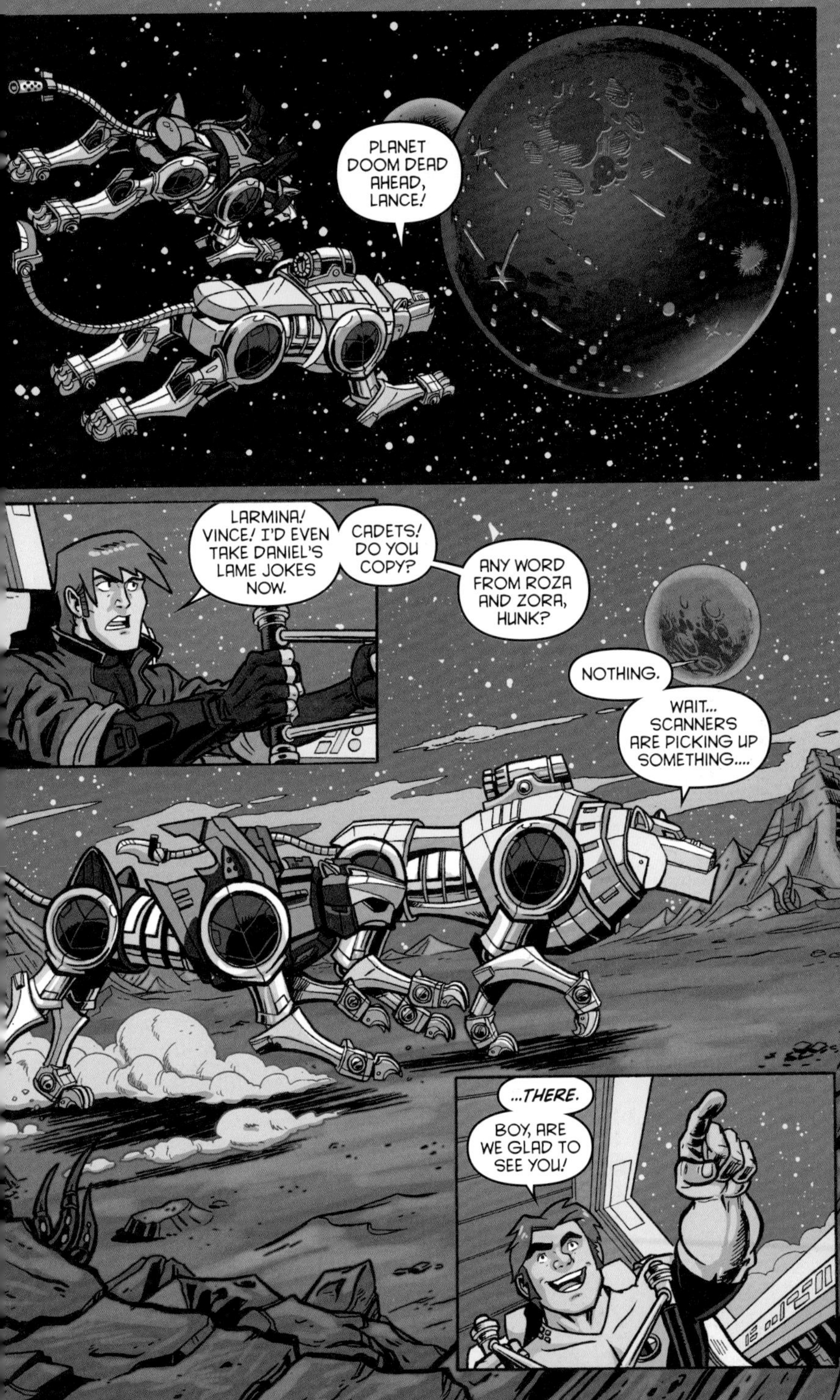
PLANET DOOM DEAD AHEAD, LANCE!
LARMINA! VINCE! I'D EVEN TAKE DANIEL'S LAME JOKES NOW.
CADETS! DO YOU COPY?
ANY WORD FROM ROZA AND ZORA, HUNK?
NOTHING.
WAIT... SCANNERS ARE PICKING UP SOMETHING....
...THERE.
BOY, ARE WE GLAD TO SEE YOU!

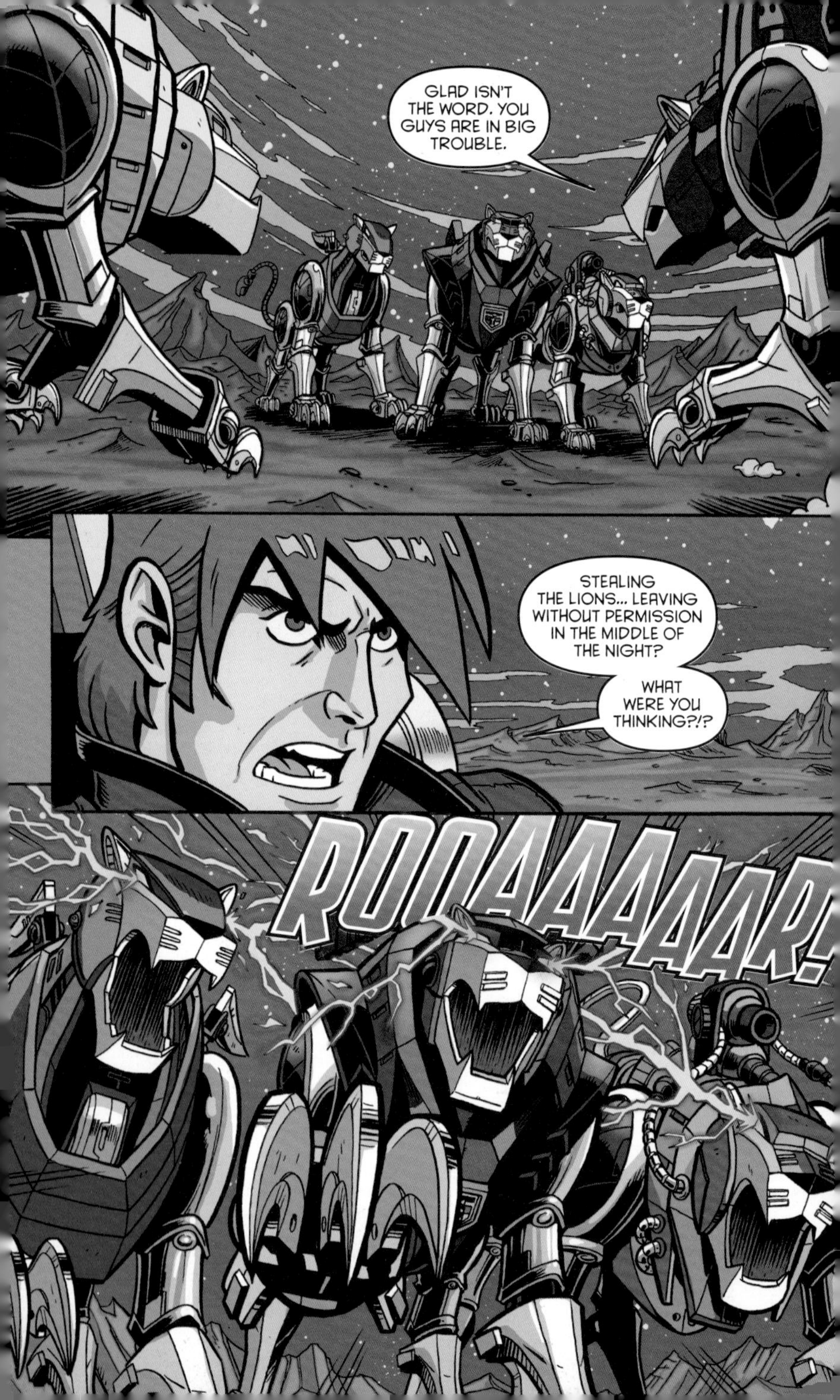
GLAD ISN'T THE WORD. YOU GUYS ARE IN BIG TROUBLE.
STEALING THE LIONS... LEAVING WITHOUT PERMISSION IN THE MIDDLE OF THE NIGHT?
WHAT WERE YOU THINKING?!?
ROOAAAAAAR!

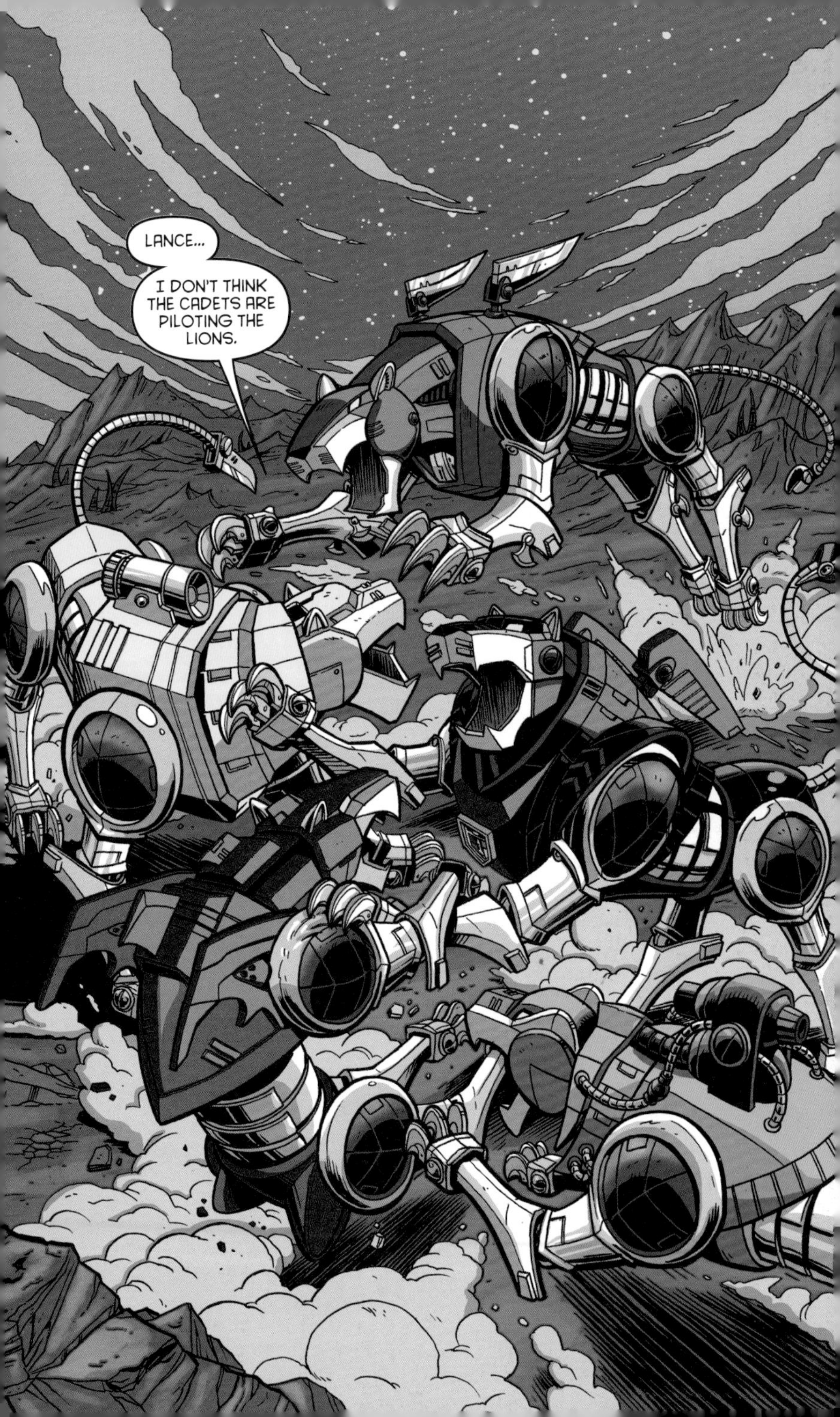
LANCE...
I DON'T THINK THE CADETS ARE PILOTING THE LIONS.

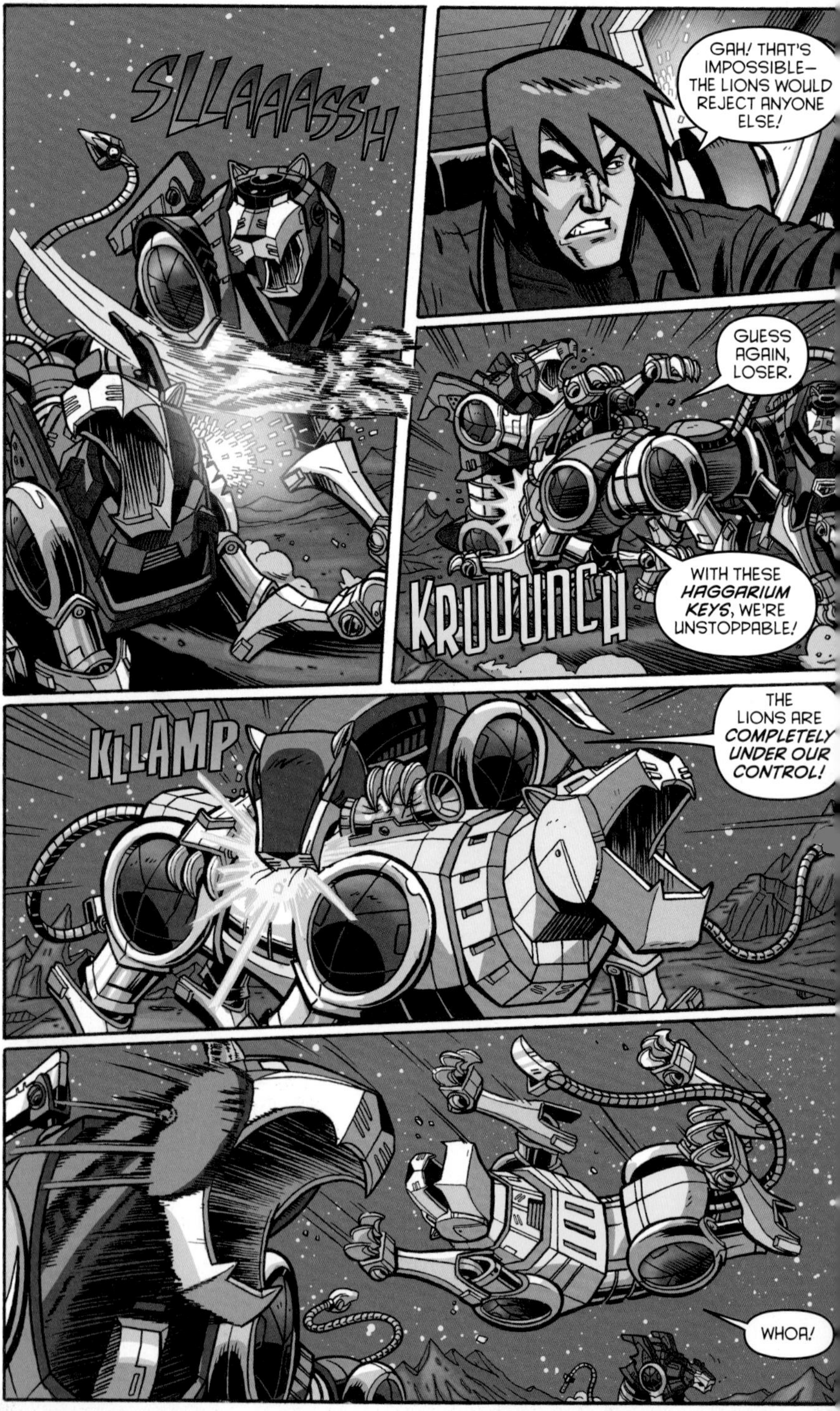
SLLAAASSH
GAH! THAT'S IMPOSSIBLE— THE LIONS WOULD REJECT ANYONE ELSE!
GUESS AGAIN, LOSER.
KRUUUNCH
WITH THESE *HAGGARIUM KEYS*, WE'RE UNSTOPPABLE!
KLLAMP
THE LIONS ARE ***COMPLETELY UNDER OUR CONTROL!***
WHOA!

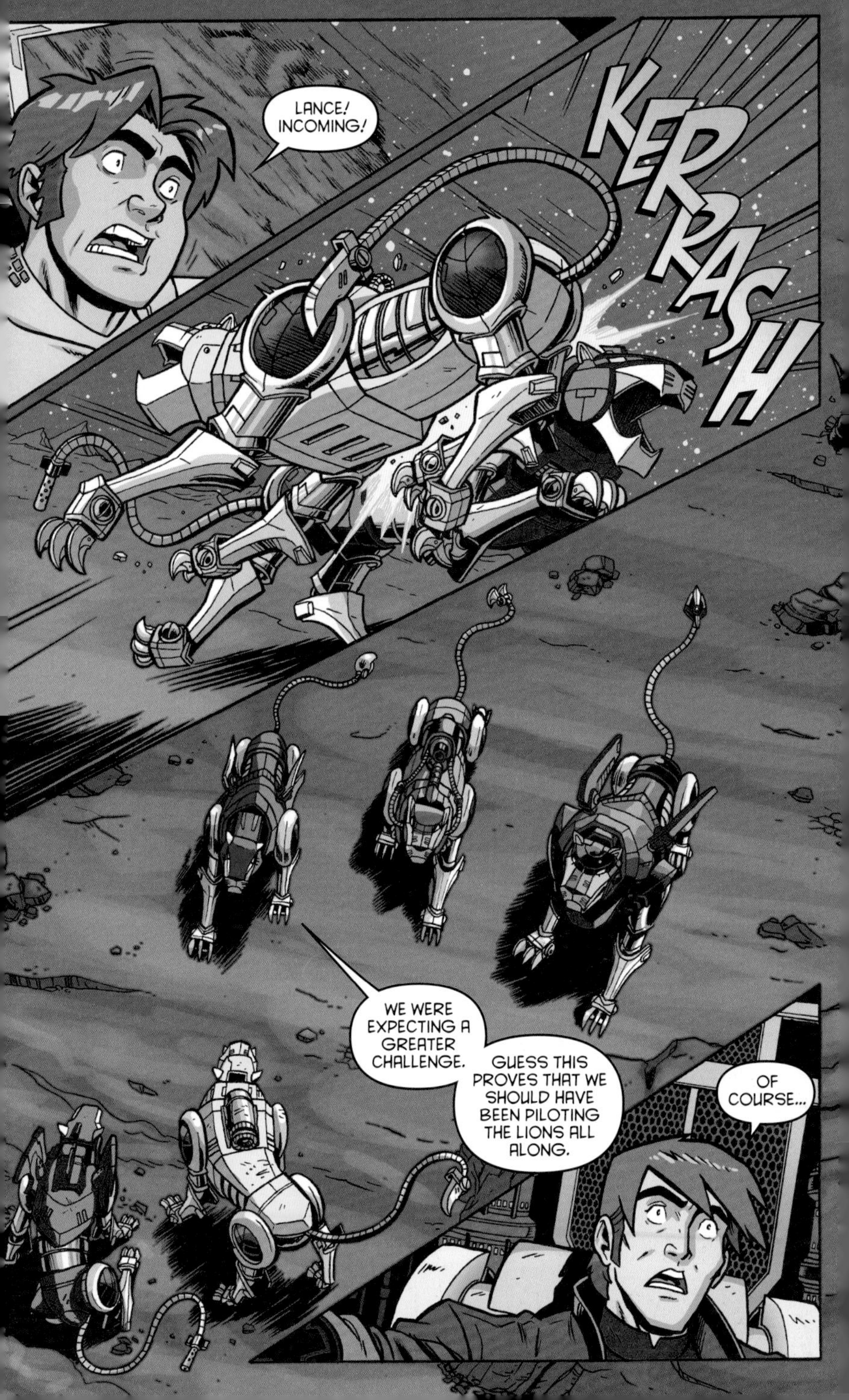
LANCE! INCOMING!
KERRASH
WE WERE EXPECTING A GREATER CHALLENGE.
GUESS THIS PROVES THAT WE SHOULD HAVE BEEN PILOTING THE LIONS ALL ALONG.
OF COURSE...

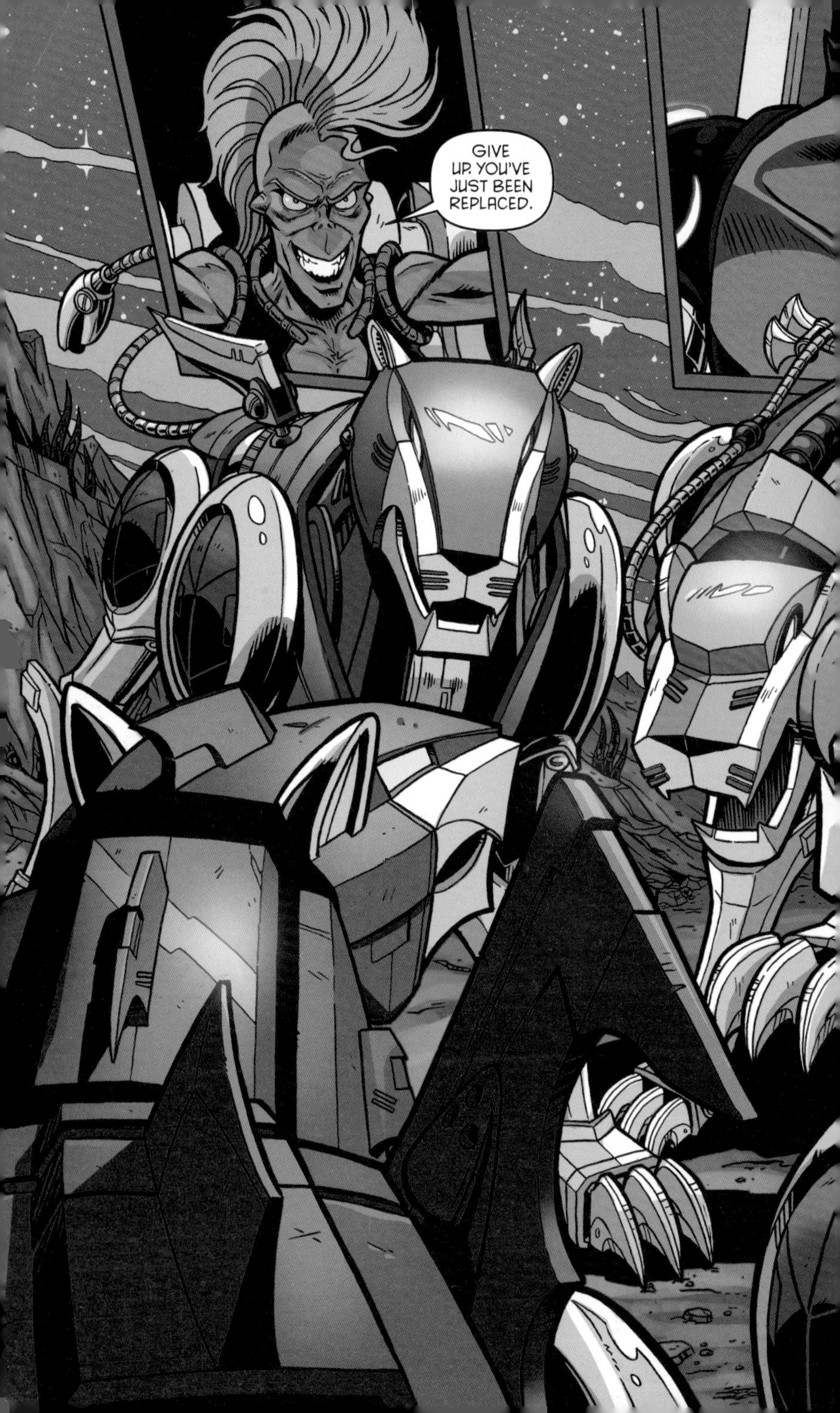
GIVE UP. YOU'VE JUST BEEN REPLACED.

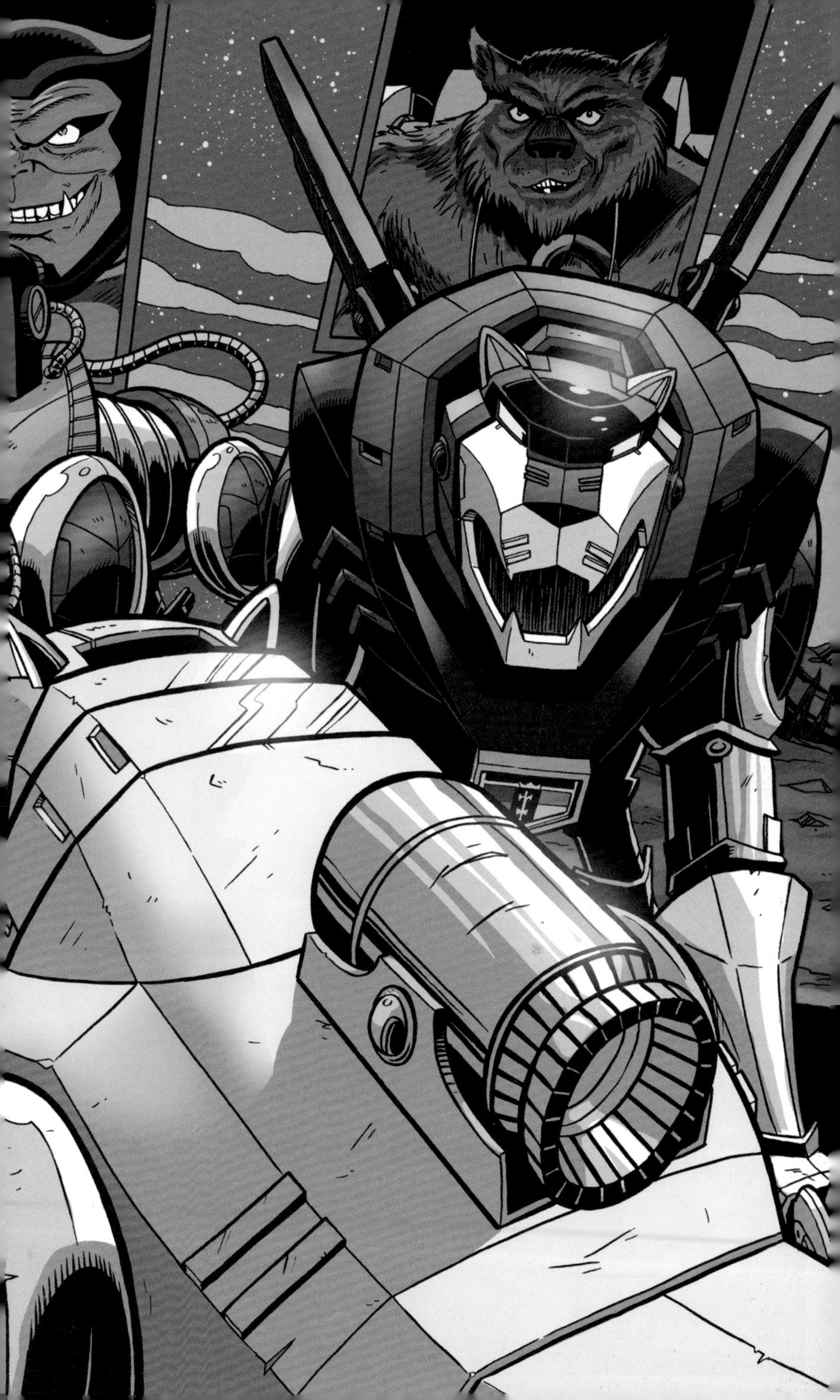

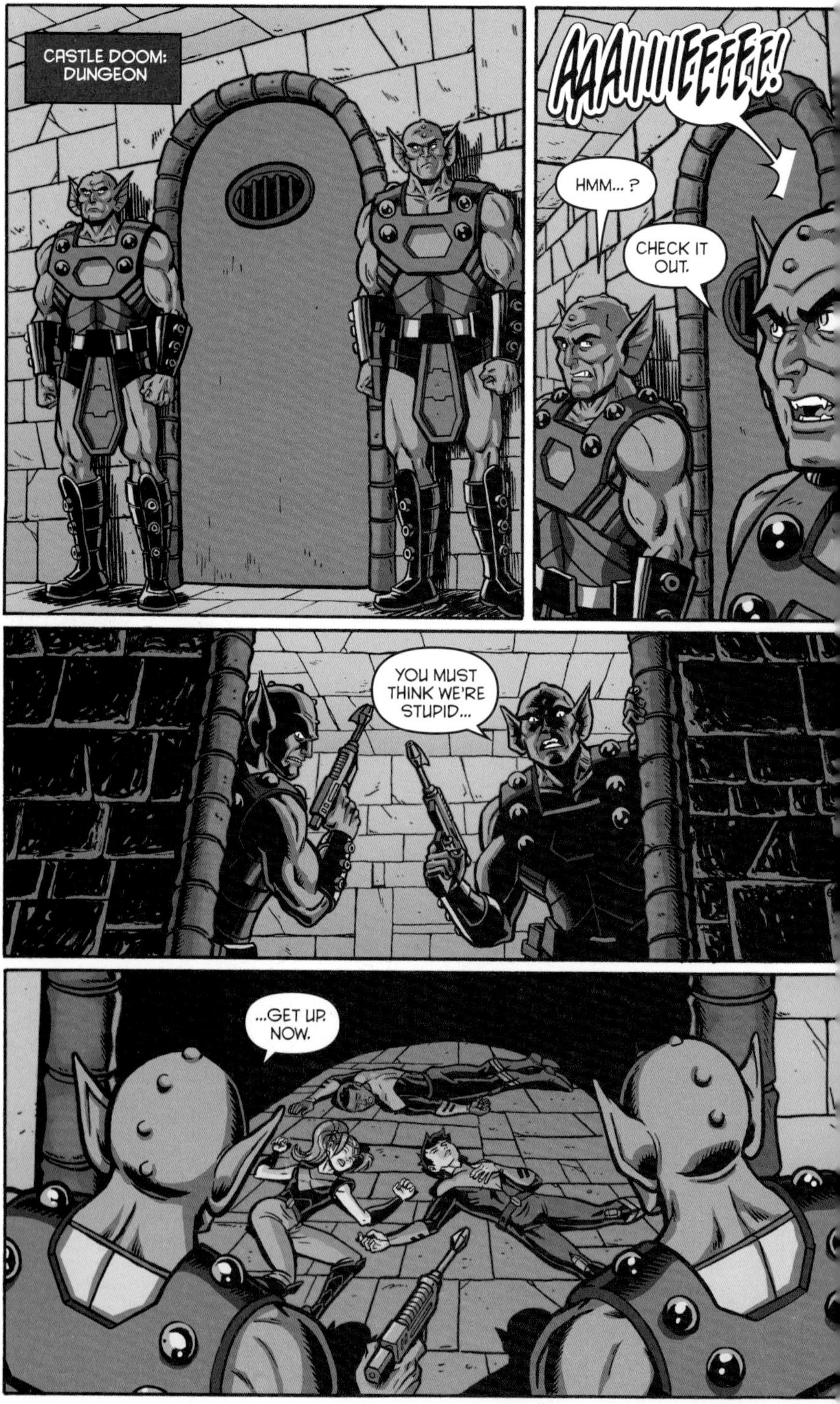
CASTLE DOOM: DUNGEON
AAAIIIIIEEEEE!
HMM... ?
CHECK IT OUT.
YOU MUST THINK WE'RE STUPID...
...GET UP. NOW.

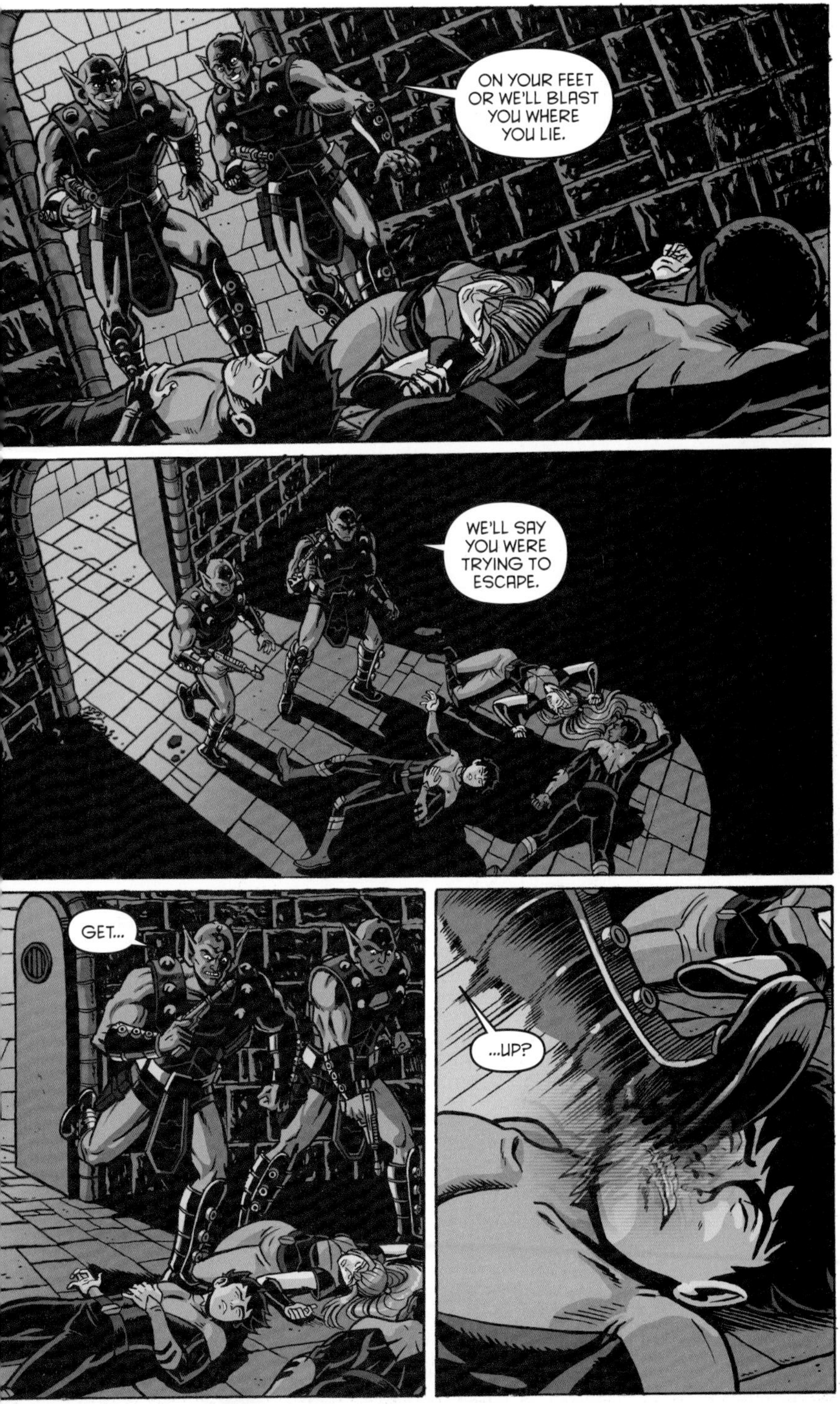
ON YOUR FEET OR WE'LL BLAST YOU WHERE YOU LIE.
WE'LL SAY YOU WERE TRYING TO ESCAPE.
GET...
...UP?

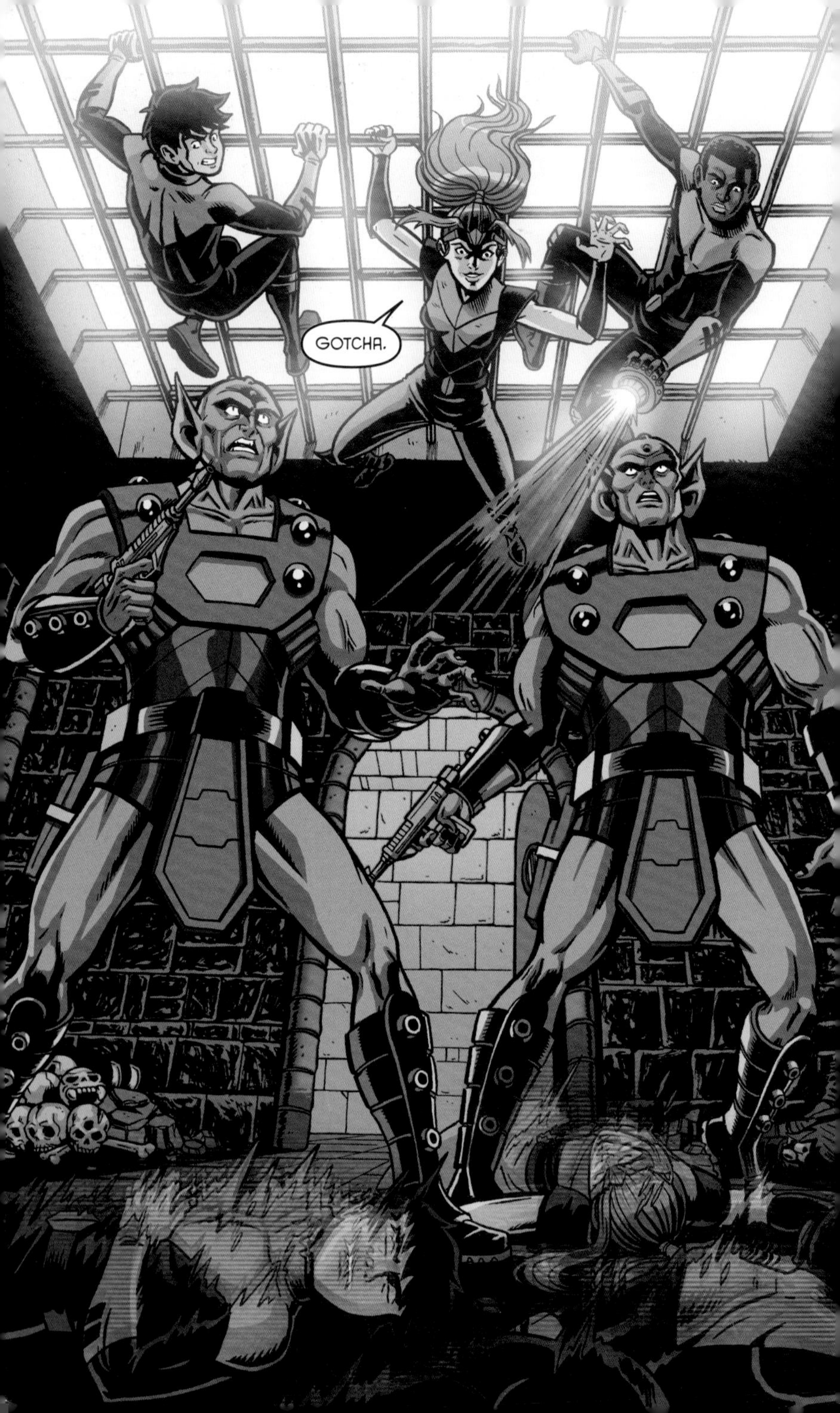
GOTCHA.

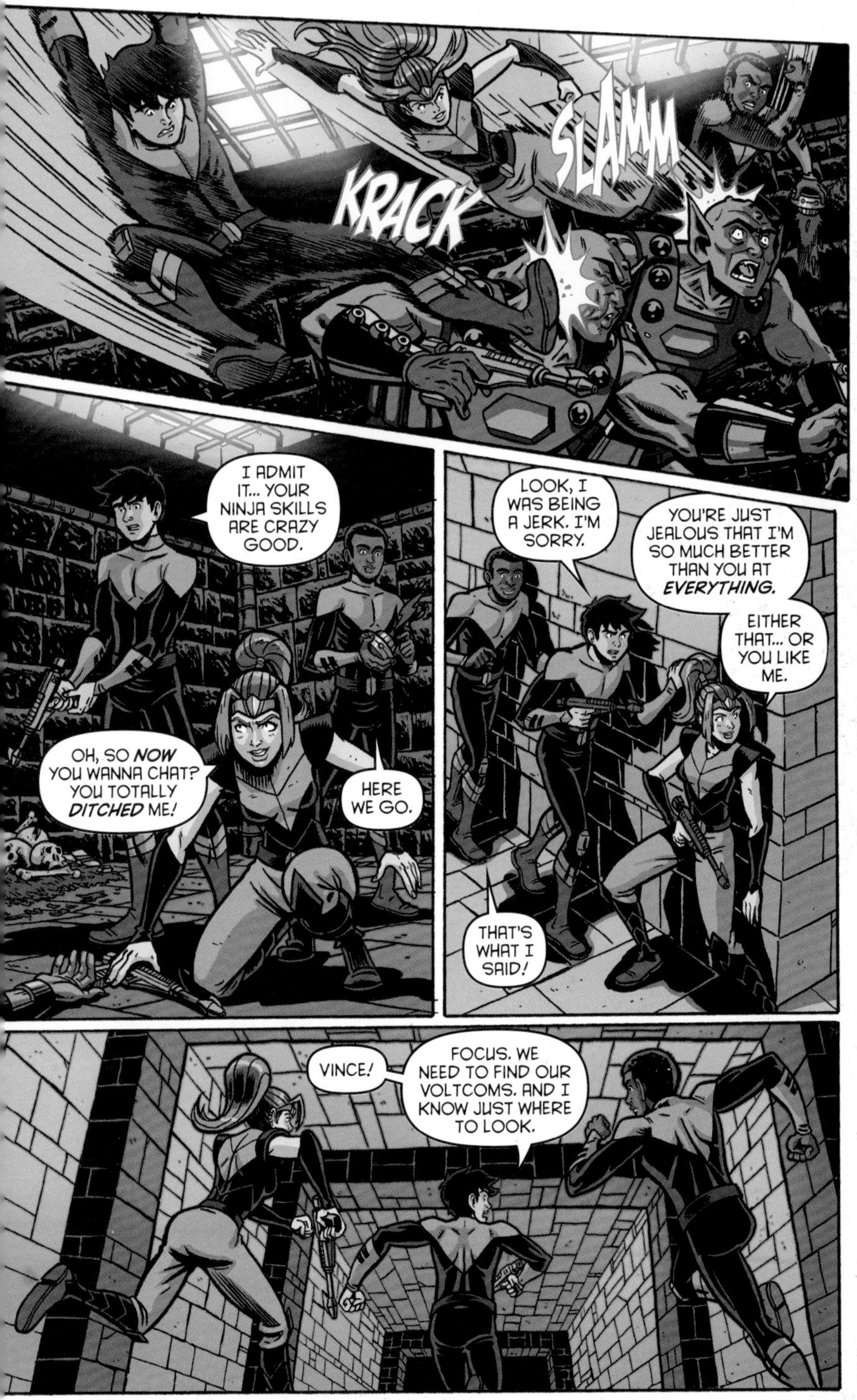
KRACK
SLAMM
I ADMIT IT... YOUR NINJA SKILLS ARE CRAZY GOOD.
OH, SO *NOW* YOU WANNA CHAT? YOU TOTALLY *DITCHED* ME!
HERE WE GO.
LOOK, I WAS BEING A JERK. I'M SORRY.
YOU'RE JUST JEALOUS THAT I'M SO MUCH BETTER THAN YOU AT *EVERYTHING.*
EITHER THAT... OR YOU LIKE ME.
THAT'S WHAT I SAID!
VINCE!
FOCUS. WE NEED TO FIND OUR VOLTCOMS. AND I KNOW JUST WHERE TO LOOK.

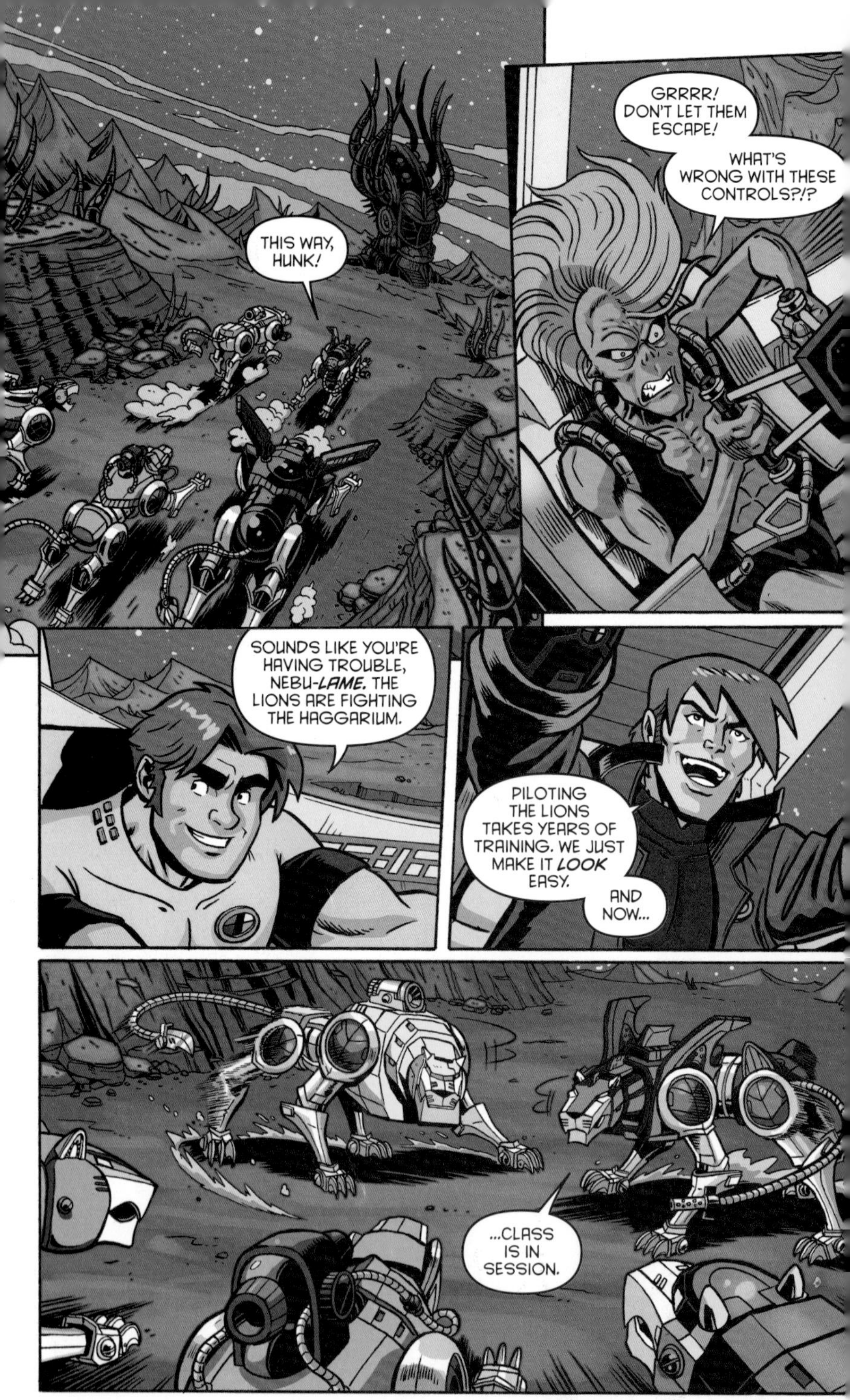

THIS WAY, HUNK!
GRRRR! DON'T LET THEM ESCAPE!
WHAT'S WRONG WITH THESE CONTROLS?!?
SOUNDS LIKE YOU'RE HAVING TROUBLE, NEBU-*LAME.* THE LIONS ARE FIGHTING THE HAGGARIUM.
PILOTING THE LIONS TAKES YEARS OF TRAINING. WE JUST MAKE IT *LOOK* EASY.
AND NOW...
...CLASS IS IN SESSION.

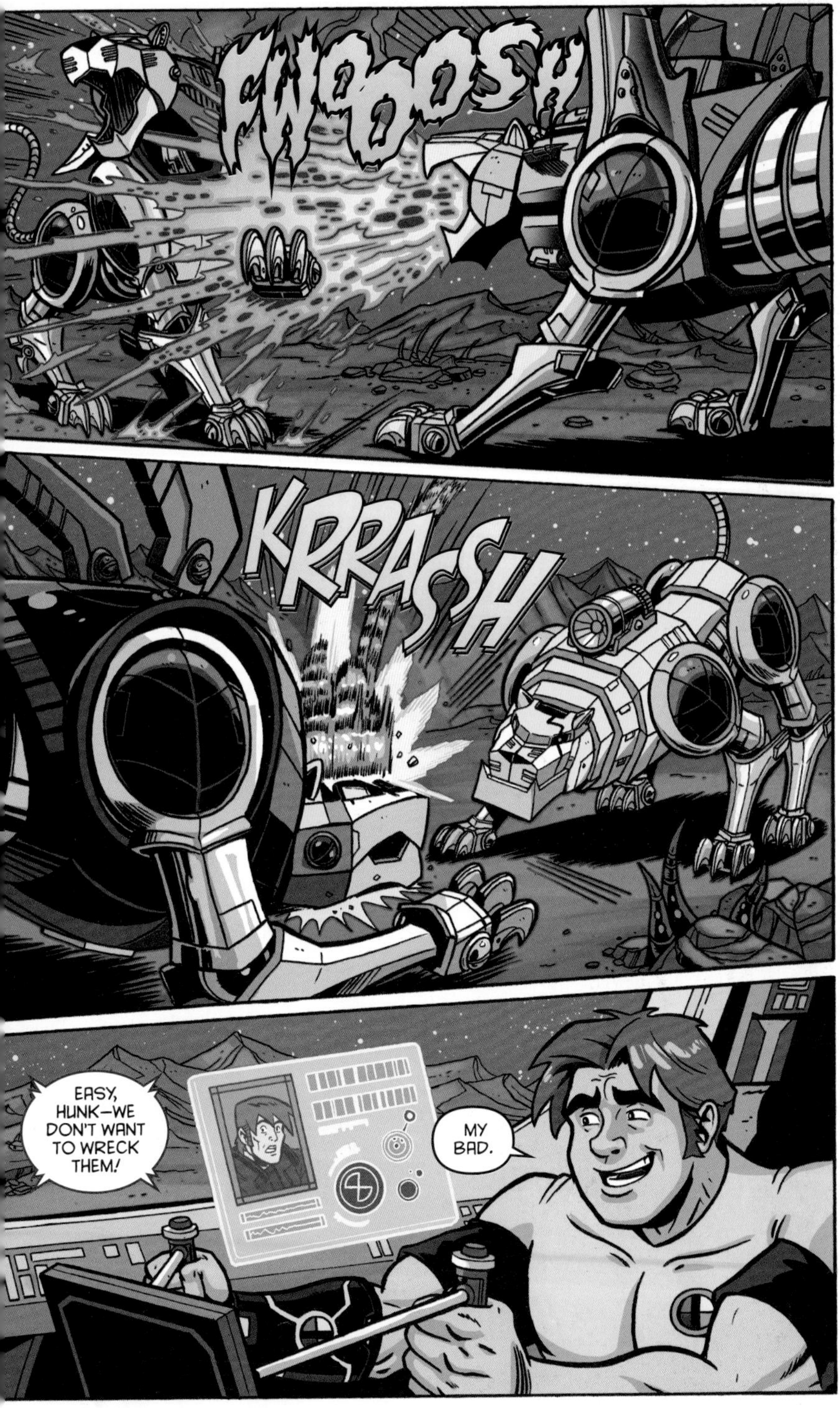
FWOOSH
KRRASH
EASY, HUNK—WE DON'T WANT TO WRECK THEM!
MY BAD.

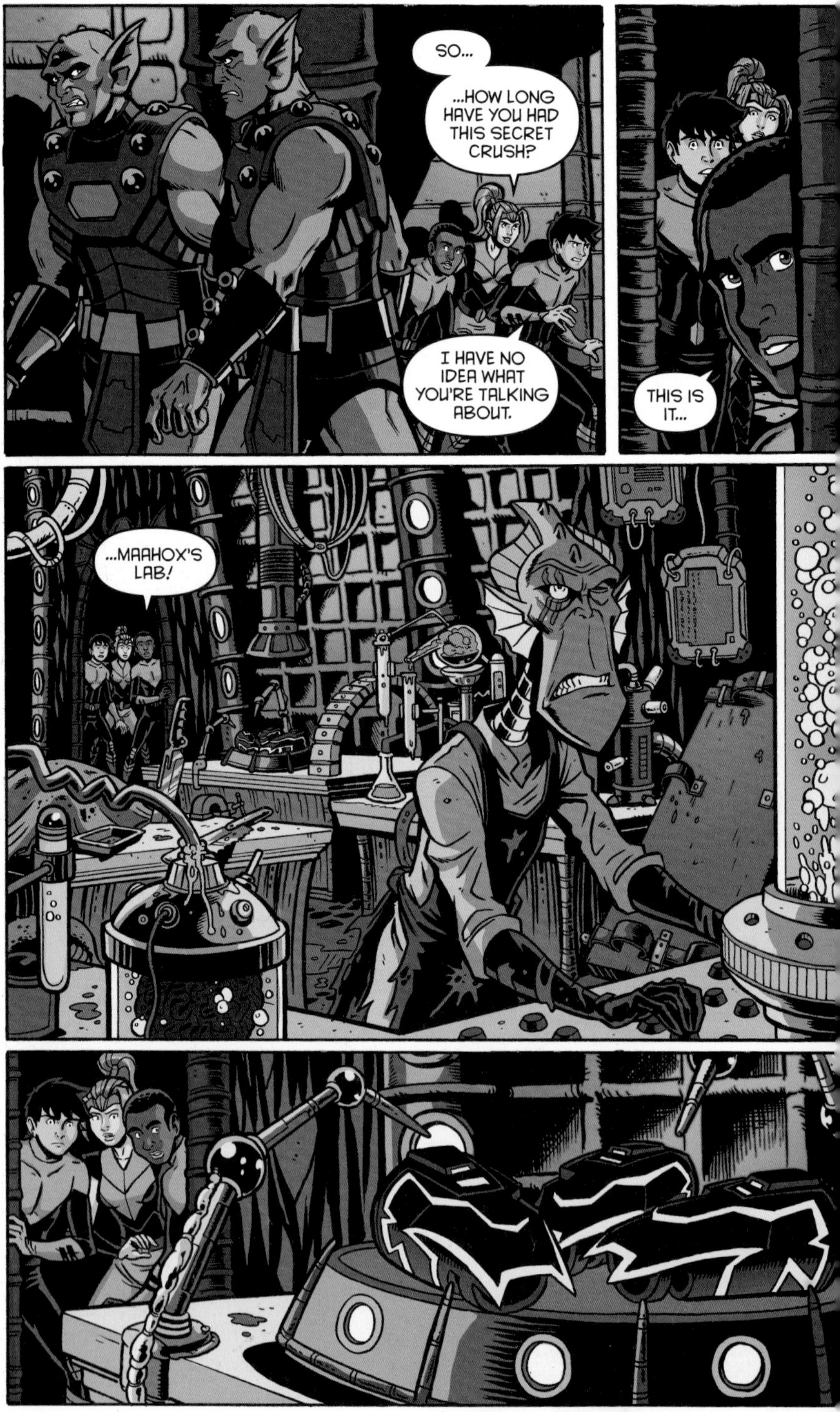
SO...
...HOW LONG HAVE YOU HAD THIS SECRET CRUSH?
I HAVE NO IDEA WHAT YOU'RE TALKING ABOUT.
THIS IS IT...
...MAAHOX'S LAB!

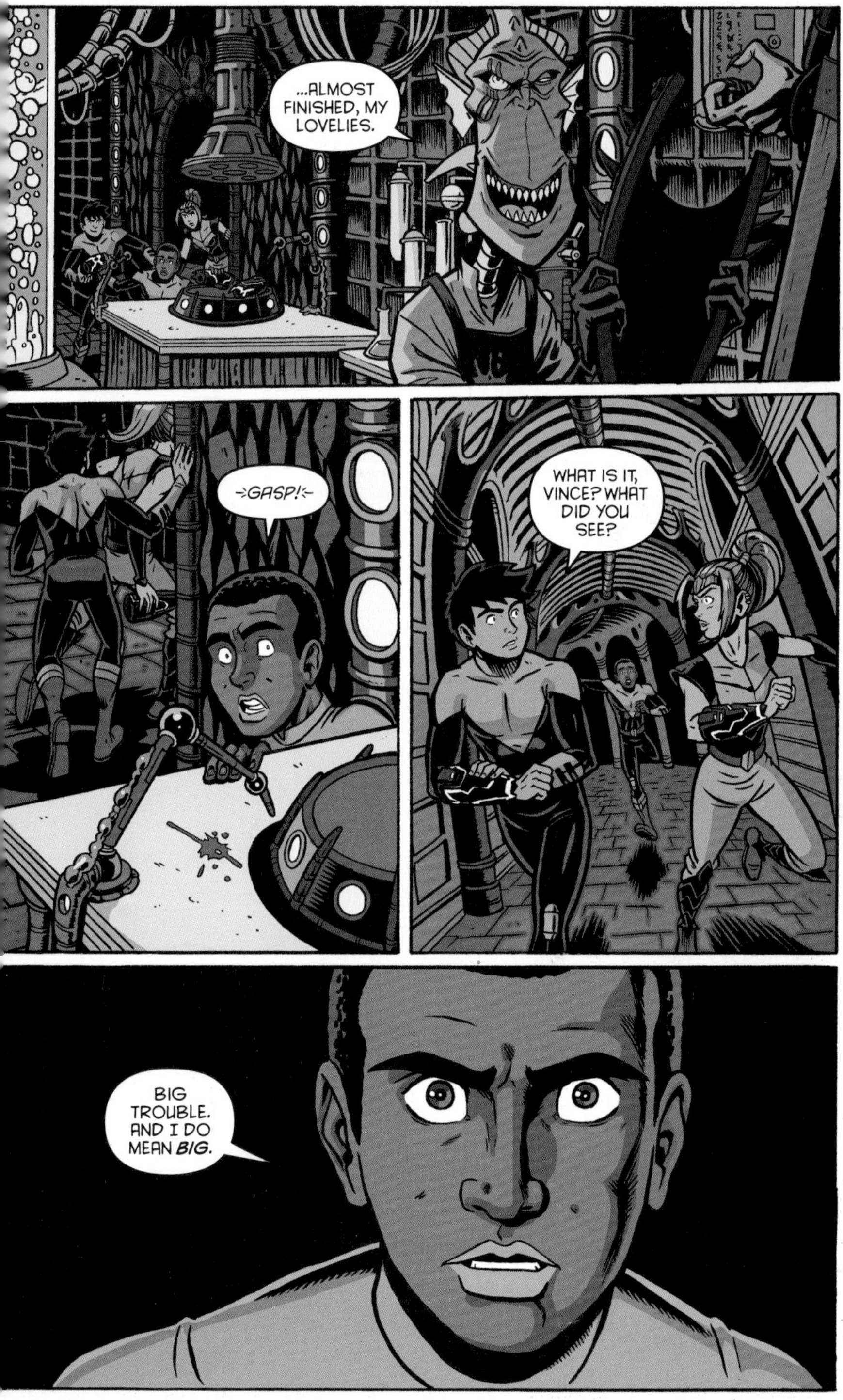
...ALMOST FINISHED, MY LOVELIES.
->GASP!<-
WHAT IS IT, VINCE? WHAT DID YOU SEE?
BIG TROUBLE. AND I DO MEAN *BIG*.

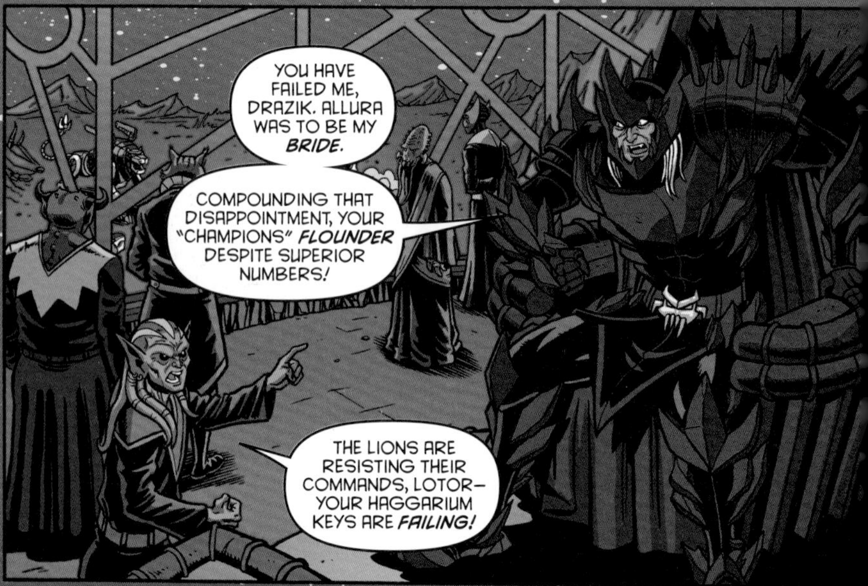
YOU HAVE FAILED ME, DRAZIK. ALLURA WAS TO BE MY BRIDE.
COMPOUNDING THAT DISAPPOINTMENT, YOUR "CHAMPIONS" FLOUNDER DESPITE SUPERIOR NUMBERS!
THE LIONS ARE RESISTING THEIR COMMANDS, LOTOR— YOUR HAGGARIUM KEYS ARE FAILING!

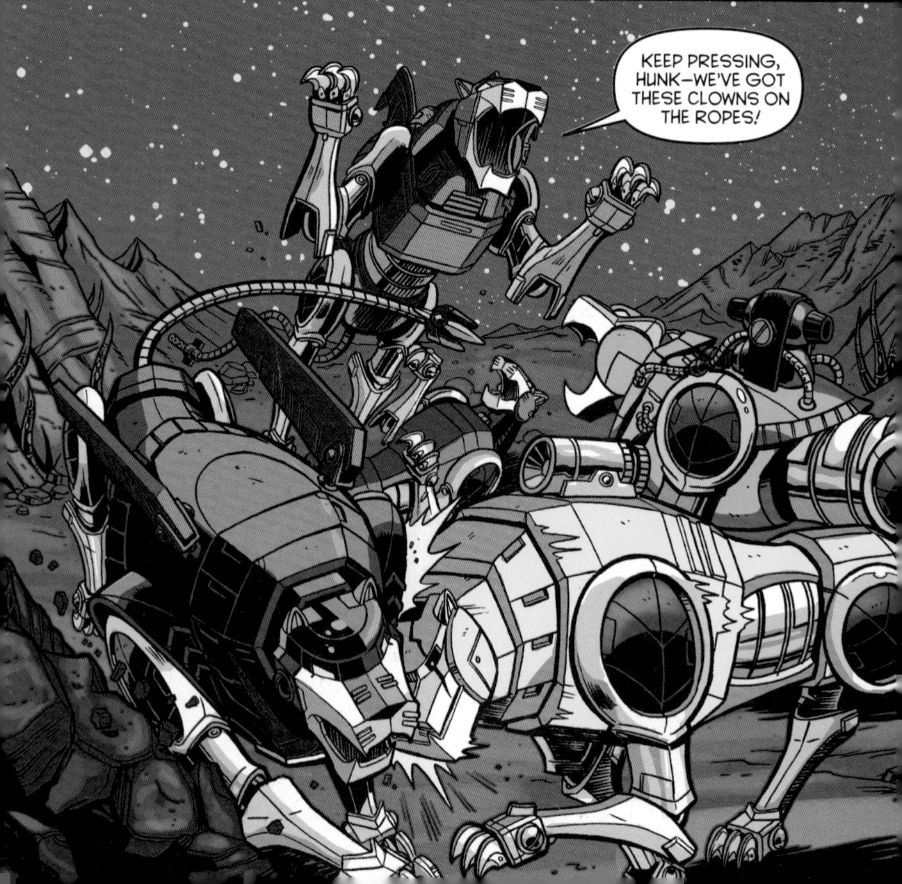
KEEP PRESSING, HUNK—WE'VE GOT THESE CLOWNS ON THE ROPES!

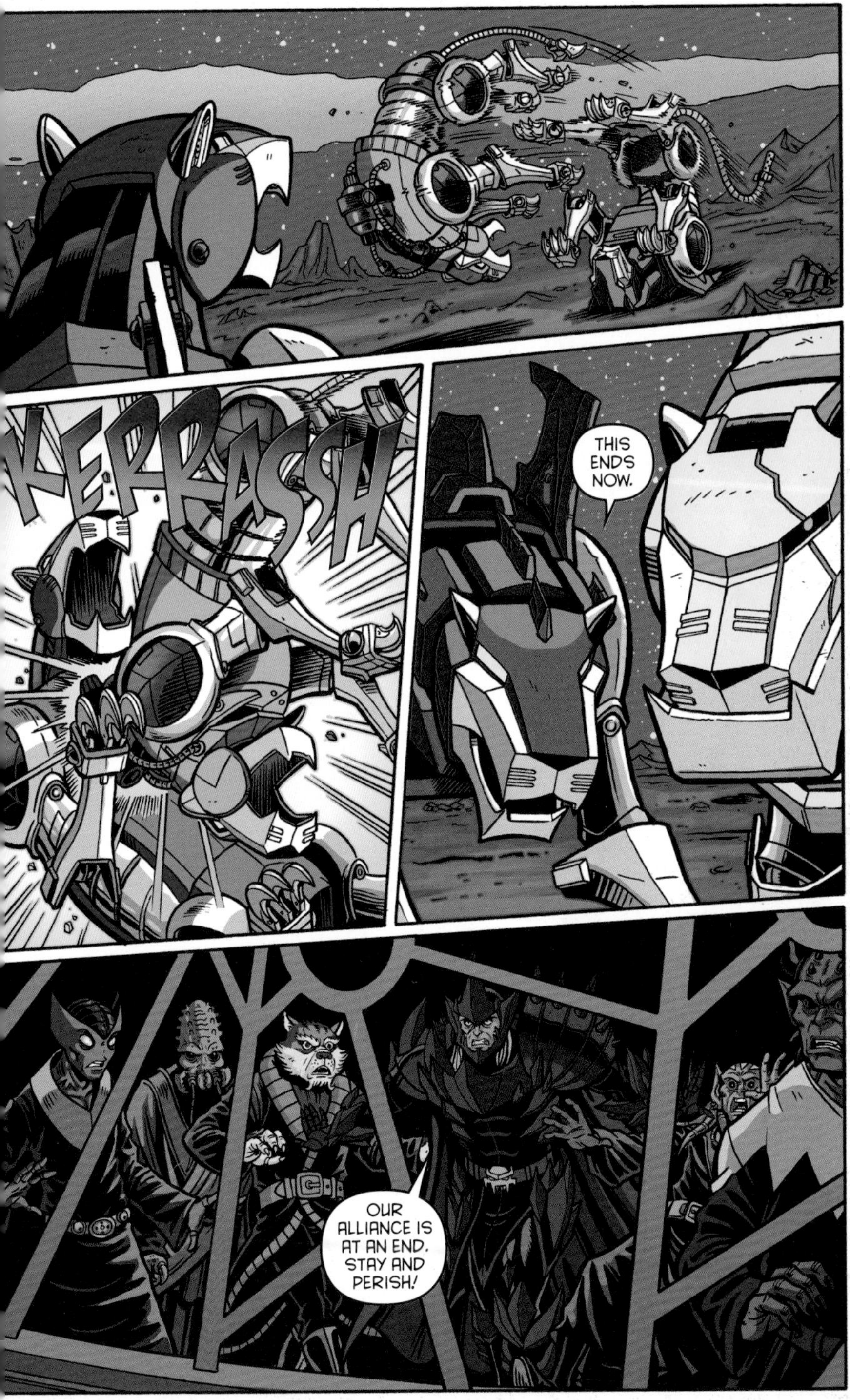
KERRASSH
THIS ENDS NOW.
OUR ALLIANCE IS AT AN END. STAY AND PERISH!

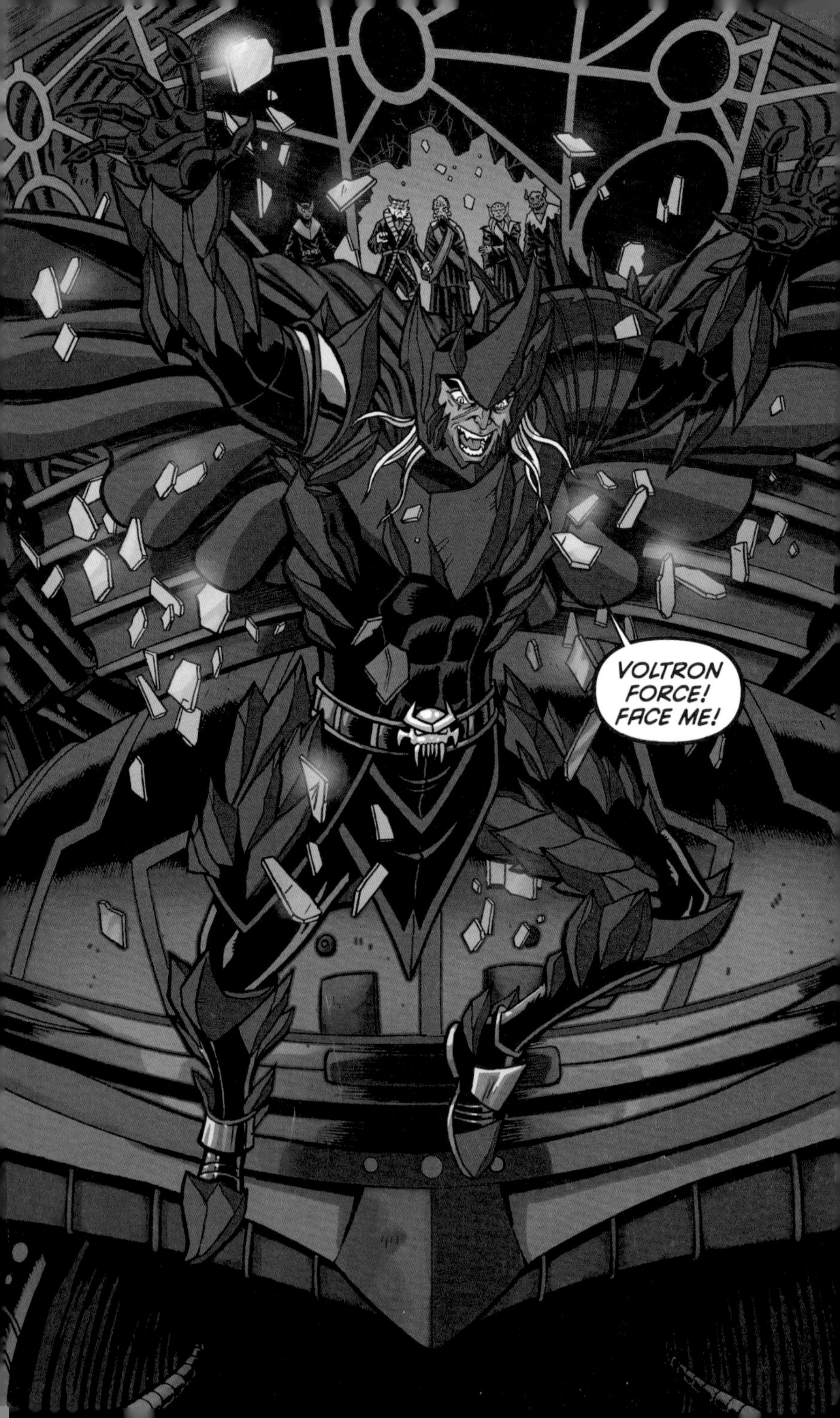
VOLTRON FORCE! FACE ME!

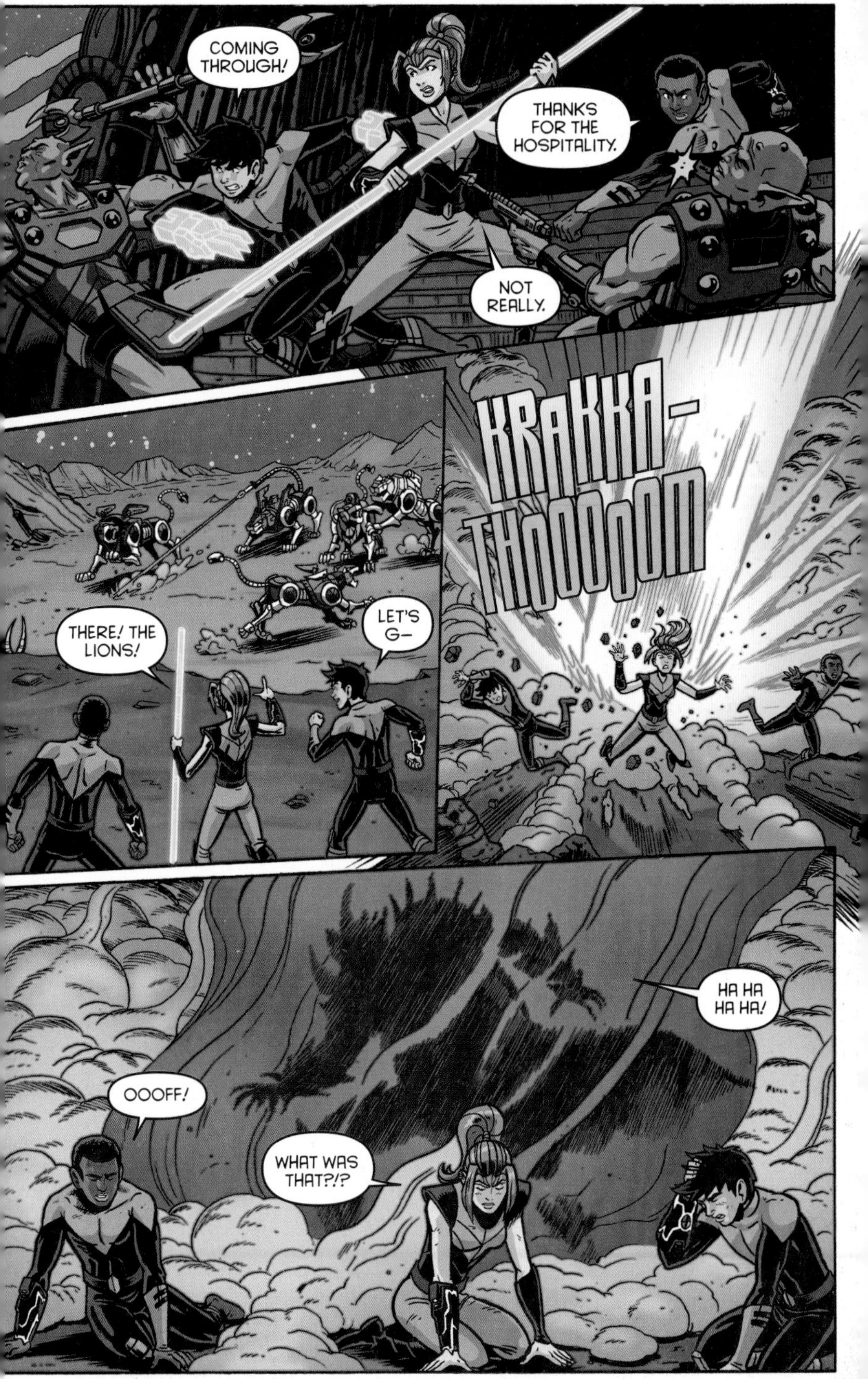

COMING THROUGH!
THANKS FOR THE HOSPITALITY.
NOT REALLY.
THERE! THE LIONS!
LET'S G—
KRAKKA-THOOOOOOM
HA HA HA HA!
OOOFF!
WHAT WAS THAT?!?

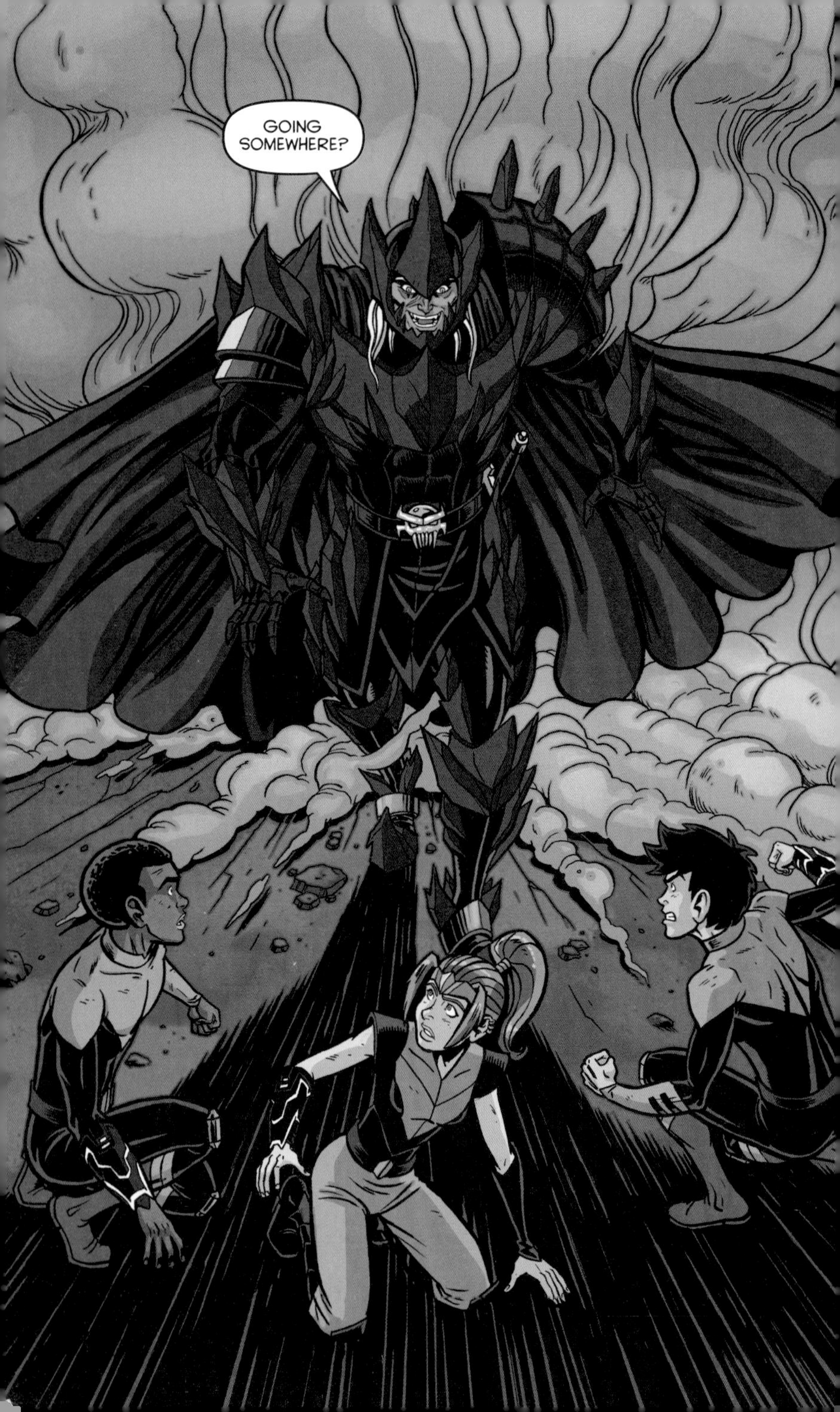
GOING SOMEWHERE?

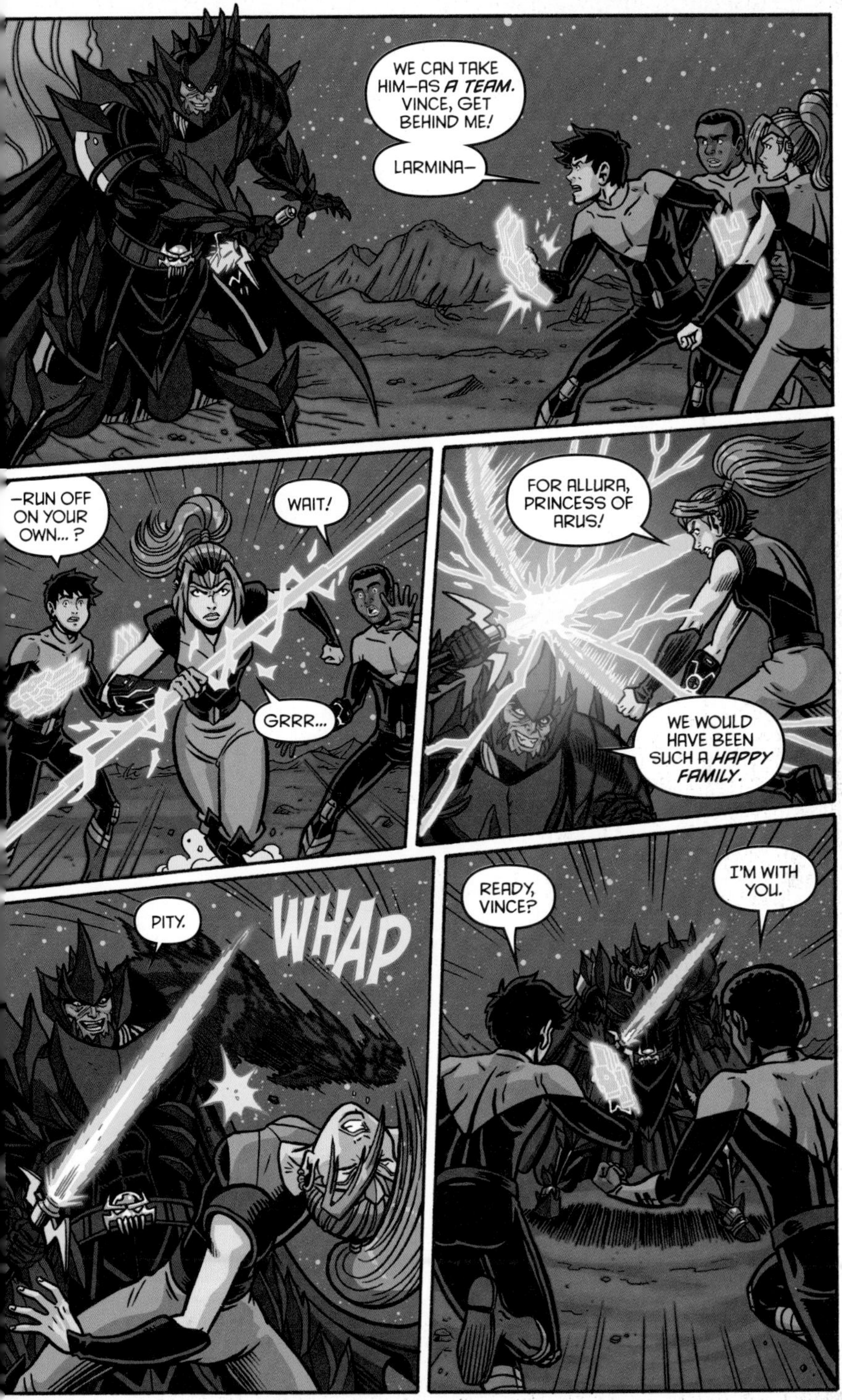
WE CAN TAKE HIM—AS A TEAM. VINCE, GET BEHIND ME!
LARMINA—
—RUN OFF ON YOUR OWN... ?
WAIT!
GRRR...
FOR ALLURA, PRINCESS OF ARUS!
WE WOULD HAVE BEEN SUCH A HAPPY FAMILY.
PITY.
WHAP
READY, VINCE?
I'M WITH YOU.

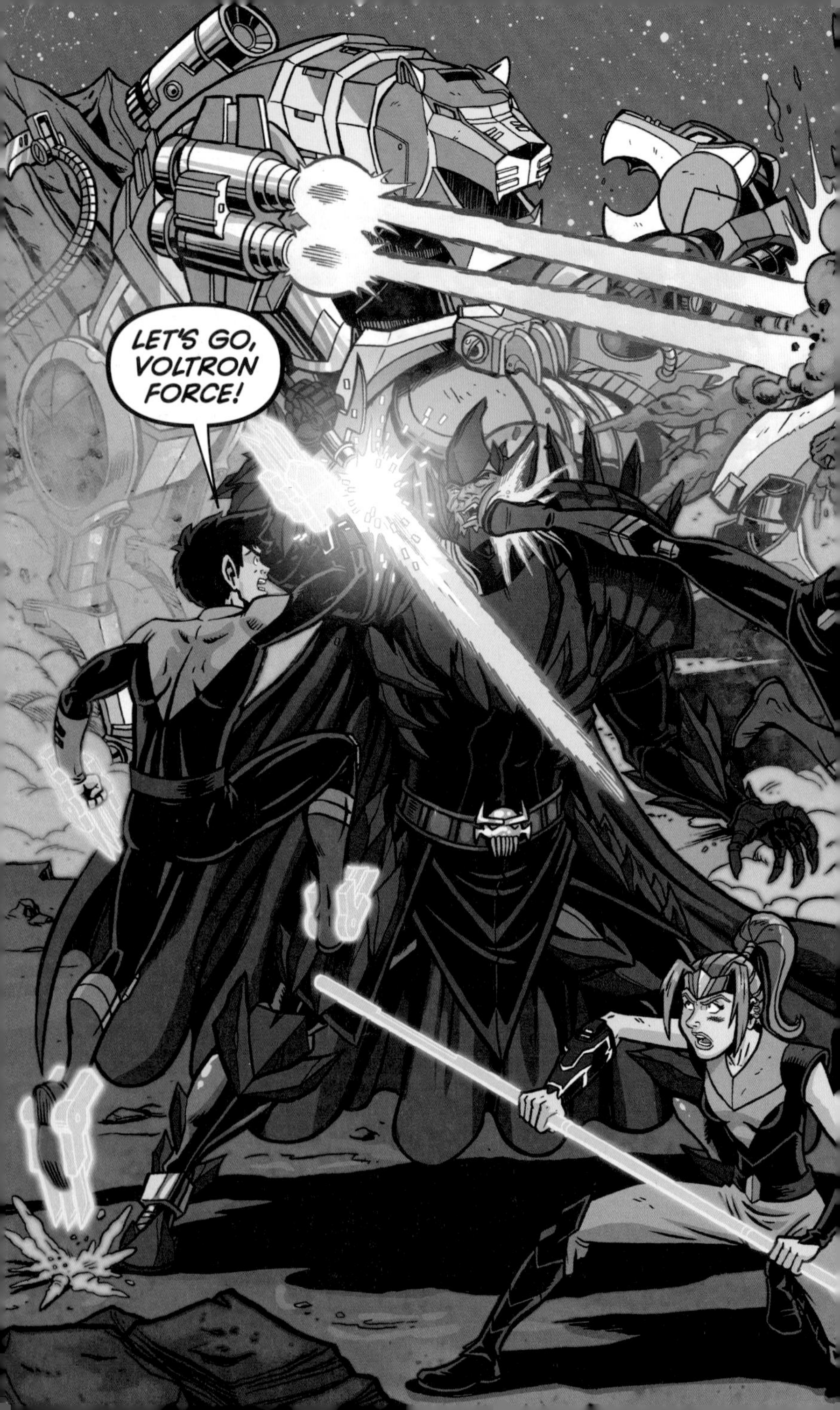
LET'S GO, VOLTRON FORCE!

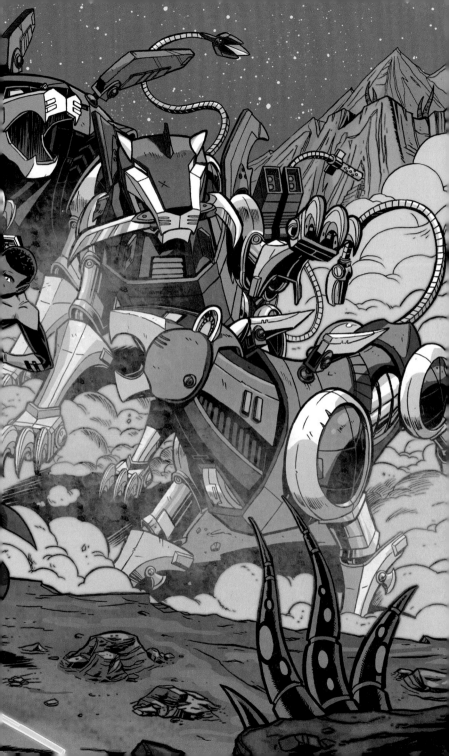

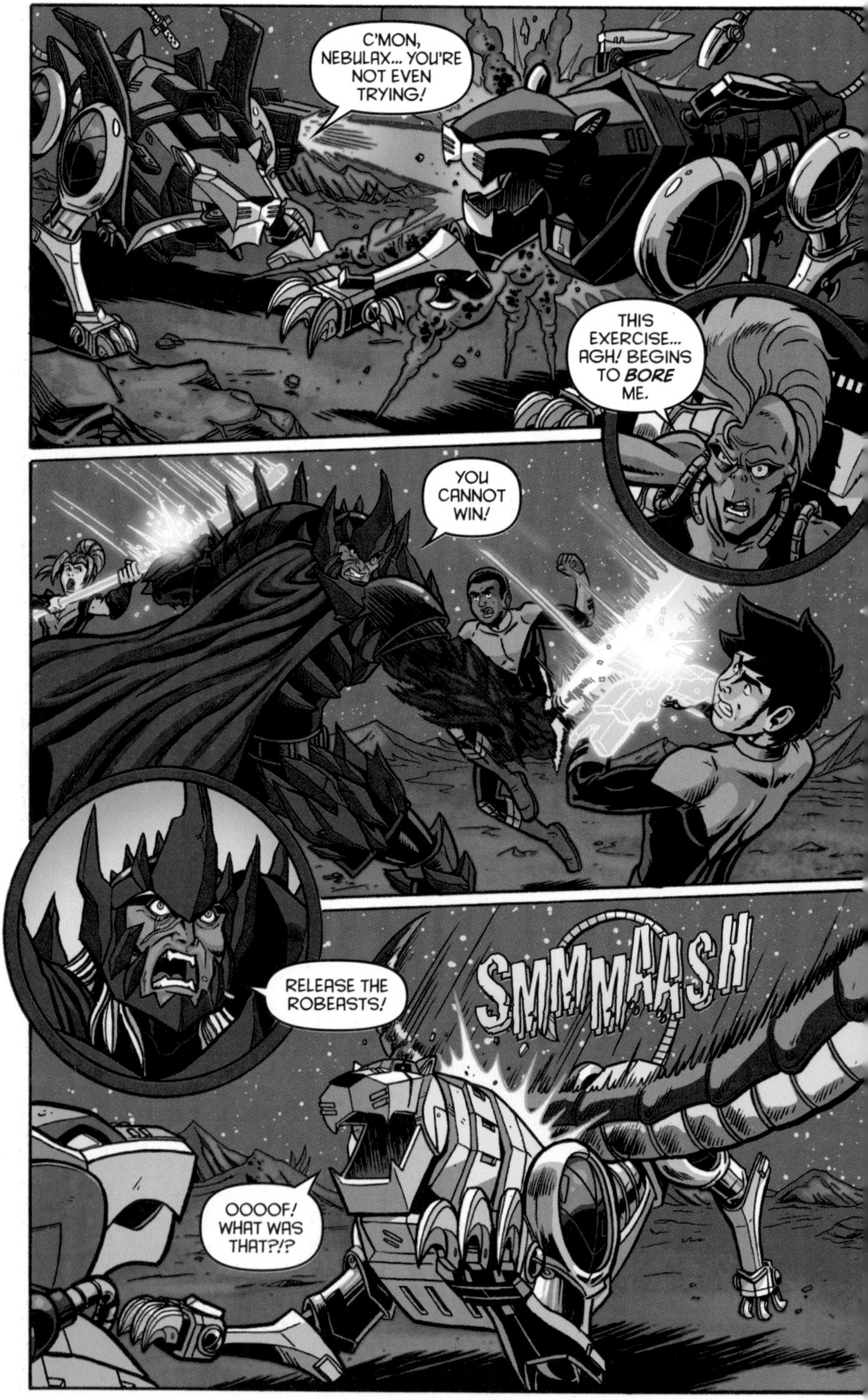

C'MON, NEBULAX... YOU'RE NOT EVEN TRYING!
THIS EXERCISE... AGH! BEGINS TO BORE ME.
YOU CANNOT WIN!
RELEASE THE ROBEASTS!
SMMMAASH
OOOOF! WHAT WAS THAT?!?

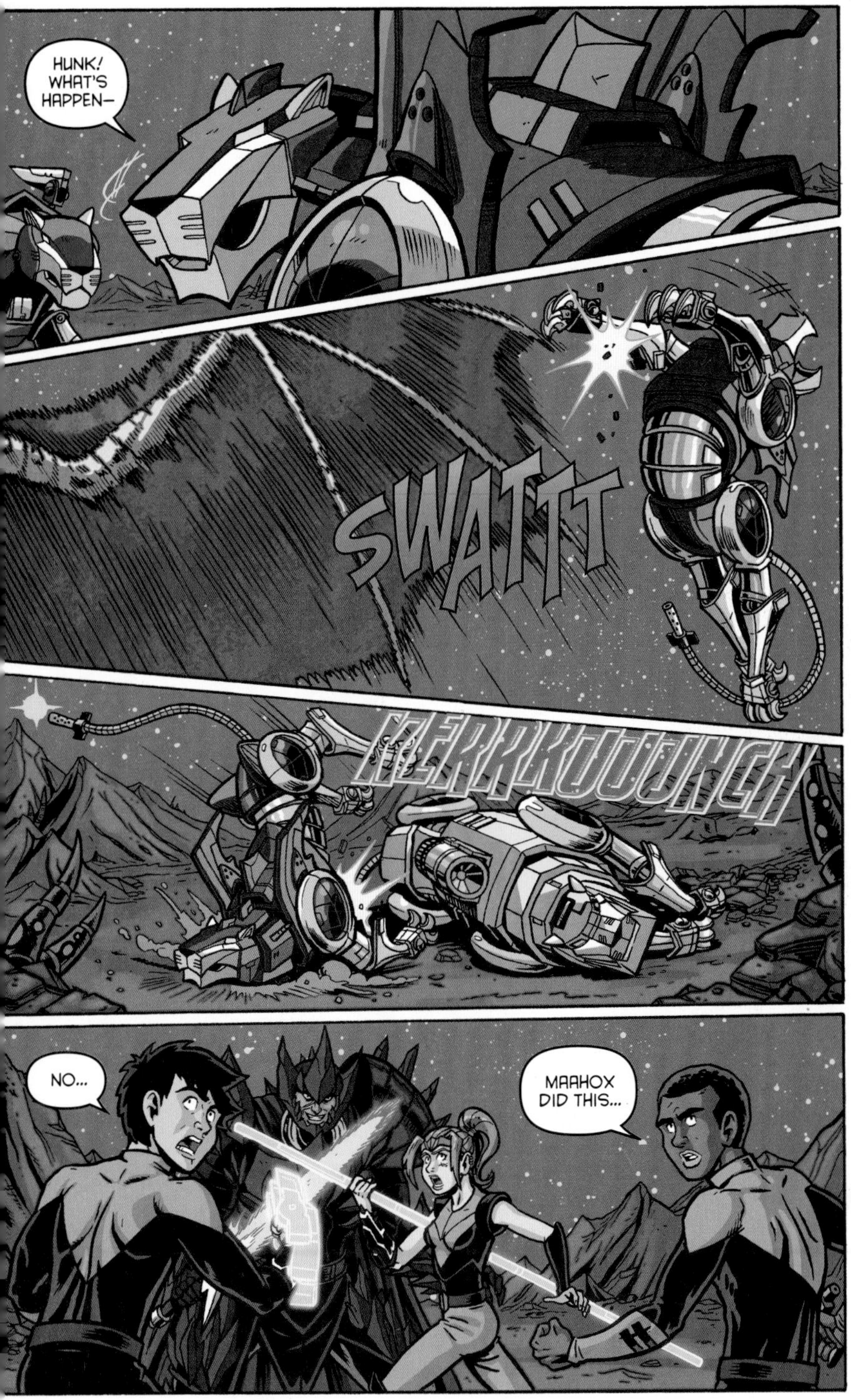
HUNK! WHAT'S HAPPEN—
SWATTT
KERRKOOOONCH
NO...
MAAHOX DID THIS...

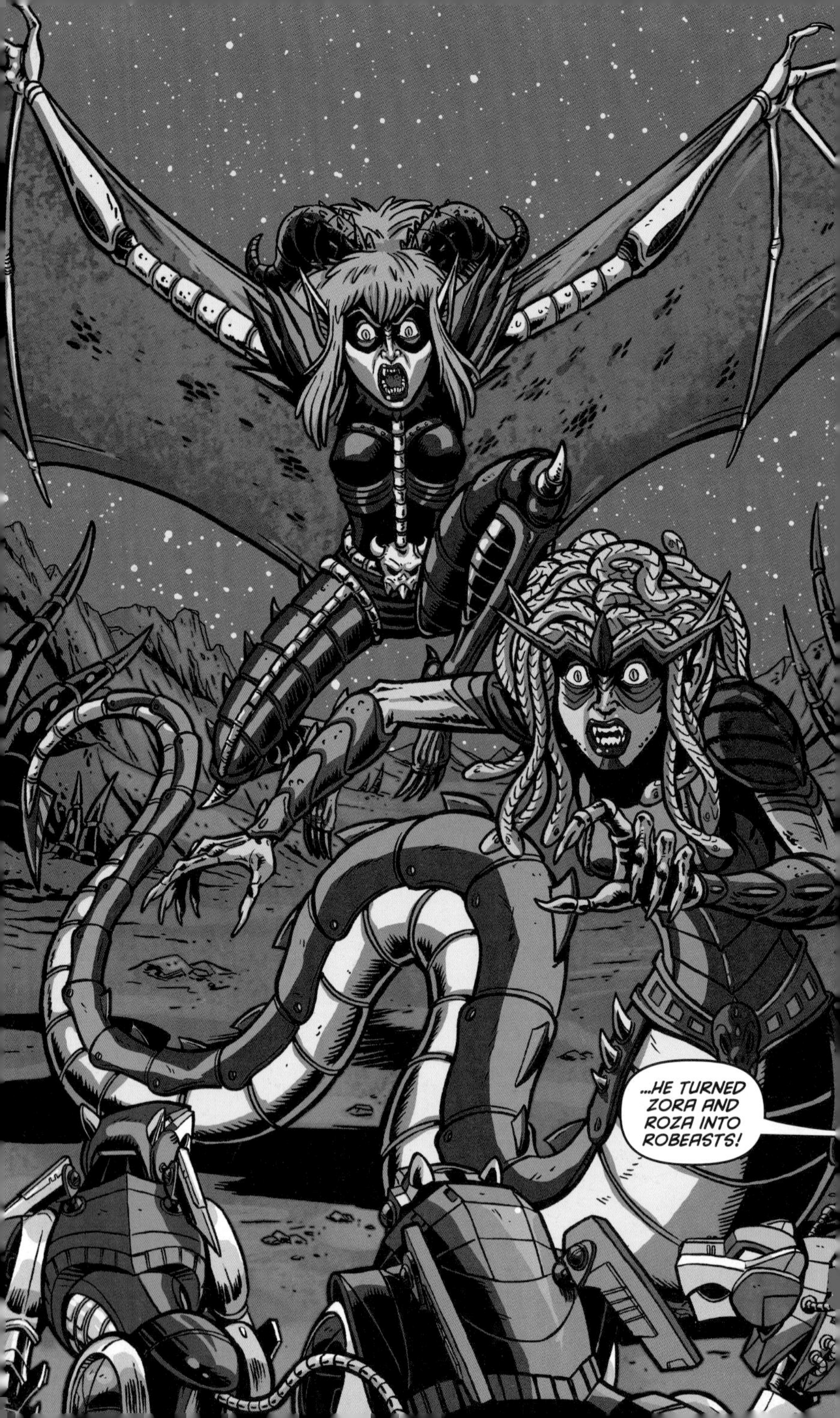
...HE TURNED ZORA AND ROZA INTO ROBEASTS!

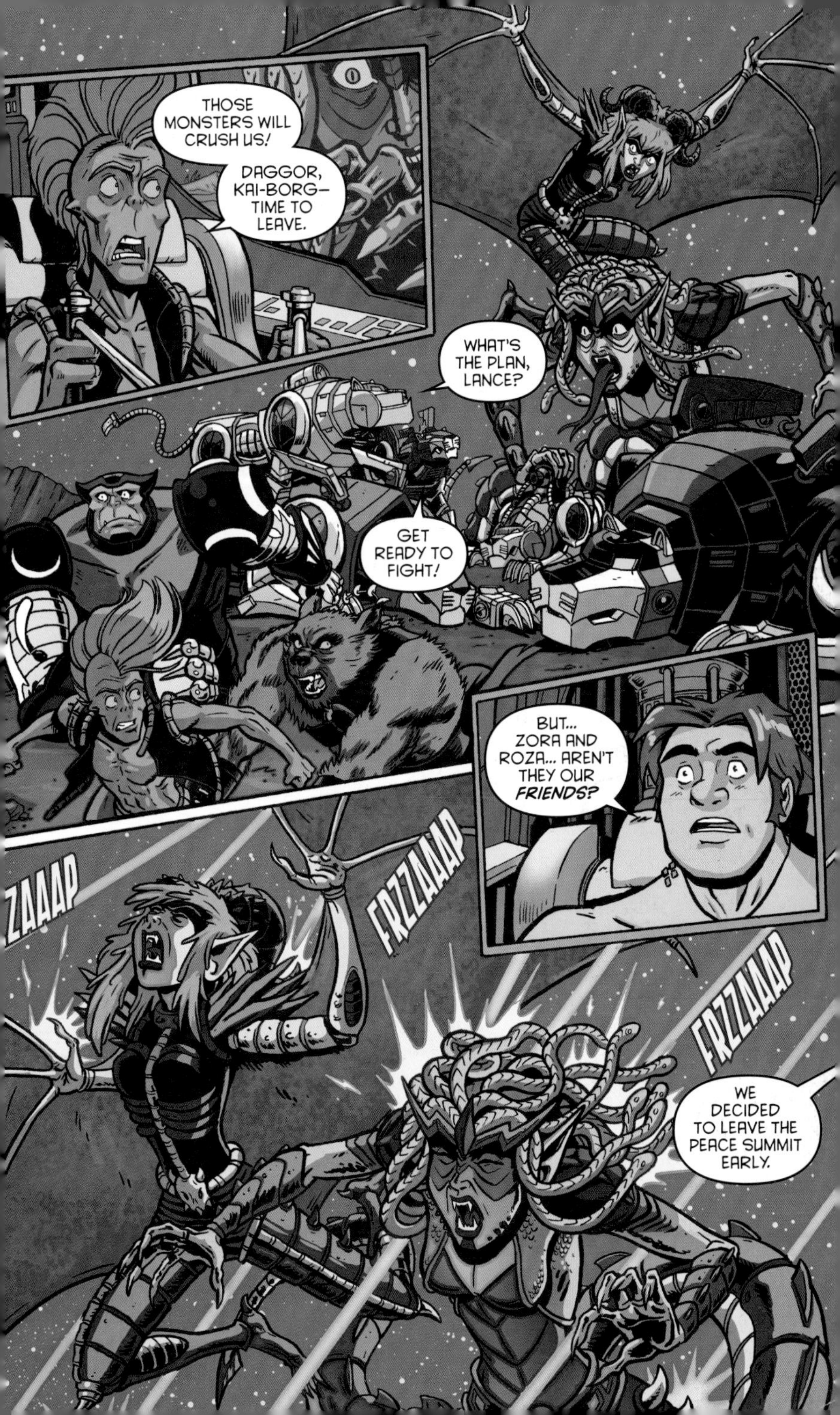
THOSE MONSTERS WILL CRUSH US!
DAGGOR, KAI-BORG— TIME TO LEAVE.
WHAT'S THE PLAN, LANCE?
GET READY TO FIGHT!
BUT... ZORA AND ROZA... AREN'T THEY OUR *FRIENDS?*
ZAAAP
FRZZAAAP
FRZZAAAP
WE DECIDED TO LEAVE THE PEACE SUMMIT EARLY.

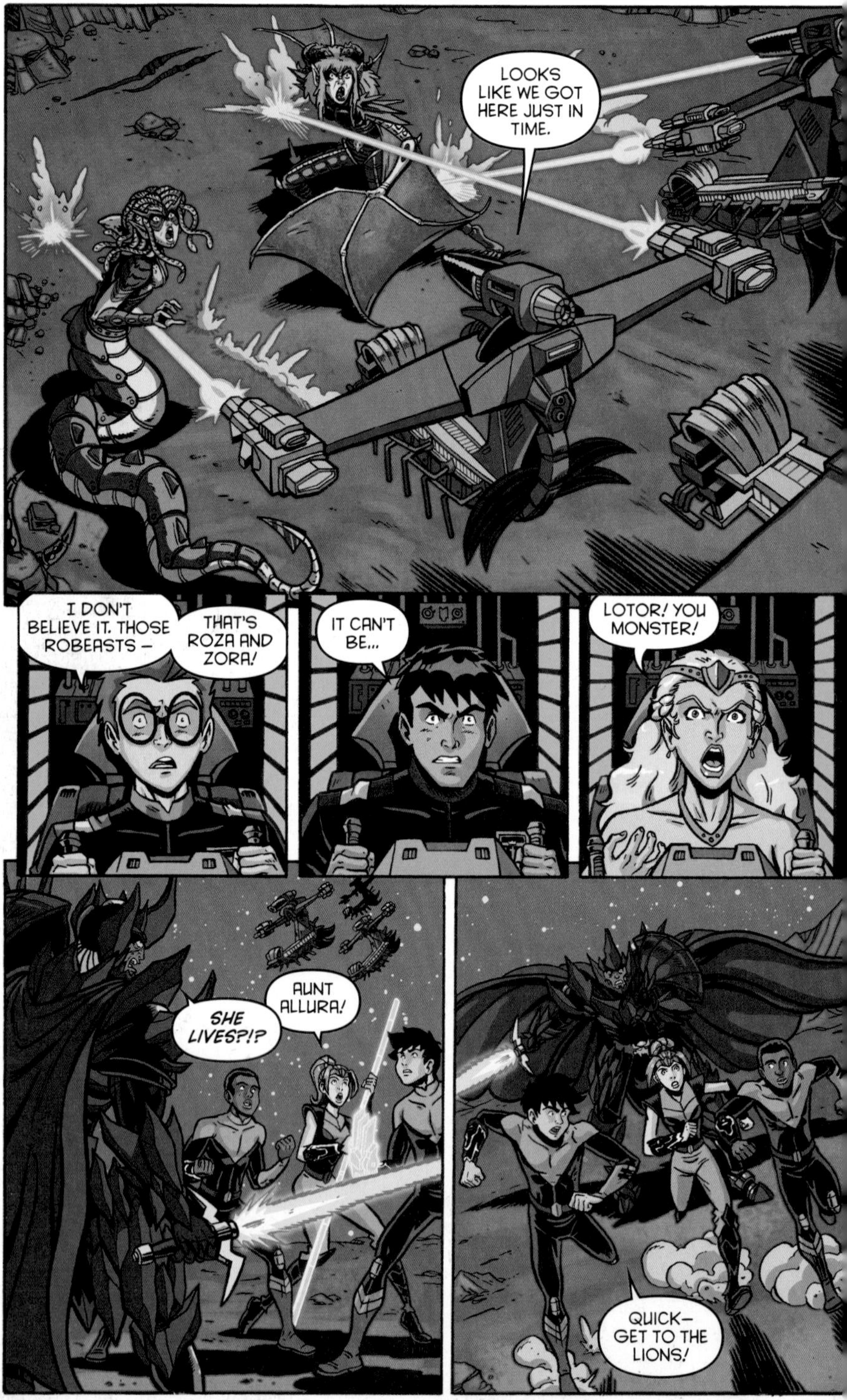
LOOKS LIKE WE GOT HERE JUST IN TIME.
I DON'T BELIEVE IT. THOSE ROBEASTS –
THAT'S ROZA AND ZORA!
IT CAN'T BE...
LOTOR! YOU MONSTER!
SHE LIVES?!?
AUNT ALLURA!
QUICK– GET TO THE LIONS!

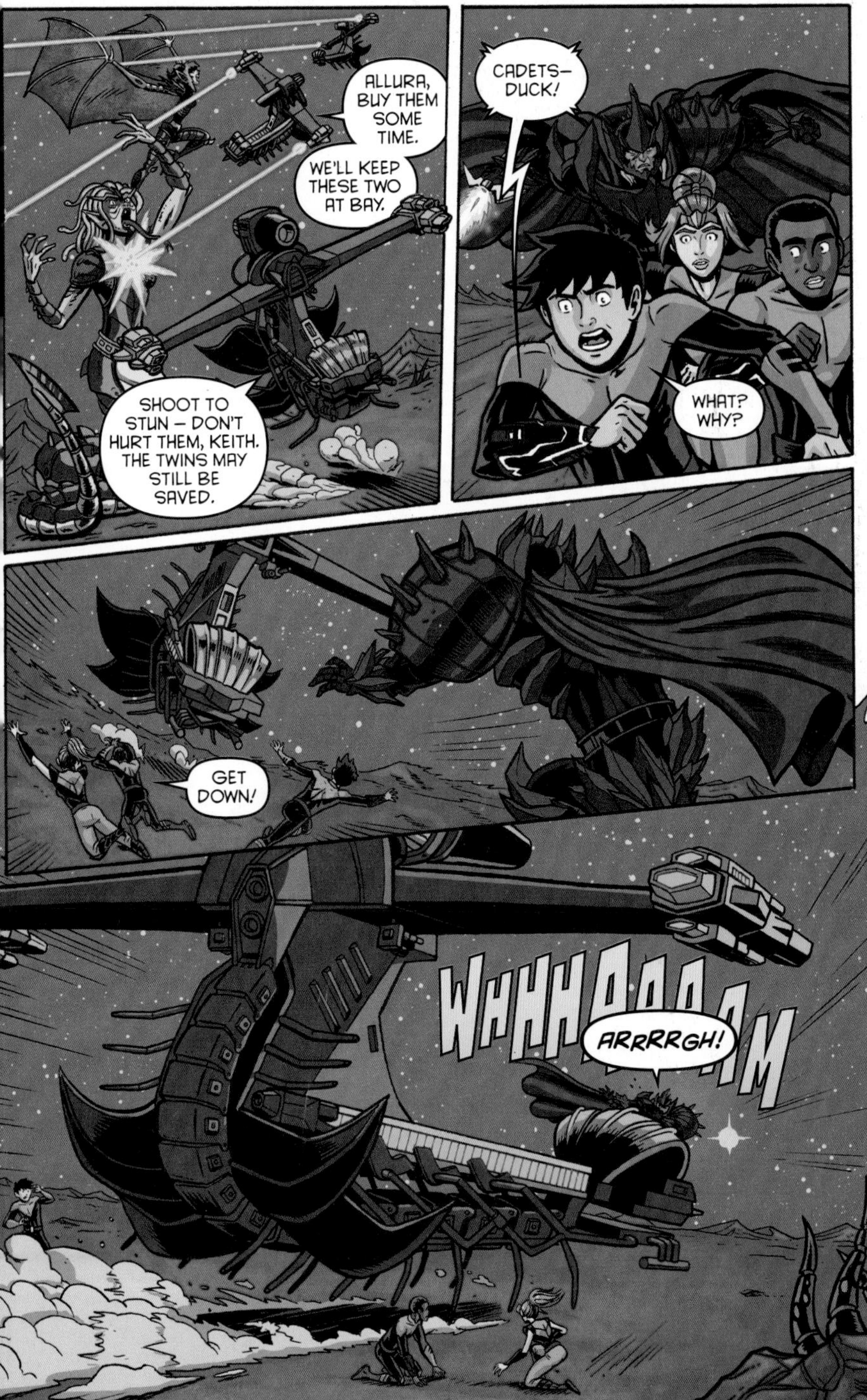
ALLURA, BUY THEM SOME TIME.
WE'LL KEEP THESE TWO AT BAY.
SHOOT TO STUN — DON'T HURT THEM, KEITH. THE TWINS MAY STILL BE SAVED.
CADETS— DUCK!
WHAT? WHY?
GET DOWN!
WHHHAAAAM
ARRRRGH!

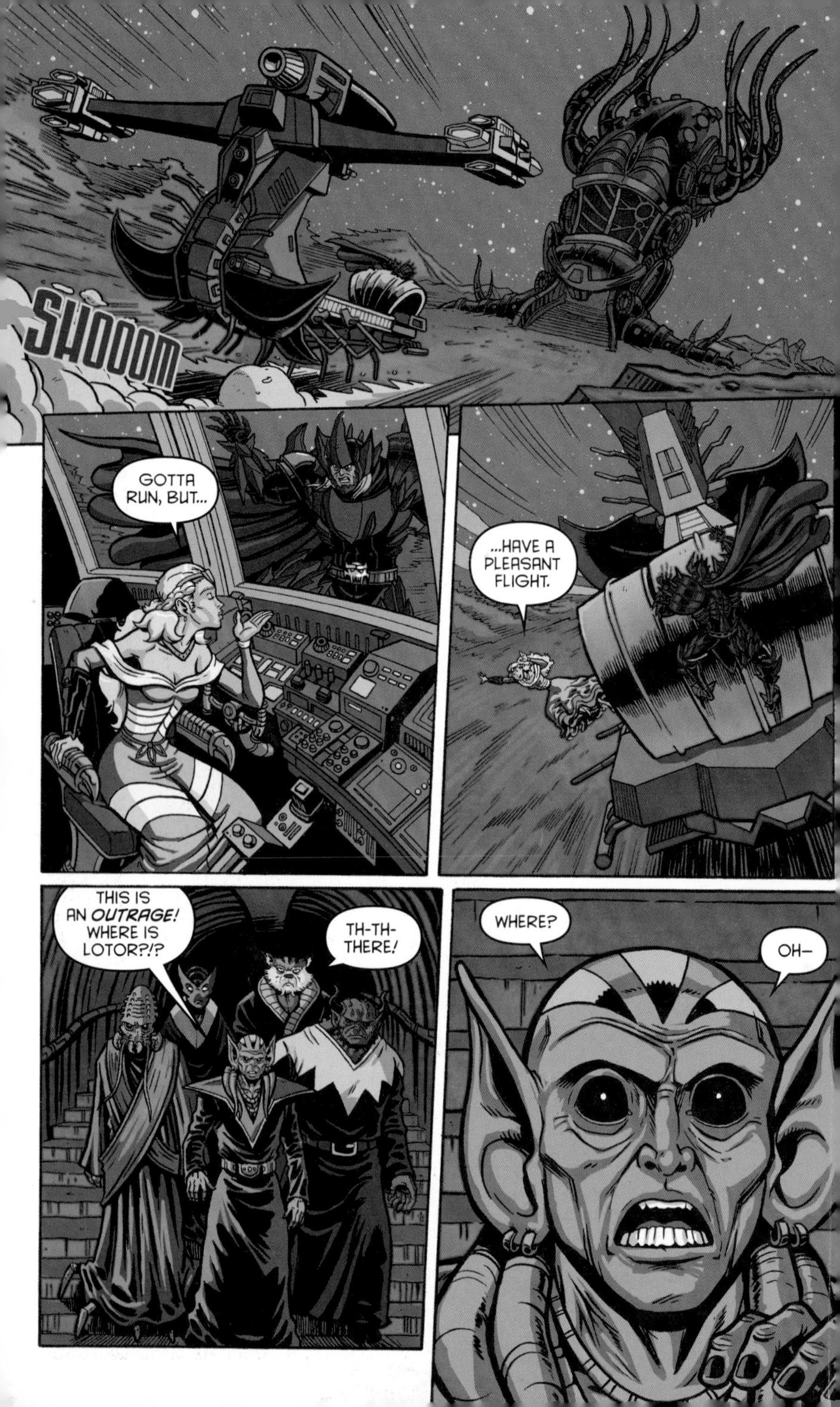
SHOOOM
GOTTA RUN, BUT...
...HAVE A PLEASANT FLIGHT.
THIS IS AN *OUTRAGE!* WHERE IS LOTOR?!?
TH-TH-THERE!
WHERE?
OH—

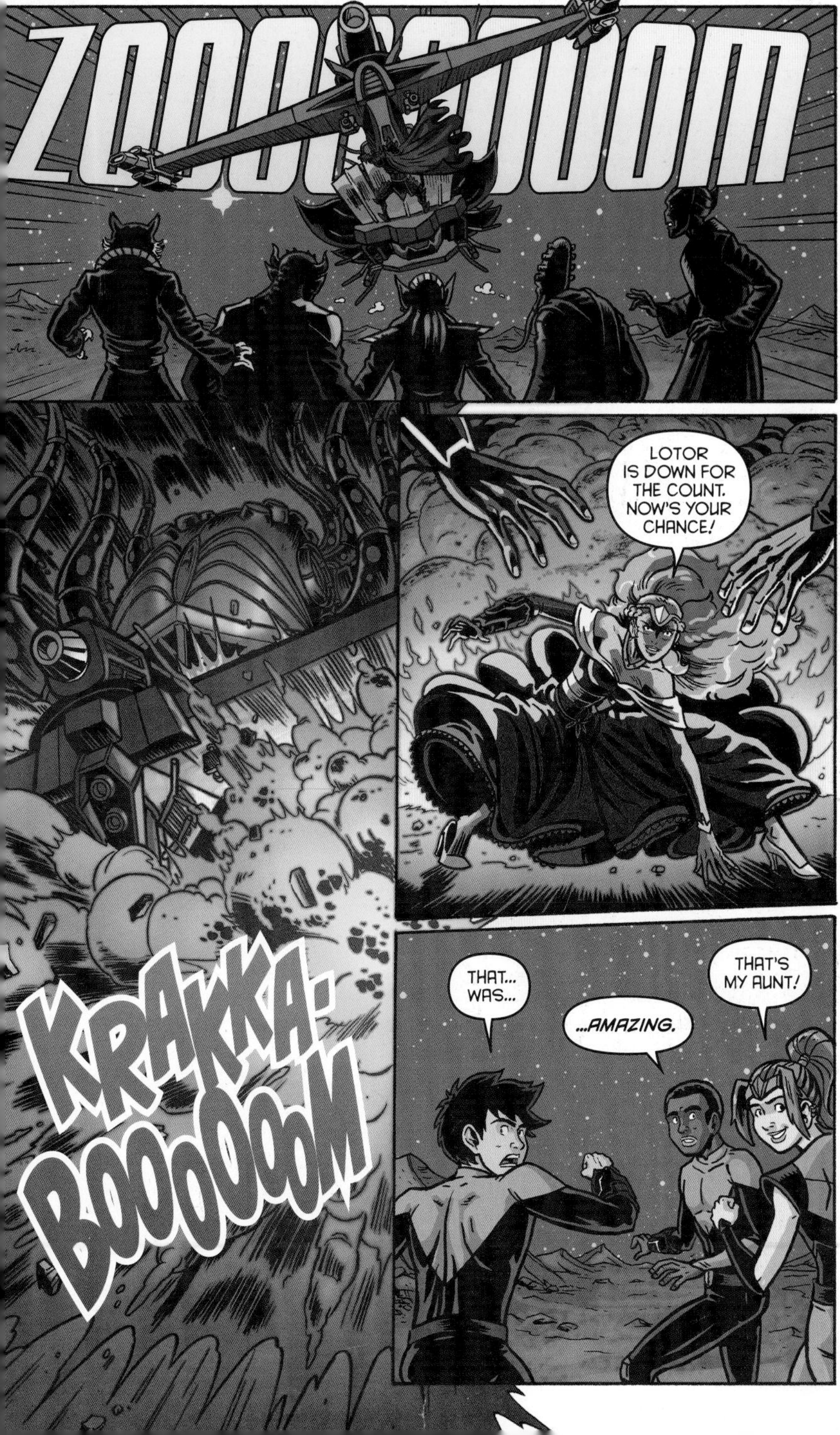
ZOOOOOOOOM
LOTOR IS DOWN FOR THE COUNT. NOW'S YOUR CHANCE!
KRAKKA-BOOOOOOM
THAT... WAS...
...AMAZING.
THAT'S MY AUNT!

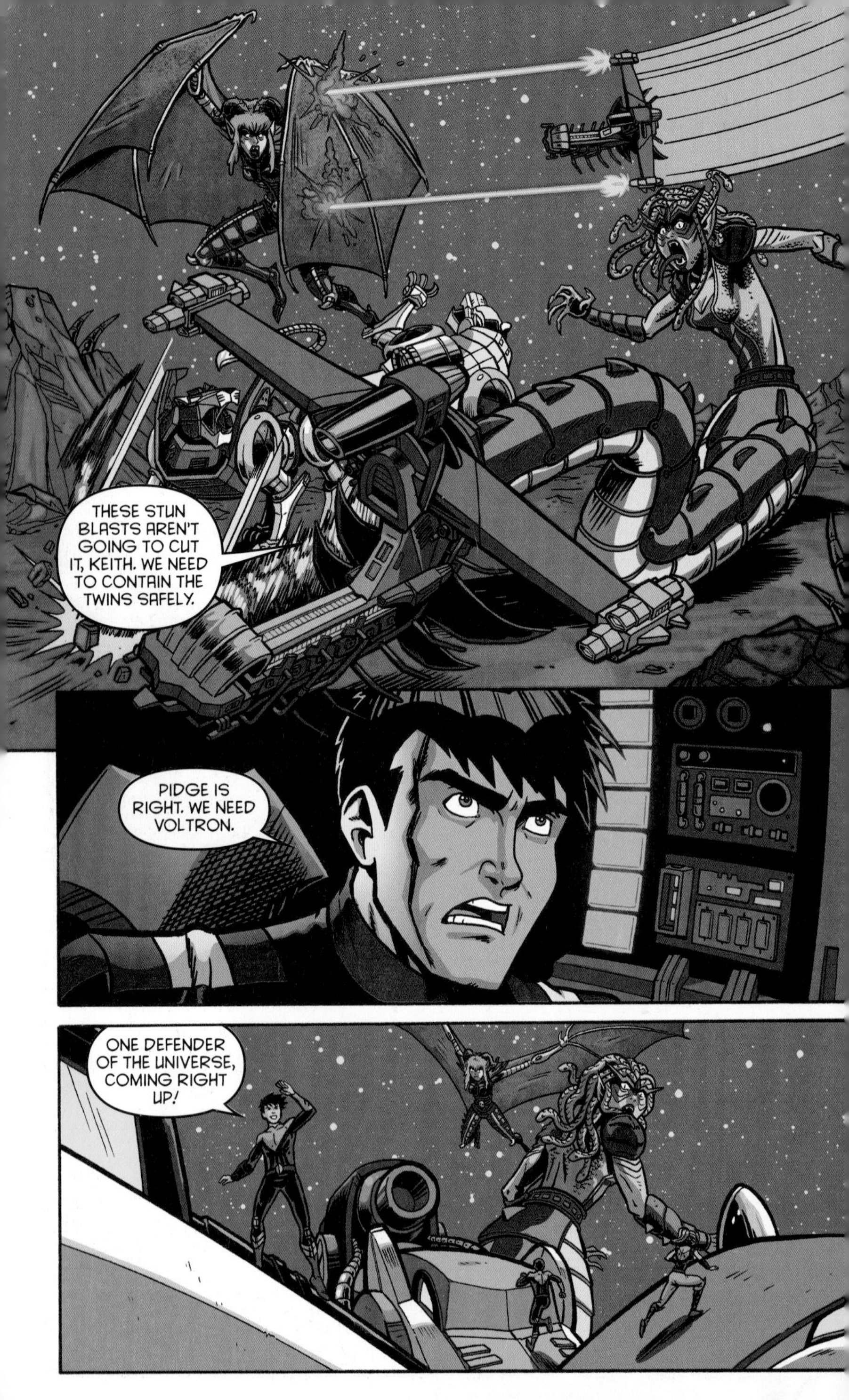
THESE STUN BLASTS AREN'T GOING TO CUT IT, KEITH. WE NEED TO CONTAIN THE TWINS SAFELY.
PIDGE IS RIGHT. WE NEED VOLTRON.
ONE DEFENDER OF THE UNIVERSE, COMING RIGHT UP!

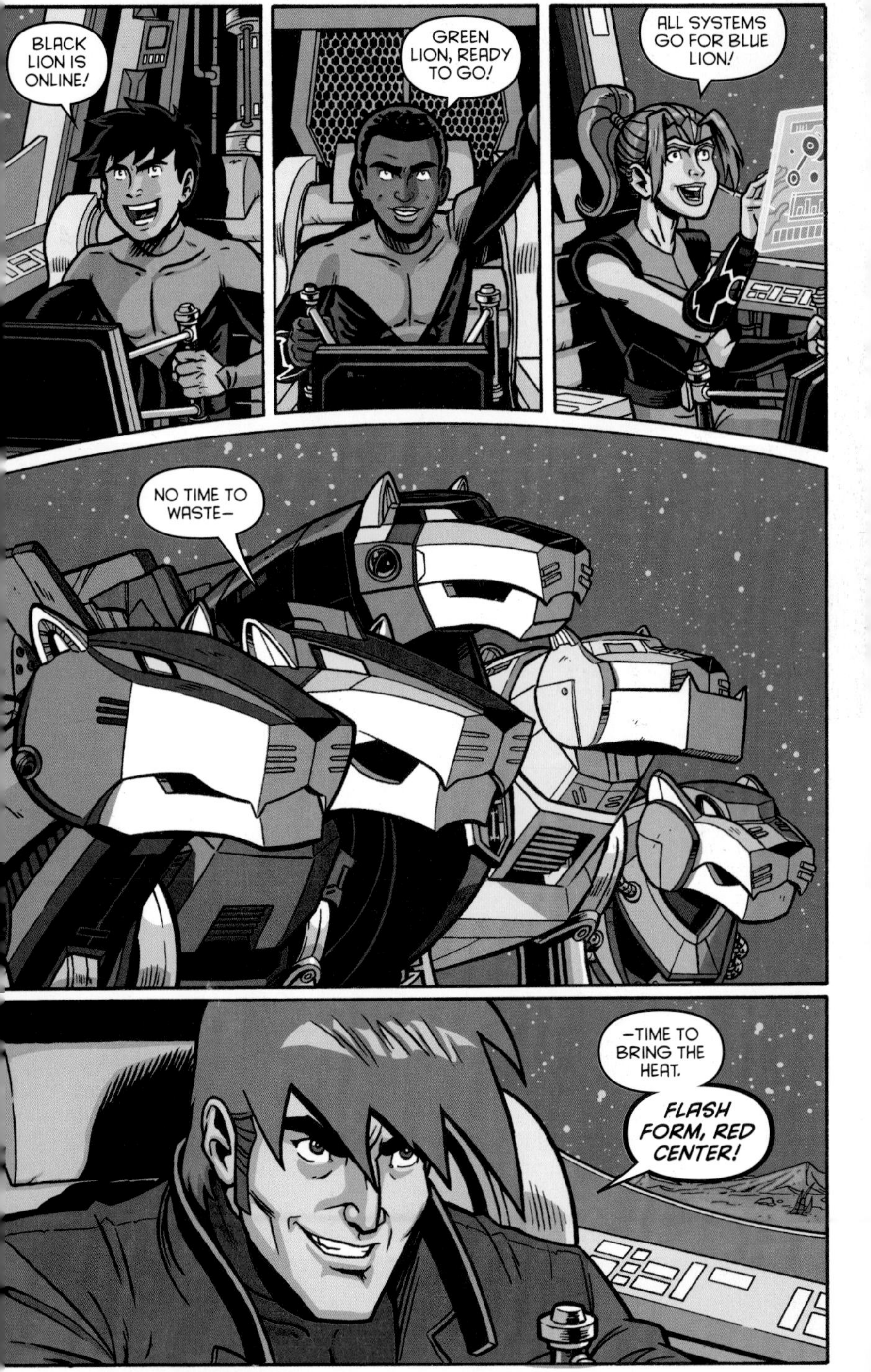
BLACK LION IS ONLINE!
GREEN LION, READY TO GO!
ALL SYSTEMS GO FOR BLUE LION!
NO TIME TO WASTE—
—TIME TO BRING THE HEAT.
FLASH FORM, RED CENTER!

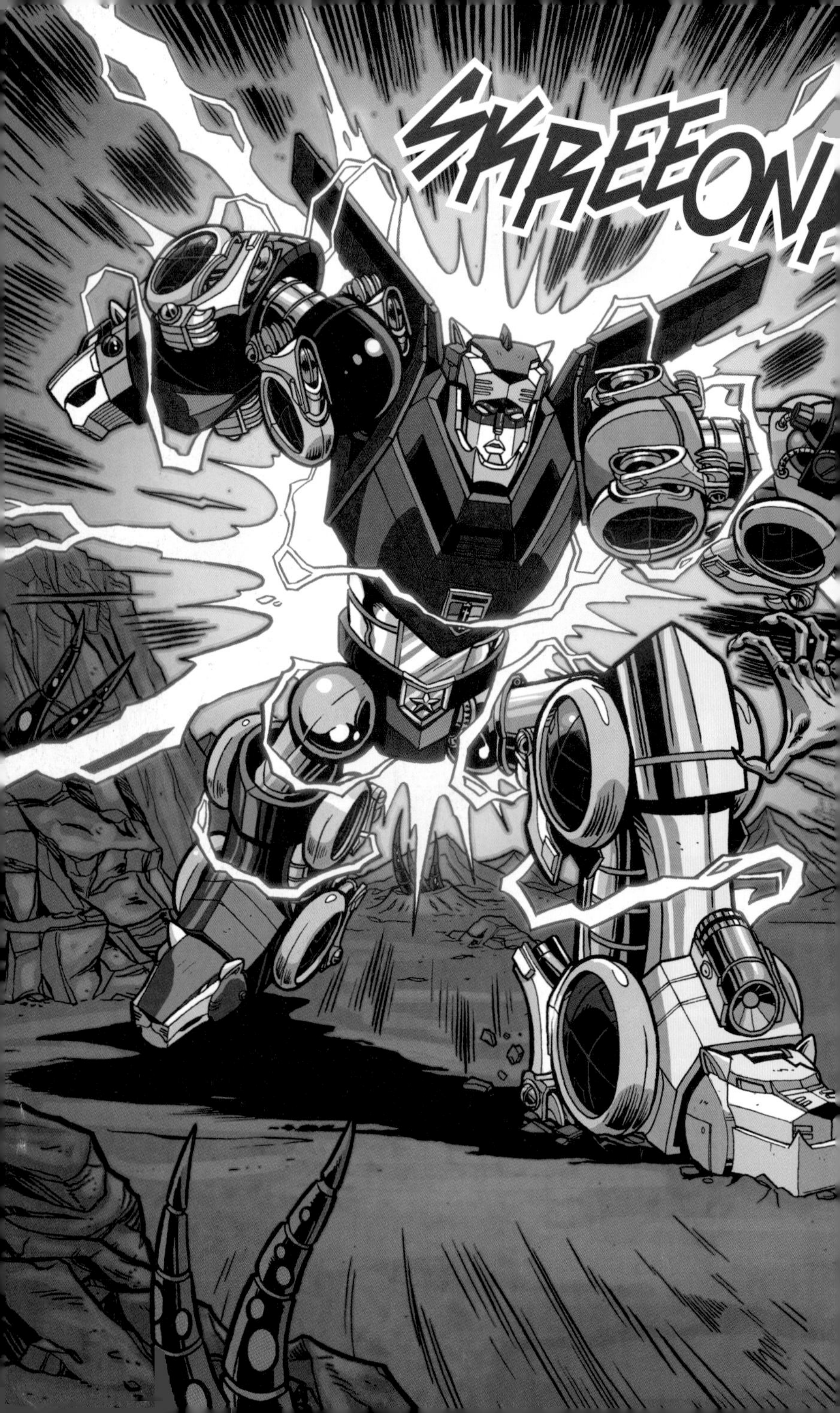
SKREEON!

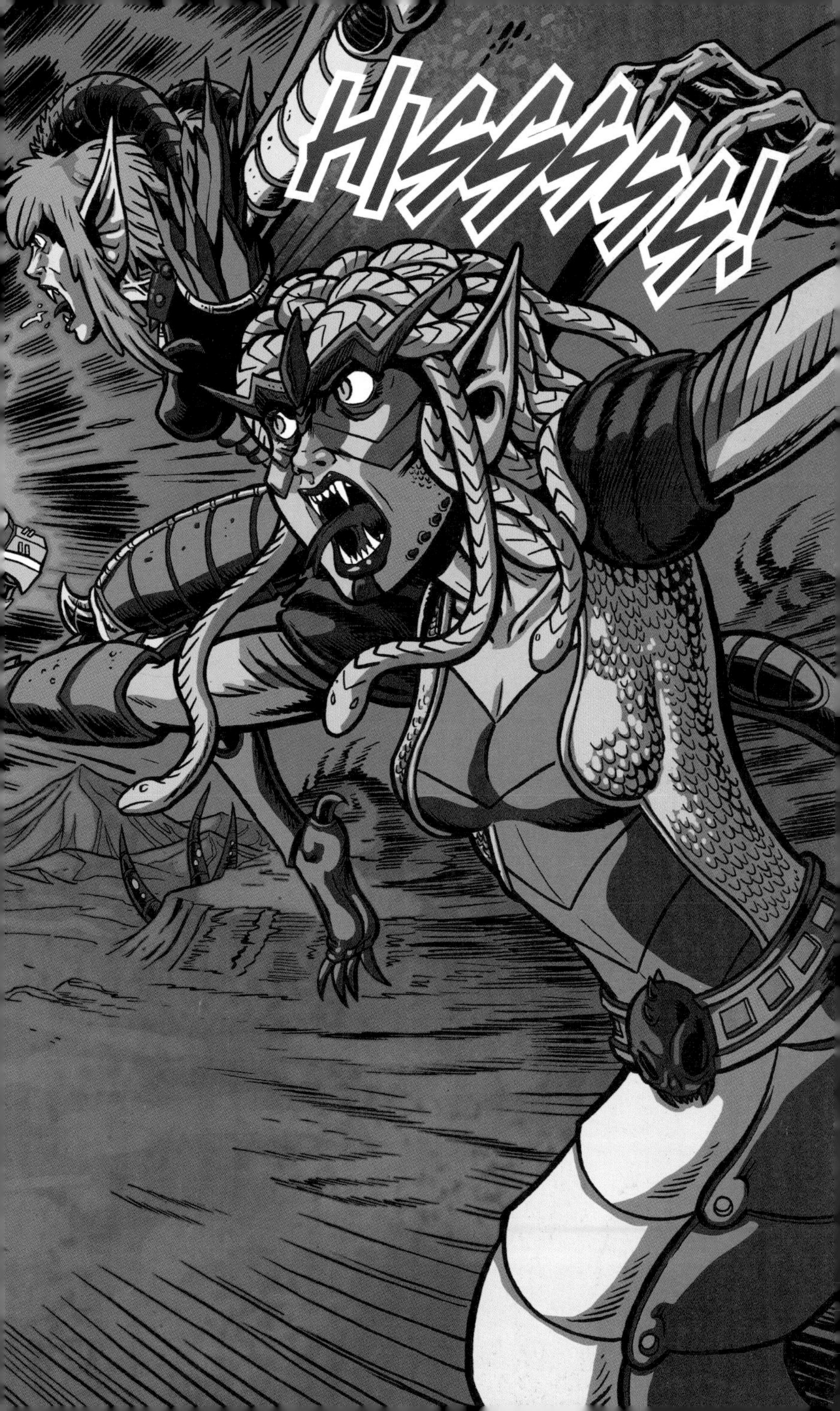
HISSSSS!

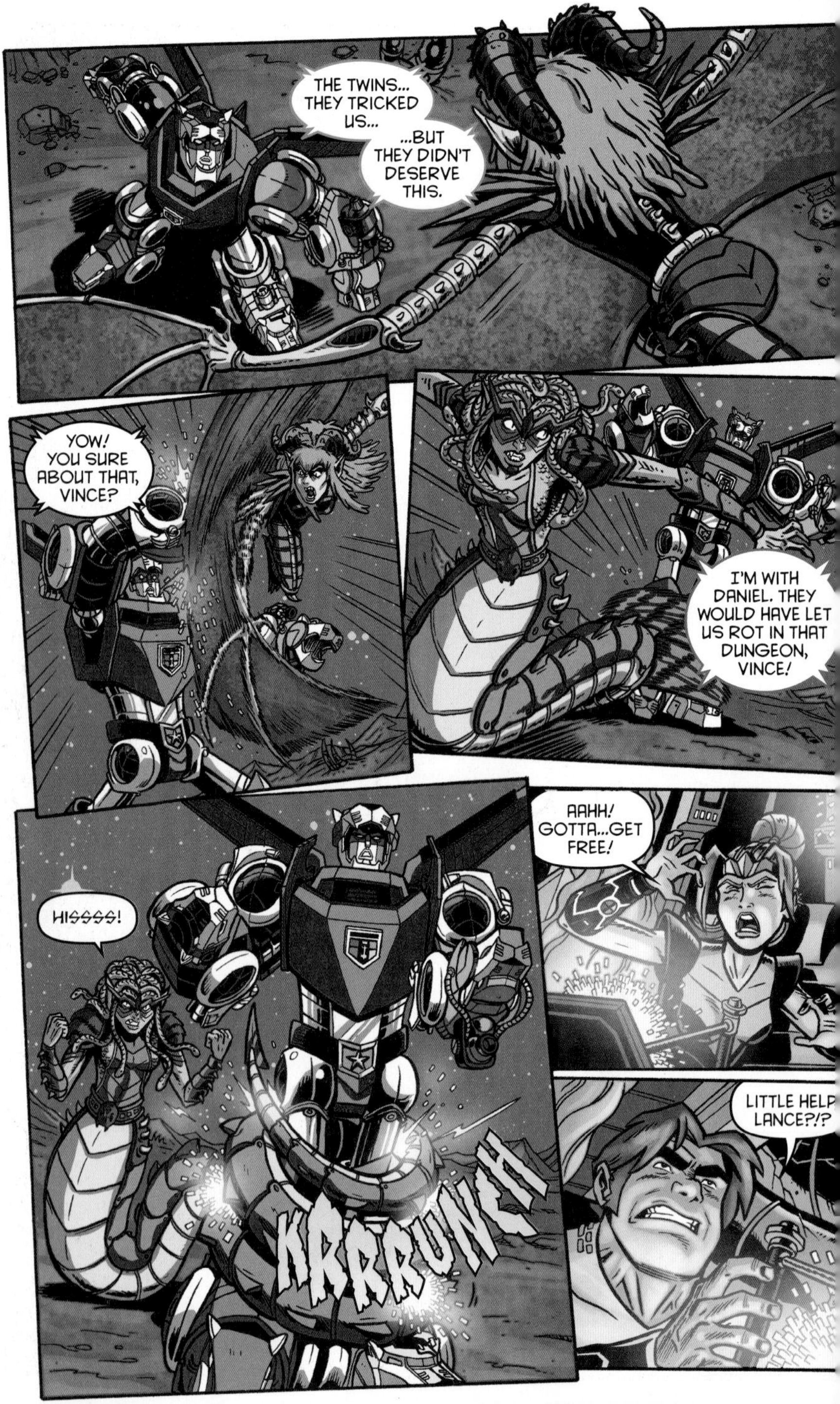
THE TWINS... THEY TRICKED US...
...BUT THEY DIDN'T DESERVE THIS.
YOW! YOU SURE ABOUT THAT, VINCE?
I'M WITH DANIEL. THEY WOULD HAVE LET US ROT IN THAT DUNGEON, VINCE!
HISSSS!
KRRRUNCH
AAHH! GOTTA...GET FREE!
LITTLE HELP LANCE?!?

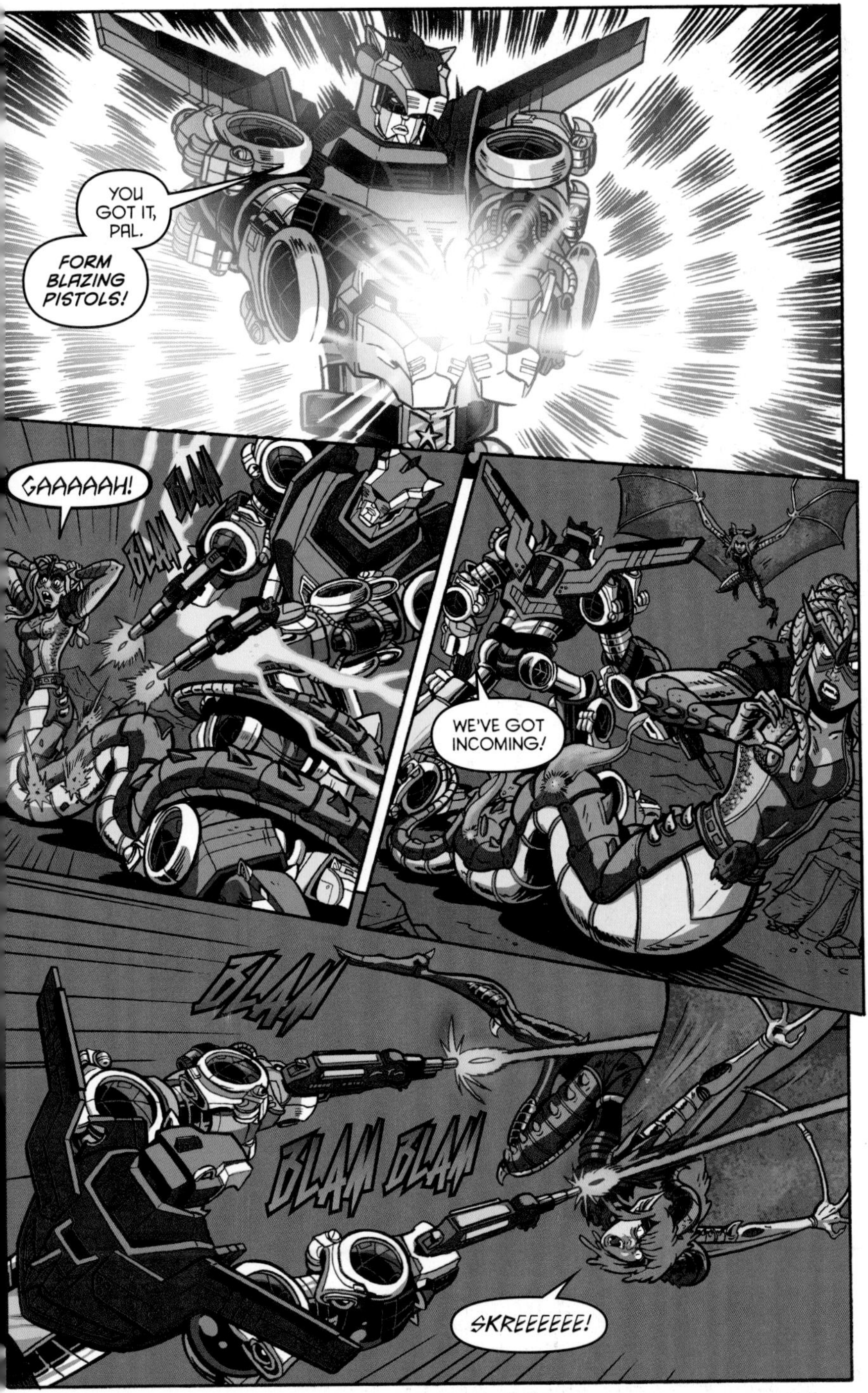
YOU GOT IT, PAL.
FORM BLAZING PISTOLS!
GAAAAAH!
BLAM BLAM BLAM
WE'VE GOT INCOMING!
BLAM
BLAM BLAM
SKREEEEEE!

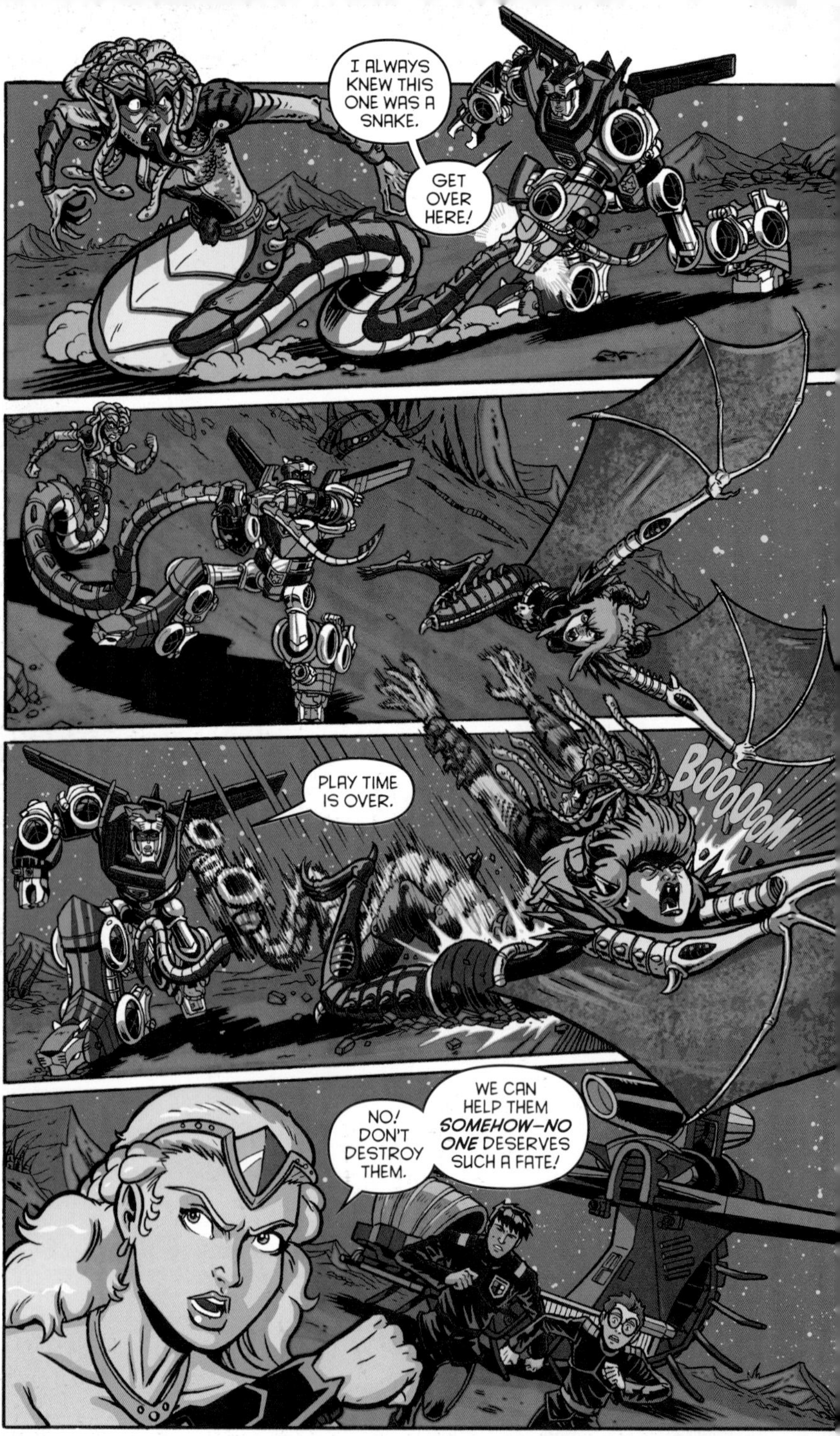

I ALWAYS KNEW THIS ONE WAS A SNAKE.
GET OVER HERE!
PLAY TIME IS OVER.
BOOOOOOM
NO! DON'T DESTROY THEM.
WE CAN HELP THEM *SOMEHOW*—*NO ONE* DESERVES SUCH A FATE!

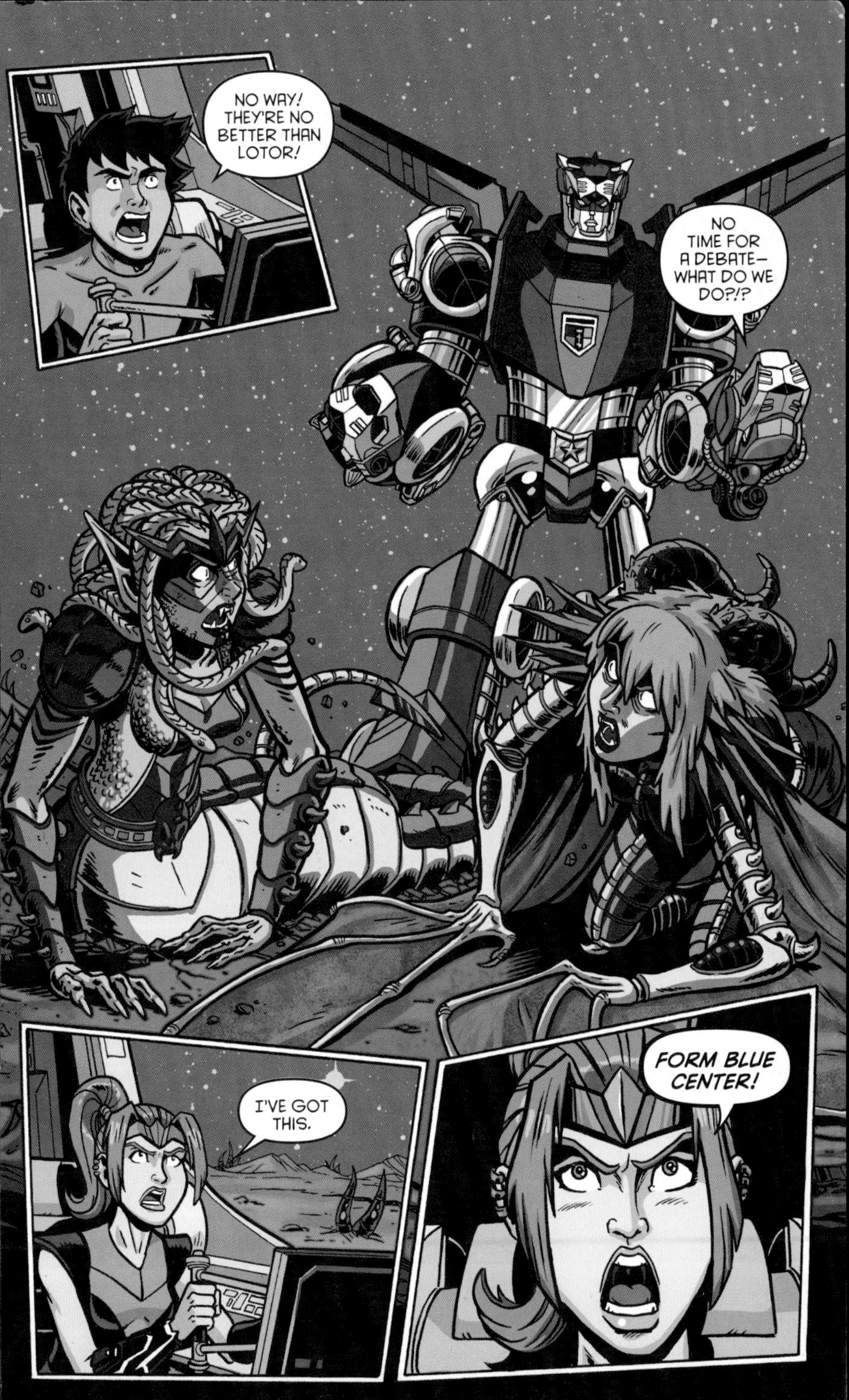
NO WAY! THEY'RE NO BETTER THAN LOTOR!
NO TIME FOR A DEBATE— WHAT DO WE DO?!?
I'VE GOT THIS.
FORM BLUE CENTER!

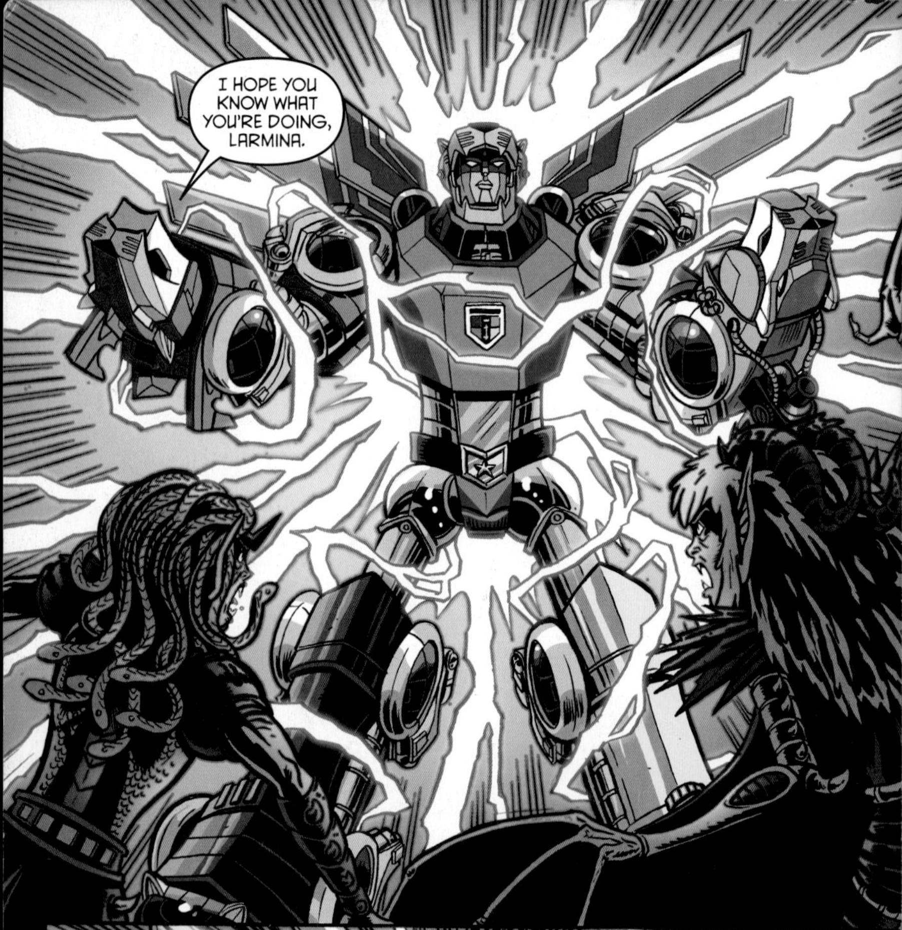

I HOPE YOU KNOW WHAT YOU'RE DOING, LARMINA.

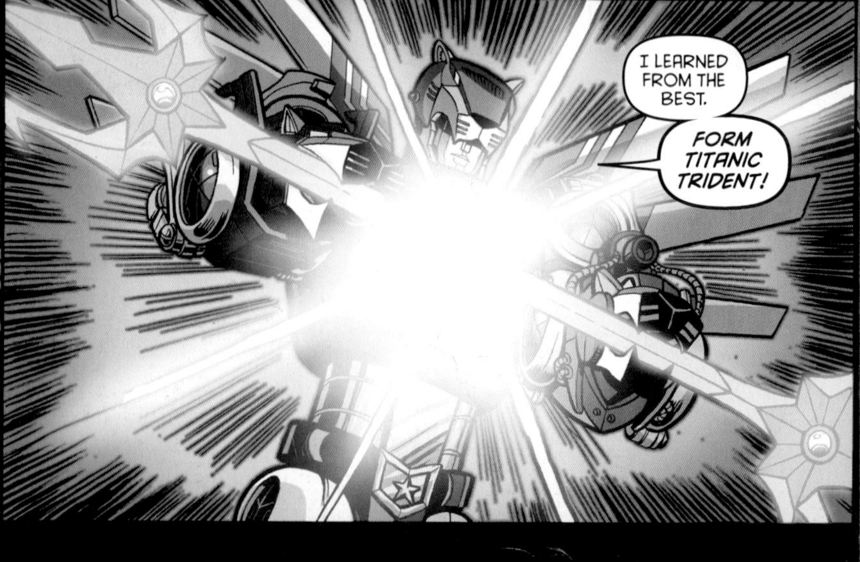

I LEARNED FROM THE BEST.
FORM TITANIC TRIDENT!

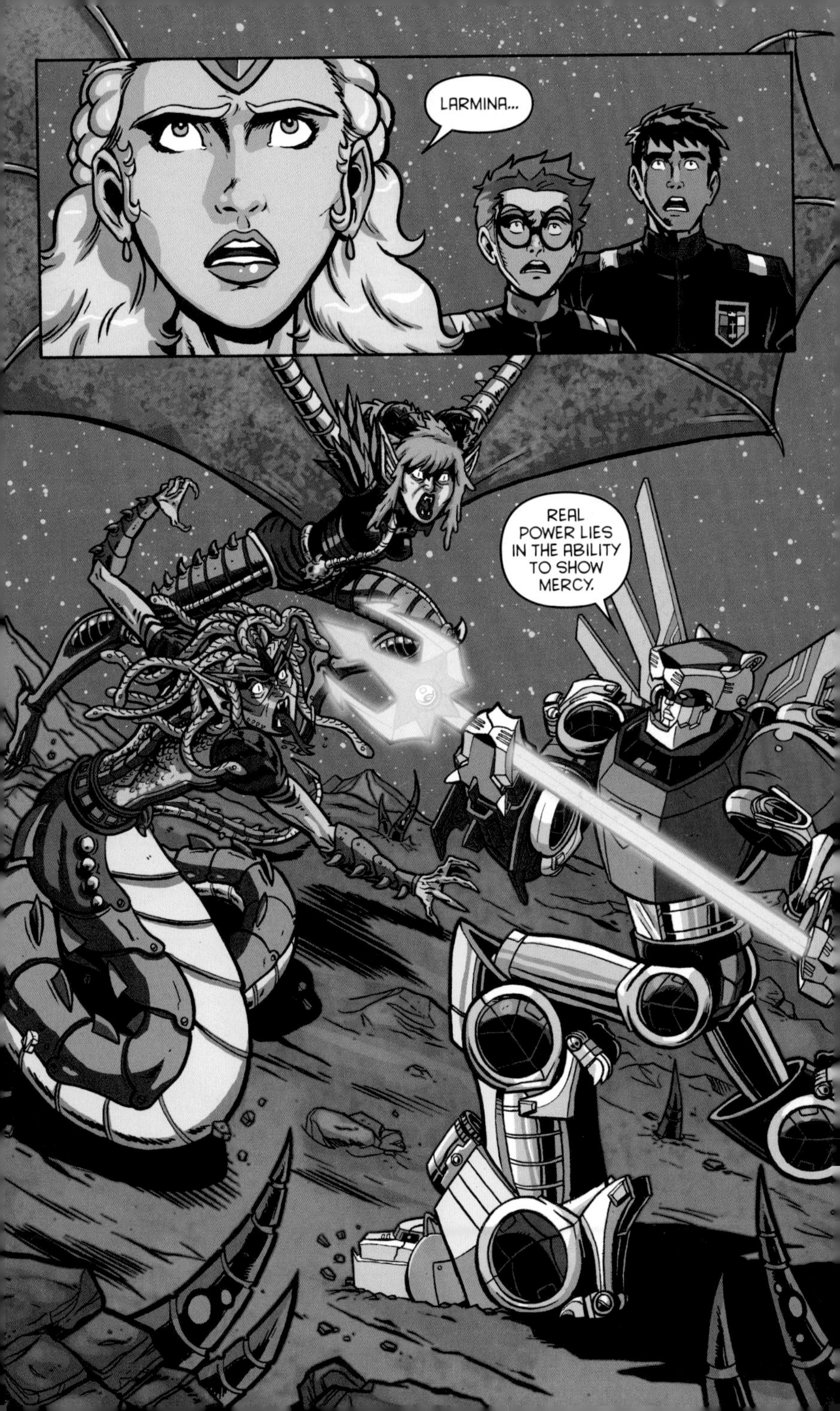
LARMINA...
REAL POWER LIES IN THE ABILITY TO SHOW MERCY.

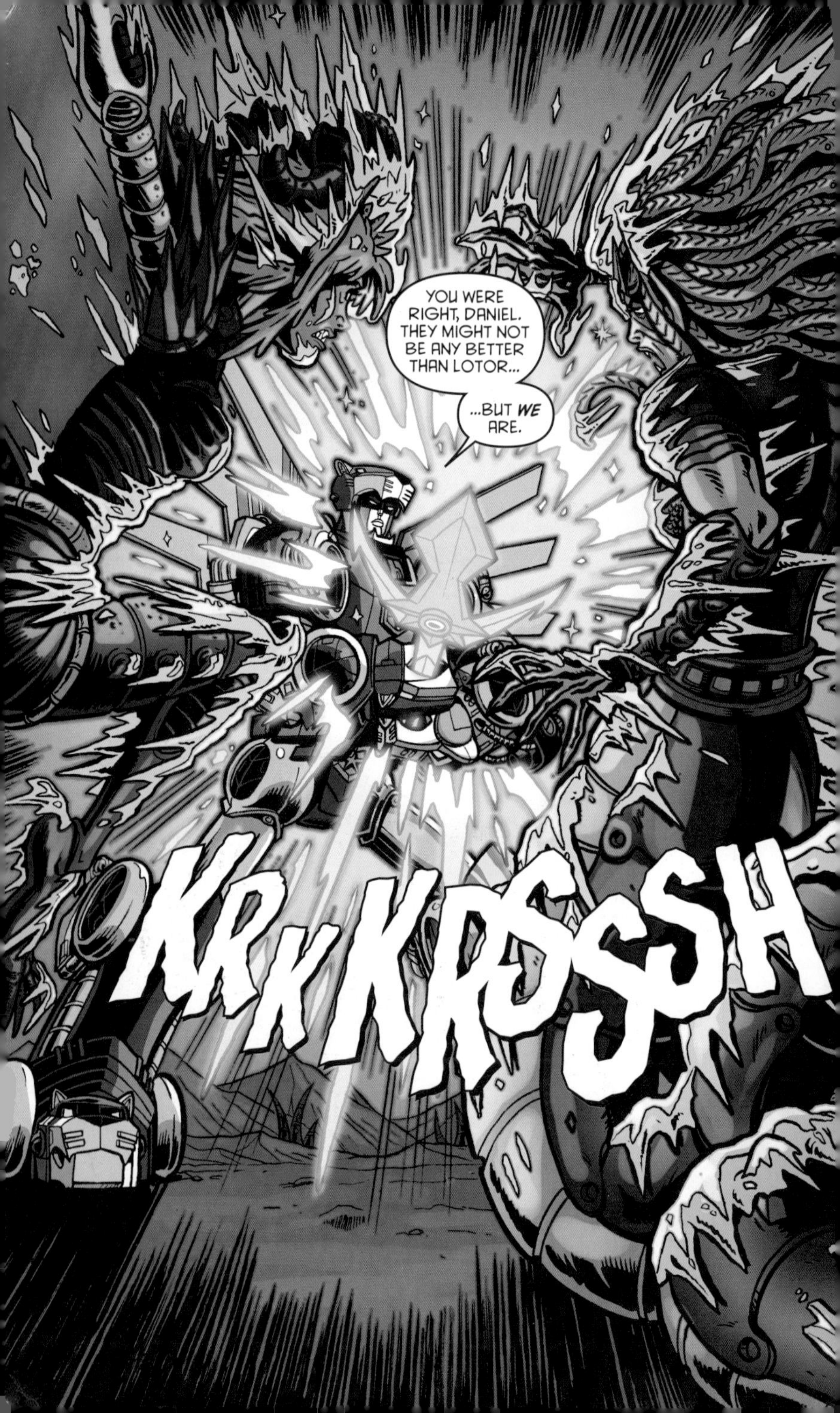
YOU WERE RIGHT, DANIEL. THEY MIGHT NOT BE ANY BETTER THAN LOTOR...
...BUT WE ARE.
KRKKRSSSH

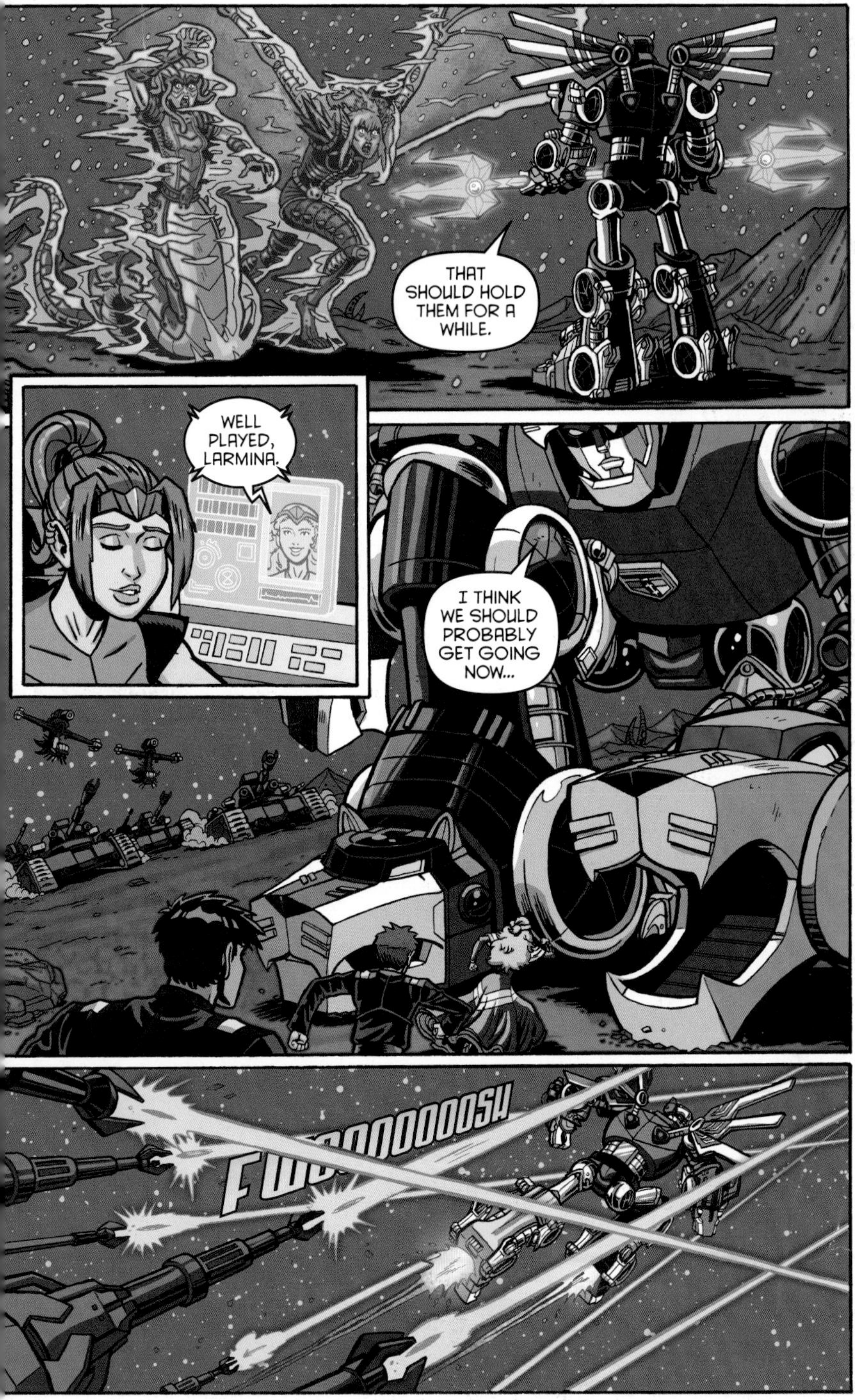
THAT SHOULD HOLD THEM FOR A WHILE.
WELL PLAYED, LARMINA.
I THINK WE SHOULD PROBABLY GET GOING NOW...
FWOOOOOOOOSH

CEASE FIRE, YOU FOOLS!

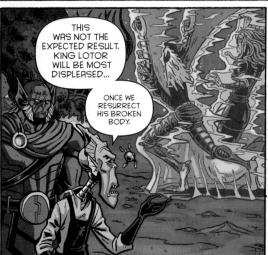

THIS WAS NOT THE EXPECTED RESULT. KING LOTOR WILL BE MOST DISPLEASED...

ONCE WE RESURRECT HIS BROKEN BODY.

TAKE YOUR TIME GATHERING HIM UP.

LET'S NOT GET BOGGED DOWN WITH WHO SNUCK OUT WHERE WITH WHAT LION...

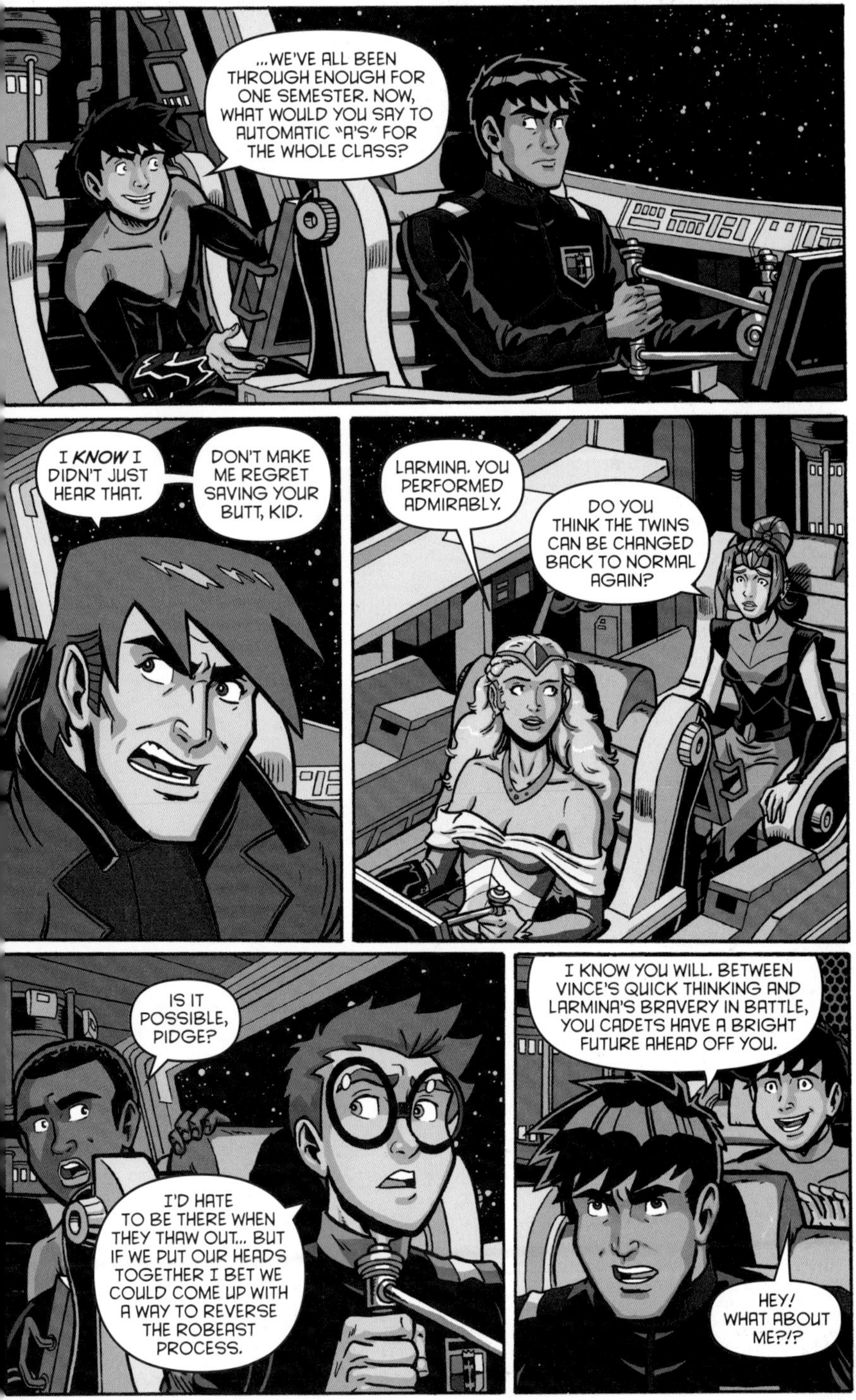
...WE'VE ALL BEEN THROUGH ENOUGH FOR ONE SEMESTER. NOW, WHAT WOULD YOU SAY TO AUTOMATIC "A'S" FOR THE WHOLE CLASS?
I KNOW I DIDN'T JUST HEAR THAT.
DON'T MAKE ME REGRET SAVING YOUR BUTT, KID.
LARMINA. YOU PERFORMED ADMIRABLY.
DO YOU THINK THE TWINS CAN BE CHANGED BACK TO NORMAL AGAIN?
IS IT POSSIBLE, PIDGE?
I'D HATE TO BE THERE WHEN THEY THAW OUT... BUT IF WE PUT OUR HEADS TOGETHER I BET WE COULD COME UP WITH A WAY TO REVERSE THE ROBEAST PROCESS.
I KNOW YOU WILL. BETWEEN VINCE'S QUICK THINKING AND LARMINA'S BRAVERY IN BATTLE, YOU CADETS HAVE A BRIGHT FUTURE AHEAD OFF YOU.
HEY! WHAT ABOUT ME?!?

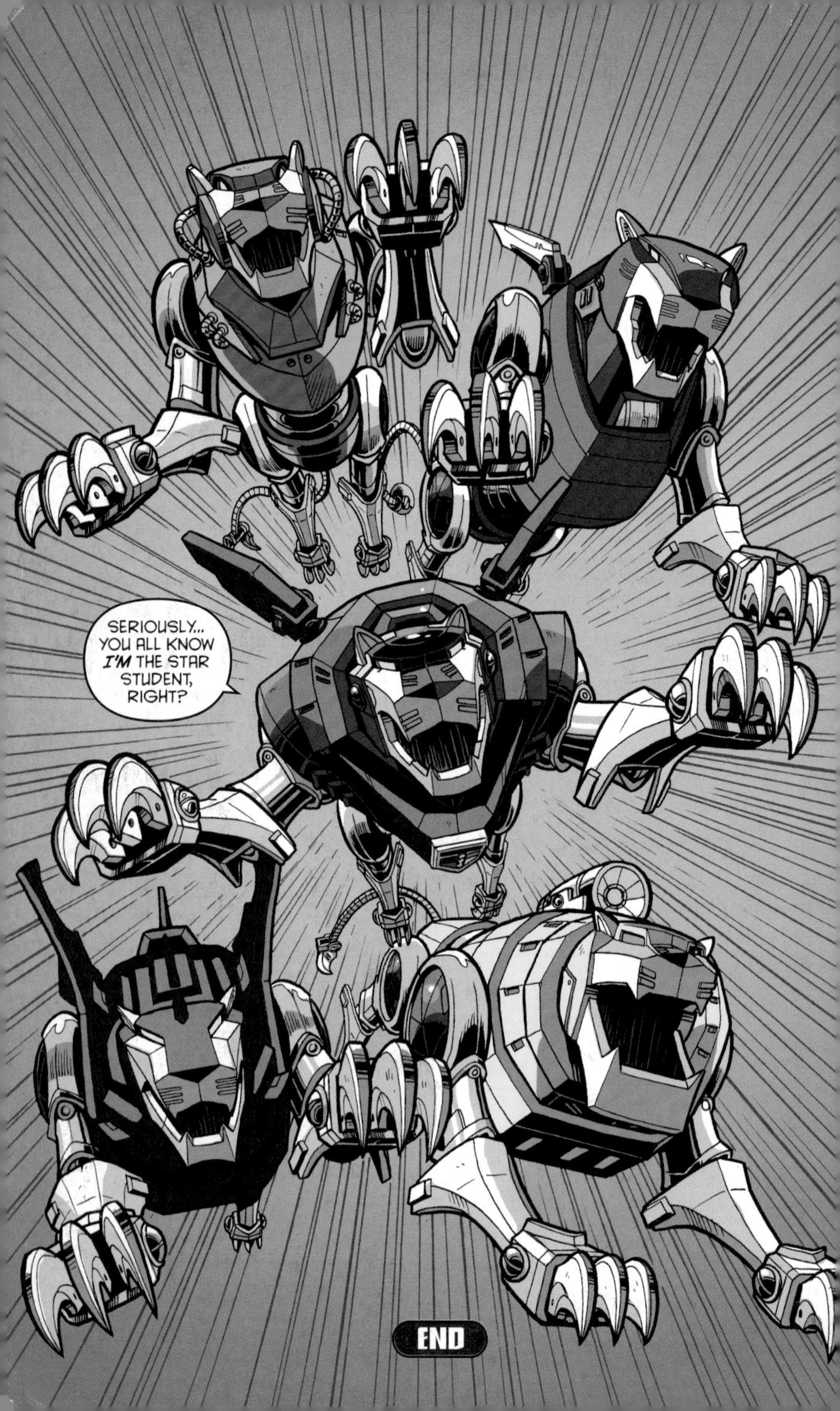
SERIOUSLY... YOU ALL KNOW *I'M* THE STAR STUDENT, RIGHT?
END

BRIAN SMITH

Brian Smith is a former Marvel Comics editor. His credits include *The Ultimates*, *Ultimate Spider-Man*, *Iron Man*, *Captain America*, *The Incredible Hulk*, and dozens of other comics. Smith is the co-creator/writer behind the *New York Times* best-selling graphic novel *The Stuff of Legend*, and the writer/artist of the all-ages comic *The Intrepid EscapeGoat*. His writing credits include *Finding Nemo: Losing Dory* from BOOM! Studios and *SpongeBob Comics* from Bongo.

Smith is also the illustrator of *The Adventures of Daniel Boom AKA LOUDBOY!*, named one of The Top 10 Graphic Novels for Youths 2009 by Booklist Online. His illustration clients include *Time Out New York Magazine*, *Nickelodeon*, *MAD Kids Magazine*, Harper Collins, Bongo Comics, Grosset & Dunlap, and American Greetings.

JACOB CHABOT

Jacob Chabot is a New York City-based cartoonist and illustrator. His comics have appeared in publications such as *Nickelodeon Magazine*, the now discontinued *Mad Kids*, *Savage Dragon*, and in various Marvel Comics. He has also done design work for such companies as Marvel, American Greetings, and The Princeton Review. Jacob is probably best known for his comic *The Mighty Skullboy Army*, which has been published in a series of minicomics as well as compiled in a graphic novel published by Dark Horse Comics. *The Mighty Skullboy Army* graphic novel was nominated for an Eisner Award in 2008 for Best Book for Teens. More examples of Jacob's work can be found at www.beetlebugcomics.com.

MICHAEL E. WIGGAM

Michael E. Wiggam is a professional comic book colorist whose work includes *Buffy the Vampire Slayer* and *Star Wars: Clone Wars* for Dark Horse Comics, Raymond E. Feist's *Magician Master: Enter the Great One* for Marvel Comics, *Amber Atoms* for Image Comics, *R.P.M.* and *I.C.E.* for 12 Gauge Comics, as well as other various publications. He was born and raised in Florida but has lived in Europe and seven U.S. states. His seventh birthday cake was Voltron themed.

COLLECT THEM ALL!